Badge

Art Edwards

Brian.
I'm grateful.
Lso is Badge.

Thirteenth
Note

Published by Thirteenth Note

ISBN-13: 978-0-9799066-8-8
ISBN-10: 0-9799066-8-7

Jacket photographs and design by Raquel
Edwards
www.raqueledwards.com

Badge

1970

Badge pushed the headphones into his ears so he could hear the music better, and the rest barely at all.

His mom and dad had been yelling in the front room for a minute, an hour, as long as he could remember. He eventually quit pretending to sleep and went to the stereo console in the dining room, put on his dad's copy of *Blow by Blow* by Jeff Beck, listened. His dad had taught him how to put the record on, how to use AUTO, to let the machine do its job. If you didn't, the needle would scratch it. Badge never sat down in front of the stereo, never looked at the brown tweed speaker or even at the album art. The music came from the needle and the spin. That was all he needed.

His dad had other records—Iron Butterfly, Savoy Brown, Mountain—but Badge liked *Blow by Blow*. It was all guitar, but guitar you could sing along with. He never sang out loud, just in his head. The notes felt like they were being stored there, like he might need them someday. He liked to think of a future where they had value, like money.

"Get out," his mom yelled, loud enough for him to hear. His dad said something back. Badge turned up the volume, pushed the speakers into his ears. The front door opened, slammed.

His mom came around the corner, stopped when she saw

him standing there in his headphones and pajamas. She was a tiny woman but looked even tinier in her nightshirt. Tears streaked her face.

"I was just—"

She motioned for the headphones. The music quickly diminished, but the sound still came from the headphones in her hand.

She knelt in front of him, hugged him. "Your dad is going away. To live somewhere."

The hug felt too close, stuttered breaths, warm tears on his shoulder. The headphones sounded at his back.

She looked at him, worried. He hated the worry more than anything.

"Do you understand?"

The record wouldn't stop until it was done. The needle was a diamond.

Part I

The New Lucky Bastard

I

Badge was once again a soldier for rock music—a guitarist as always, a sideman this time—stepping out of a cab on Sunset Boulevard on his way to rehearsal, his Stratocaster cased and in his hand, his boots laced to the top. In his eight years away from the business—the real business, the one that didn't involve playing for tips during Albuquerque happy hours, or laying tracks *pro bono* for singer-songwriter types, or aping covers at some Indian casino just off I-25—the only difference so far was the style of key that got him into his hotel room, this new one a credit card type, an ad for a local pizza joint on its back. *You weren't done, and you're back now, and that's all there is to it. When you're really done, the world will let you know.* If a soldier is only a soldier at war, a musician is only a musician in L.A.

Earlier that day, Badge had called Glen from his hotel room.

"You're to meet Betty at the Band Bungalow at eight o'clock," Glen said. "You remember where that is?"

"Sure," Badge said. "It hasn't been that long."

"Eight years is an eternity in this business. You know Britney Spears?"

"Yeah."

"She was in the Brownies the last time you did a job for me."

Badge smiled. He'd always liked Glen, in the masochistic way you can like someone for being clever enough to dupe you. "Eight o'clock. Got it."

"You need anything else?"

"Yeah." It had to be said, if only so they could get past it, like offering condolences to a friend after a death in the family. "I need to thank you for getting me this gig."

"You called, didn't you?"

"Yeah, but with the way things ended with– You could've easily–"

"Forget it," Glen said. "If I took it personally every time a musician lost his mind I wouldn't have anyone to hire."

The Band Bungalow, two rows of storage units that ran up both sides of an alley off Vine, had gotten even more run-down since Badge had last seen it. White paint flaked off its gutters, and the lower half of the office door was missing, replaced inexactly with a piece of plywood. It amazed Badge that the Bungalow still did enough business to stay open, still housed bands. The music scene had changed so much in the last few years. Now, in the first month of a new millennium, boy bands, pop princesses, pretty faces ruled. But Badge could hear rock music coming from these rooms, the noise of drums and guitars, singers crooning ad hoc lyrics, bassists adding foundation. It reminded Badge of something. *Hope* was the only word he could come up with. Nobody here was on the back end of anything.

The air was cool and still, SoCal, but January nonetheless. Badge didn't know which room housed No Fun Intended. A kid carrying a guitar case, his blond hair poking out of the center of a modified stocking cap, walked by and Badge stopped him.

"You know where I can find Betty?"

The kid smirked. One rivet-like post stuck out from his lip, what looked like the result of a construction project gone awry. "You in her band?"

Badge nodded.

"So," the kid said. He set his guitar down. "You're the new lucky bastard."

"Lucky bastard?"

"Girl's got an attitude. I was her guitar player when she started the record. After everyone saw her, they called me the lucky bastard. By my count, you're the fifth lucky bastard."

"What's the deal with her?" Glen had given him the basics. Young girl, debut record past due, enough money to keep Badge fed and his kid in child support. What more did he need to know?

The slam of a door came from up the alley. Two men—one tall with a grey beard that came all the way to his crotch; the other short with bleach-blond hair like Billy Idol's—marched towards the entrance. Badge recognized the bearded one. It was Les McKay—*the* Les McKay—the flannel-shirted bass player who'd been showing up on records in Badge's collection for twenty years. Les carried a guitar case, and his brow cut deep into the line of his eyes. His demeanor was like a farmer about to exact revenge on a barn burner. The blond one loped behind, carrying a drum case.

The kid shook his head. "Looks like she's at it again."

"Wait," Badge said. "Les McKay's in Betty's band?"

"'Was' might be the better word. She's in space fifteen." The kid ambled away. "And be careful. She always smells blood when someone new's around."

Each storage room had a metal door, and between the doors overgrown bougainvilleas crawled up the wall. Their fuchsia petals littered the alley. They were just like the bush at Holly and Malcolm's place—what used to be his place too, now just his ex-wife and son's. During summers, Holly had to sweep the walk to keep the three of them from tracking petals into the house. The bush had only grown more out of hand since the divorce, spreading like kudzu until Holly hired a crew to trim it back. Still, she never had it removed.

No sound came from space fifteen. A large padlock, undone, hung from its hinge. Badge took a breath. Luckily, his nearly four decades had yet to tarnish his looks—tall body just south of lanky, dark hair to his shoulders, brown eyes that seemed calm even when he was losing his shit. His looks, combined with his playing, had opened many musical doors in Albuquerque, but this was L.A. Bigger factors were at work here, none of which cared two shits about him. Badge used the nose of his guitar case to push the door open.

A black light, the tube a purple fluorescence, cast its glow over everything. A guitar—Gretsch hollowbody, 6120, Filtertron pickups—slanted up from a stand. A drum set glistened. A Patti Smith poster hung above a line of amplifiers, and a couch stretched along the far wall. A girl, her face glowing an almost ethereal white, sat on the couch and held what looked like a publicity photo, which was on fire, the blue flame expanding from its lowest corner.

She was barely adult, twenty or so by Badge's guess, and her hair featured beads and dreadlocks, a new style that seemed a deliberate attempt to look trampy. Her legs, sticking out from her miniskirt, held the light like marble. Upon Badge's entering, Betty eyed him like she might an opponent who'd just entered the ring, then continued to follow the flame. "I threw them out," she said.

"I hear you like to do that."

"Who do I have to thank for your high opinion of me? Glen?"

Badge set his case down. It could very well be over already, his day of travel wasted. At least the Fender Super Reverb amp had made it. His only goal was to get plugged in. He could accept any decision after that. "What did they do?"

"Nothing." She dropped the photo to the floor, snuffed it out with her combat boot. Her voice had just the hint of a rasp, a high school cheerleader after a night of smoking cigarettes. "They offered nothing, and they left with nothing."

"Maybe it was your attitude."

Betty looked surprised, the same cheerleader after getting cut from the team for a less popular girl. "Excuse me?"

"Those guys are better than you think. You might've tried listening to them."

"You're serious."

"I am."

"My sidemen are going to tell me how to make my record."

"Records need rhythm sections, and good ones."

"I'll get a good one."

"When? June? This thing was due six weeks ago."

Anger flushed Betty's face, and Badge didn't care. If he were turning around and flying home, she'd hear it from him first.

"What exactly did you want from them?" he said.

Betty glared from the couch, her feet spread, offering a view of her underwear, a perfect V of Scottish plaid. He didn't know if this was emblematic of a true ambivalence or some attempt to manipulate him. He doubted she knew either. "I wanted them to have soul."

"Soul," Badge repeated. He eased down into what must've been a nice papasan chair at one point. It smelled musty, like the inside of a laundry bag. "You mean like James Brown?"

"Good Christ." Betty flopped back onto the couch. "You should just go now before this gets humiliating for both of us."

"Come on. Tell me what soul is."

"You'll take it personally."

"You already have me kicked out of the band. What more do I have to lose?"

"That's it." Betty snapped her fingers, sat up again. The beads in her hair tapped together. "I need people to play like they have nothing to lose, like their very lives depend on it. Those cream puffs in here before only cared about lunch breaks and union scale. I'm trying to do something real, and everyone else pushes me toward the safe and mundane."

"Who pushes you?"

Betty rolled her eyes. "My biggest mistake to Glen is that I was never on the Mickey Mouse Club."

"A 'great platform,' right?" Badge remembered the meetings with Glen and the Famous Dead. "Platform" was one of Glen's favorite words, as were "leverage" and "accessibility."

"Platform," Betty yelled. She got up, paced the floor. Her folded arms accented the curve of her neck. If Glen was looking for someone to compete with the pinups of the day, he'd done well. "If I had one real musician in here for every time that guy said *platform*."

"Glen's a marketer. If you didn't want that, why team up with him?"

Betty stopped pacing. She glanced at Badge, then away. "He was the only one who wanted me."

The desperate songwriter, the wily manager. It was a familiar story. Hopefully she hadn't signed over her publishing. "We don't get to pick and choose in this business."

"I don't need the guy forever. I'm ready to do it all myself as soon as I have a fan base. You're not gonna do squat if people don't know you first."

And you're not gonna do squat by yourself even if they do. As a hired-gun player, Badge had seen dozens of songwriters go it alone, and each project ended with broken dreams, maxed-out credit cards, and boxes of product stuffed in a closet. Like it or not, being with people like Glen was the litmus test that determined success or failure. It was how Elvis and the Beatles and KISS and Zeppelin and Van Halen and U2 and Nirvana all got started. Name one who wasn't.

"Well," Badge said. He grabbed his case, flipped it on its

back. "I came all the way from New Mexico to play with you. It'd be nice of you to at least hear me before you decide I'm not the guy."

Betty looked askance at him. "Why should I?"

Badge took out his Stratocaster—sea foam green, white pick guard, chrome accents—and a familiar, cocked feeling grew inside him. Coming to L.A., playing in a new project, he loved this part. If she tried to throw him out, he'd refuse to go. If she tried to leave, he'd tackle her. "Because your only other option tonight is to go home, lie around and wonder how your songs could've sounded." He snapped his case closed. "Or pick up that Gretsch and let's get down to it."

Betty couldn't quite stifle a smile, but instead of grabbing her guitar she reached for a cardboard box, removed a photo. "Tell me what you think of this." She handed it to him.

It was a publicity shot of Betty, her head slightly tilted, her face looking straight into the camera. A fisheye lens gave the effect of roundness to her features, and her eyes looked huge, like a baby bird's as its mother drops food into its mouth. In short, the photo didn't look like it would influence anyone to do anything.

"I'm no expert," he said, handing the photo back.

"Didn't say you were," Betty said, not taking it. "What do you think?"

Badge looked again. He knew what she wanted to hear which, lucky for him, was the truth. "I think you should burn every one of them, and I think you should tell Glen not to worry about head shots until he knows what he's selling."

A smile crept across Betty's face, more revealing than lingerie. "Then we can jam," she said and reached for her Gretsch.

2

The pointy-haired, nose-pierced, studded-belt clientele at the Tiki Bar gawked as Badge and Betty walked in. Badge knew why. Not only was Betty probably the hottest item that drank at the Tiki, she was also the only one with a record contract. L.A.'s the second largest city in the country, but everyone knows everyone else's business. It was worse in Albuquerque, where Badge's past tried to ambush him around every corner. That was okay. He was here now, where no one was left to remember.

And how did the Tiki crowd see Badge? The older guy moving in on their territory, no doubt. Too bad, suckers. Try spending more time practicing, less time at the tattoo parlor.

If Betty was aware of the attention, she didn't show it. She sauntered past the onlookers, moved out of the way of a pool cue, hopped onto the lone free barstool. The girl had it. Sultry voice, and her songs weren't bad either, not the noise-for-noise's-sake Badge half expected. Cut a few intros, add a bridge here or there, and you never know. Every boy in America could have her name carved on the underside of his skateboard.

Badge knew the Tiki Bar, knew it too well. It had always been the dive of choice for the musicians that rehearsed at the Bungalow, and the Famous Dead were no different. The place had hardly changed. The stage still sat across from the bar, a six-inch rise that had once featured novelty acts. No one performed tonight. The bar owner probably had traded live music for the jukebox in the corner. It was a common occurrence. Whittle down entertainment to the cheapest offering. The sign above the bar promoted "Karaoke Mondays."

"What're you havin'?" Betty said. She'd gotten the bartender's attention.

Badge sidled up. "Club soda."

Three people—Betty, the bartender, and a third guy with a bleached mohawk—looked at Badge like he'd just proclaimed his undying love for Hootie and the Blowfish.

"Hey, I'm an old man."

"You diabetic?" Betty asked.

"No, I don't drink."

"Not at all?"

"Not at all."

"Not ever?"

"Not in years."

"I've heard of people like you," the mohawked guy said.

"Can it, Poltergeist," Betty said. "I think there's a wuss convention up the street you're missing out on."

Poltergeist shrugged, turned to the girl who sat to his other side.

Betty looked away. Badge could sense her uncertainty, like she worried he was trying to sell her a bill of goods, like sobriety was some gimmick meant to impress her. "Why don't you drink?"

Badge glanced at the liquor bottles behind the bar, familiar names mixed with others. "Because I tend to wreck things when I drink."

"What did you wreck?"

The bartender came back with his club soda, along with something tall, red and in a frosted glass for Betty. Badge squeezed the almost completely dried-out lime into his glass. "What didn't I wreck?"

"Your band?"

Badge hit his club soda.

"Your marriage?"

Badge grimaced.

"Anything else?"

"What else is there?"

"Your health? Career? Lifelong friendships?"

All of it, more or less. "How do you think we sounded in the practice room?"

Betty sipped her drink. The red and white lights, strung Christmas-style above the bar, gave her cheeks a candy-like glow. "I don't think it's going to work," she said.

"Hm?" Badge thought their jam had gone well, the tug of his melodies pushing her songs to places they needed to go, conjuring emotions she wouldn't have gotten to on her own. *If you didn't like it, why ask me out for a drink?*

"The way you play," she said. "It screws me up."

"What do you mean?"

"I always start with this song, and somehow it's never enough. Someone always has to come in and make it into something else."

"That's rock music," Badge said. "Bring people together, see what happens."

"Mick and Keith."

"And all the rest."

"I can't do Mick and Keith."

Badge put his back against the bar, looked out at the room. *Apparently the Rolling Stones aren't good enough.* He wouldn't let her pull him in. This was her roller coaster, he wasn't coming along for the ride. The only consolation to being a sideman is, when it comes right down to it, you don't have to give a shit. "Then make a solo record. Play all the guitars yourself."

"Glen won't have it."

"Tell Glen to take a hike."

She turned back towards the bar, started to drink but stopped. She looked like a teenager, the curve of her neck and head, her upright posture on the chair. Beads and dreadlocks notwithstanding, she could've been at a soda fountain in 1955, nursing her drink, anxious for the attention of some boy. "I guess I was afraid he was right. Then you come along and prove him right."

Badge sighed. If this was what he got for making her songs better, fine. He sucked down his club soda. "I came here because I was asked to come. If you didn't want me, I wish you would've said something sooner." He set down his drink and left.

Badge emerged into a West Hollywood night that was just beginning to percolate. Traffic eased by, people safe behind glass. Three rockabilly types smoked cigarettes at the curb, one looking for something coming from the east.

"Hey," he heard from behind him.

Badge kept walking.

"Where are you going?" Betty said.

"Back to Albuquerque."

"What for?"

"You don't want me here."

"Who said that?"

Badge stopped, shook his head, started again.

"It's not like I said no."

"Maybe I'm saying no."

She hustled in front of him, stopped him in his tracks. "Why?"

"You want everything to come from you," Badge said, "but good music doesn't happen that way. It comes the other direction."

"You think I don't know that? You heard my songs."

"Your songs are good. They need to be better."

Betty scoffed, but Badge could tell he'd landed one, the way her eyes slanted, many steps from tears but on the same path. "I don't have to listen to this."

"That's right. You can get another guy in here in thirty seconds, and he'll jump every time you say so, but that's not how to make a good record."

"Oh, tell us, Great Badge from Albuquerque. How does one make a good record?"

"You really want to know?"

"Of course." She was being sarcastic, but he could tell she was curious. It was rare someone told you the truth in this town.

"For one, you need someone in your band who isn't going to take your shit."

"Oh, and that's you, I suppose."

"You're damn right it's me. Second, you need to get Les McKay back in the practice room."

"What?"

"Les McKay is the best you or I will ever do on this planet."

He expected her to snap back, but instead her forehead wrinkled. "Why do you think he's so good?"

"The guy played with Sam and Dave, Elton John, Joni Mitchell."

"That's funny," she said. "He only took this job because no one else would hire him."

"What?"

"Too old. He hasn't worked in months."

"No way."

"I don't think he'll come back anyway."

"Why not?"

She grinned. "I called him a crazy old jackal."

Badge shook his head.

"He has this weird smile when he plays." She demonstrated, her eyes big, her head bobbing, her teeth exposed.

Badge couldn't help but laugh. "You're kidding."

"No. And he chews gum all the time."

"What about the drummer?"

"Flip," Betty said. "He won't quit talking about his last band, the Gentlemen's Septet, a swing band that tours up the coast."

"Awesome." Badge loved playing with swing drummers, had recorded with one just a few months ago. They made everything more groovy, and no one ever argued with more groove. "Get them both back in the room, and we can start again tomorrow."

"Wait," she said. "I make the calls around here."

She was right. He needed to step back, leave the window open, give the bird a chance to fly away.

Betty stood there, her arms crossed, looking into the distance at a future she didn't know, couldn't control. She glanced away. "What if I don't like it?"

"Then you don't like it. You set the tapes on fire and send me home on the next plane."

By afternoon the next day, both Les and Flip were back in the practice room. Badge got there early for a quick word before Betty showed up.

"We were all fired yesterday," he said, "but Betty wants to give us another chance."

The pair stared at him. Flip sat on his throne, holding his sticks. Tattoos covered both of his arms, and his face was as evenly tan as a plastic doll's. Les, in a dishrag thin flannel shirt, leaned against his amp.

"If we want one," Badge said.

"I got no problem being fired," Les said. His voice was more Southern than Badge had expected, with a thinness that completely cut against the thick, muscular tone of every bass note on every recording he'd ever played. "I been fired by James Brown, okay? Cried for a week. Once you been fired by James Brown, nothing else matters. But if I stick it out, what's to keep her from doing it again?"

A forty-year veteran on bass; a seasoned, touring swing drummer; the four of them would simply sound too good to mess with. "If she fires anyone in this room, I'll leave right behind you."

"Why would she care?" Les said.

Why would she care? "She wouldn't, but I think once she hears us, there won't be any more talk of firing."

Les cleared his throat. Flip spun a drum stick.

"And if there is, I'll still leave right behind you."

"Will we get paid for yesterday?" Flip said.

Drummers. They can never see past the next paycheck. "Probably," Badge said. "Either way, with six weeks in the studio plus the road afterwards, there's potential to get paid for a long time."

"I'm in," Flip said and pulled his snare from its case.

"Great," Badge said. "Les?"

Les sighed, a pro baseball coach weary of a rookie's enthusiasm. He took a jumbo pack of gum from his shirt pocket, slid out a stick, unwrapped it, popped it into his mouth. "Okay, but if that girl gets nippy with me again I'll throw her over my knee. I can still be mean as a snake if I want to be."

Betty came through the storage room door with a bang. She carried her guitar case and held her cell phone to her ear. She sauntered right through the three jamming musicians and dropped her case—a little too hard—in front of her amp. She wore a pleated skirt that accented her curves and a black T-shirt with some strange design on the front. The band stopped playing. "That was months ago, Ryan," she said. "You know what? I really don't give a shit anymore." She saw the rest of them staring and rolled her eyes. "Listen, I gotta go. Three very old, very hairy guys are looking at me like I'm on the lunch menu ... No, I'm not fucking any of them." She wrinkled her forehead in a *Can you believe this guy?* way. "Well, that's not your problem anymore, is it ... Oka-ay ... Goodbye now ... No, we don't need to talk about it later." And she dropped the phone onto the couch.

"Everything all right?" Badge said.

Betty squatted, and with a few flicks of latches out came her Gretsch. "Rule number one." She untwisted her guitar strap. "No rock happens in this room without me."

"What do you mean?" Badge said.

"I mean don't play unless I'm here."

"Don't warm up?" Flip said.

"If that's what you were doing." Betty rustled up her cord, pushed it into her guitar.

"Doesn't sound like any way to run a band," Les said.

"It's not your choice," Betty said. She hit her amp's power switch.

"I'm not sure I like your tone," Les said.

"Nobody asked what you liked, Chewbacca."

"Man, you got a mouth on you."

"What part of 'I don't give a shit' don't you understand?"

"Wait," Badge said. "Betty, why wouldn't you want us to warm up?"

Betty looked down as she tuned her guitar. "Because I hear it when I'm coming up, and it puts me in the wrong mood."

"Why?"

She kept tuning.

Our age, our maleness, our experience, shared and otherwise. She's outnumbered, outnumbered in her own band. "Betty, you're the boss," Badge said.

"You're goddamn right I am."

"But you can't ask us not to get ready."

"Sounds like I just did."

"Fuck it," Les said, and he went to take off his bass.

"*Arrrww*," Betty groaned, Chewbacca-like.

"Listen," Badge said. "Everyone's getting their hair up before— Can we just play?"

They all got quiet. Amps buzzed into the room.

"I mean, that's what we're here for, right?"

Les crossed his arms, looked stoically into the distance.

"How about 'Yellowtail?'"

Betty wouldn't look up, bounced the toe of one combat-booted foot on the carpet.

Badge locked eyes with Flip, who picked up his sticks. "Hit it," he said.

Flip clicked *one, two, three, four,* and all of them came in on the tonic. Flip's drumming led the way. He played swing-style, the stick in his right hand bent back at nine o'clock, and something of a swing feel found its way into the groove. When Badge and Betty had played "Yellowtail" the night before, Badge imagined a more straight rhythm, but the hi-hat's lazy quarter notes nudged them forward in a way that felt good. It allowed the music to sway, the blown pipe that makes the snake dance.

Les's bass line came thick into Flip's rhythm, puffs of a hungry dragon. His notes acted as scout, moving the music from one change to the next, hinting at what was ahead. His tone shimmered at its very fringe with distortion, specks of color on rolling hills, adding brilliance.

And Betty's Gretsch and Marshall, God and the devil, one showing its neck, the other pitchfork-ready, waiting for its chance. They challenged each other right there in the scrapes of her fingers, the pick stabbing at the chords, the feedback coming with every lift of her hand. Her playing style, less studied than the rest, brought playfulness to the fore, a kid in a room full of adults, acting out the id for everyone. With just her playing, Betty already dominated the song, and she hadn't even sung a note.

After four revolutions, the rhythm making Badge's heart thump in a way that probably wasn't good for him, Betty eased up to the microphone, took in a breath, let it all out.

3

At the end of his first week of rehearsals, Badge called his son.

"Hey," Malcolm said.

"Hey, Bako," Badge said. It was a nickname he'd given Malcolm after they'd gone to a baseball game in Arizona. For some reason, Malcolm took to liking backup catcher Paul Bako, who warmed up relief pitchers in the bullpen. "Where's Bako?" "Is that Bako?" "When's Bako gonna play?" By the seventh inning Malcolm was up in the concession area playing with a group of kids, a crumpled soda cup used as a ball, claiming "I'm Bako" to anyone who would listen. It was years ago, but Badge couldn't ween himself off the nickname, even if Malcolm had moved on to worshipping Pudge Rodriguez.

"Are you rocking out with your cock out?" Malcolm said.

"Whoa," Badge said. "Where'd you hear that?"

"Around." Of course. All of these little nuggets came from "around." A ten-year-old never hears anything, and when he does, it's never said by anyone.

"Don't let your mother hear you."

"Duh."

"You taking it easy on her?" Holly had all of the Malcolm duties in Badge's absence, all the while putting in forty hours a week at the insurance agency. It was a job she'd taken as a kind of insurance against Badge missing any more support payments. He'd only missed two, and vowed never to be late again, but she kept the job anyway. He would be home the next weekend to take the kid off her hands. After that, the band would start pre-production, and he'd be dead to the world.

"Yeah," Malcolm said, which probably meant no.

"Well, make sure you do. Your mom doesn't need any more reason to be mad at me right now."

"Mm-m." Badge pictured him drifting away, probably staring at the TV in the living room. He hated not being there. Jet-setting to L.A., he'd made himself less substantial than even his own dad, who'd managed, despite the benders, to remain in his apartment on Adams Street throughout Badge's childhood.

"Is your mom there?"

"Yep," Malcolm said, and Badge heard thumping up stairs.

"Malcolm," Badge said. "Malcolm," he yelled.

"Hello, Badge," Holly said.

"Oh, hey."

"You want Malcolm back?"

"No. He always forgets to say goodbye. The instant I asked about you he's on to the next thing."

"Remind you of anyone?"

Badge sighed. It had been eight years, but it never quite went away. "You couldn't let that slide?"

Holly let out her own sigh, a rising and falling in the static that was distinctly hers, a little boat on the canal of the phone line, its cargo her resignation.

"How's he been?" he said.

"Fine." Badge heard kitchen sounds, a utensil set on the stovetop. He could see Holly standing next to the counter, the phone tucked under her long brown hair, stirring something in a pot. He'd quit imagining these scenes with anything like regret. If he still had regret, it had permanently hardened, a cookie that had been baked into a Christmas tree ornament.

"His new thing is missing the bus, so I either have to take him to school or, so he thinks, let him stay home."

"Malcolm," Badge moaned.

"He tried it twice last week."

"Put him back on."

"It's okay. I talked to him. He gets it. How's rock life treating you?"

"Good," he said. "I might get a couple of co-writes on the record. Betty's not keen on bridges, so I've been—"

"Betty's her name?"

"Yeah," Badge said. "She's just a kid, but the girl's not half bad."

"Are you mentoring her?"

"I wouldn't call it that."

"What would you call it?"

"I play in her band. She *pays* me. You'll notice the child support comes on time."

"Thanks for that. Malcolm's been clamoring for a Gameboy."

"You don't have to thank me."

"So, what's up with this Betty? Are you two going to the big game with Veronica and Jughead?"

"Wow," Badge said. "I didn't know you could still be jealous."

Something clanked on her end. "Shit. I just got sauce everywhere. I gotta go, Badge. Malcolm says bye."

The truth was Badge caught himself wanting to go to the big game with Betty. Or more to the point, Badge caught himself wanting to go to the bedroom of Betty with Betty.

She wasn't his type—too young, punk facade, lip-curl attitude—but her vitality, her rapid pulse, made Badge aware of her at all times, her proximity to him, the give and take of the air around them. Badge sometimes watched her too closely while she sang, feeling her song within him.

And Badge sensed the traffic flowed in both directions. Whenever they were alone together, Betty seemed to linger next to him, laughed at his jokes, glanced knowingly. That glance said, *I work on you, don't I.*

When Flip offered to take Badge to La Bodega, Badge jumped at the chance. There may have been other solutions to his problem, but he wasn't looking too hard for them.

The pair climbed into Flip's Previa, and Flip accelerated down Crenshaw, heading towards Venice. They drove past a pager store, a crowded Baskin-Robbins, a townhouse complex that needed painting. The CD player blared a live version of one of the Gentlemen Septet's swing classics, and Flip thumped out the beat on the steering wheel. During the first week of rehearsals, Flip's drumming had only gotten stronger, his cymbal crashes like lightning strikes followed by the rolling thunder of his snare work. The band was sounding ungodly good. Not even Betty complained. Badge motioned to the CD player. "So, what happened with you and these guys?"

Flip hit his palm against the steering wheel. Ashes from his cigarette fell onto his pants. "A while back, I may or may not have had a gambling problem."

"Really?"

"Got into trouble."

"What kind?"

"Creditors started showing up to gigs." Flip cranked the car left at an intersection, ignoring the red arrow. "After rehab, I tried to talk my way back in. Hook, the lead singer, wouldn't have it. He just said, 'We've moved on, man.'" Flip shook his head, put his cigarette in his mouth. "Good for him."

La Bodega, at the corner of 18th and Venice, looked like a UFO, a silver, saucer-like exterior with black trim. The Famous Dead had haunted this place back in the day. Browning, their singer, loved it. He used to sit at the bar all night, chin in hand, like a critic surveying an artist's work. His eyes—only his eyes— followed each girl as she strolled by. After great deliberation, he announced his choice to the bartender and disappeared with her into the famous La Bodega back rooms. He resurfaced a half hour later, a smile on his face and a story to tell. Badge was always jealous of the freedom Browning had at La Bodega. Now he had it too.

A "landing platform" entryway led from the parking lot to the main door.

"How long's it been since you been here?" Flip asked.

"Eight years."

"My first time was November. It's good for a little after-gig distraction. Know what I mean?"

"I know what you mean."

Flip crushed out his cigarette before they reached the door. "California law."

The crescent-shaped bar took up almost half the room, its two points protruding fang-like. Chairs and tables filled the dark spaces leading to the main stage, where a lady in white bent over for two ogling men. "Space Cowboy" by Steve Miller played. There were other stages and other women, but this girl caught Badge's eye, grabbed him with the force of a million little magnets.

The bartender, a tall woman in a purple nightie, pointed at Badge. "Do I know you?"

"I don't think so."

"I think I do. Did you play a cop on TV or something?"

Flip laughed.

"Sorry," Badge said. "Not me."

"Well, take it as a compliment. What can I get you boys?"

"Grey Goose," Flip said.

"Club soda," Badge said. "And I'd like to put in for the young lady on the main stage."

The woman's brow wrinkled. You would've thought Badge had asked for a stock tip, or a tire gauge, or her take on world religion. "What do you mean, 'put in?'"

"You know." Badge pointed up the hallway. "Put in for the back room."

The woman's smile evaporated. "This ain't that kinda place."

"Huh?"

"There are no back rooms."

"You sure?"

"Am I sure? You don't think I'd know?"

Badge glanced at Flip, whose eyes were as big and alive as a clown's. "Maybe times have changed."

"They do that."

"Just the club soda."

Flip let out a titter as the bartender walked away. "What the hell was that?"

"A mistake."

"It *has* been a long time since you been here."

"I thought that's what you were talking about."

"Sorry, just a strip club."

Badge shook his head. He lived in a new world, cleaner, more black-and-white, someone else's. The shades had gone up and the dark crevices were reserved for those who really needed them.

"By the way," Flip said, "if you want that, there are girls on Melrose."

"It's all right."

"It's been a while since I been there myself."

"It's all right. I just thought we were here for–"

"You sure did," Flip said, laughing. "That bartender looked ready to pop."

After three club sodas, overtipping for each one, Flip dropped Badge back at his hotel, but Badge didn't go to his room. In his room was the telephone, and Betty's number. He headed up Corvallis, away from the Strip. Blocks of homes, A-frames with short porches—surprisingly non-Hollywood-like—lined both sides of the street. Badge put his hands on his head, looked up at the obscure moon. *You know better.*

4

Pre-production, the process of nailing down songs in the rehearsal room before a band goes into the studio, had progressed to the point that no one had to think. Betty called out the numbers and the four played, their parts like racehorses past the initial jostling stage, settled into position. Les and Flip had locked tightly, their rhythms a guidebook that Betty and Badge could either rely on or ignore entirely. Betty's voice flourished over the foundation, brash and confident, like a black crow's. Badge toyed with as much as possible on guitar without committing to anything. He didn't want his parts over-ripe when they went to tape. There was still time to experiment, to leave the door open for magic to happen.

One day after rehearsal, Betty asked Badge to go for a ride with her.

"A ride?" Badge said.

"I've got a CD I want you to hear."

"I've probably heard it."

"Jesus, I'm not going to eat you. Let me give you a ride to your hotel."

She led him to her Dodge Dart, 1964, smoky grey paint job, red interior, no flaws in the body. It looked like she'd just washed it.

"Nice car," Badge said. He slid into the passenger's seat. It smelled of leather combined with a darker, more lived-in scent.

Betty plopped into the driver's seat, flipped down her sun visor, caught her keys as they fell to her lap. "It was my gift to myself when I got my advance. I always wanted one."

"You always wanted a Dodge Dart?"

"Sure, why not?"

"Where I'm from, girls only want Porsches or Jaguars or some other car they know their parents can't afford."

"This thing cost twelve-thousand."

"*Dollars?*"

"L.A. prices. You're not in Albuquerque anymore, Tito."

"Who?"

"Tito, the dog."

"You mean Toto."

Betty laughed.

"Unless you mean Tito Jackson."

"Actually, I meant Jermaine."

They cruised through traffic up Sunset, past the Safeway, the Blockbuster, the Rock and Roll Denny's. Motorists eased to anti-lock stops. Transients stood at corners, bearded and dirty. Palm trees added their bushy accents to the skyline. Instead of going in the direction of his hotel, Betty hooked right up Cahuenga, heading north.

"Where are we going?"

"You're being kidnapped. Relax."

They drove past the trees and tree-rooted cliffs of the Hollywood Hills. Badge watched gated driveways go by, formal, imposing. How long had it been since he'd entertained the idea of life on the other side of one of these gates? Probably not since the last time he was in L.A. If he had another shot at it, it would be because of this girl in the driver's seat, who, if he didn't know better, was taking him up to Mulholland to shag the starch out of him. Betty took out a CD.

"So, what are you playing me for my own good?"

"Patti Smith's *Horses*."

"Heard it," Badge said. Of course he'd heard it.

Betty slid the CD into the player. "I wanted to play this one song for you, to see if you could try something like it on 'Breakfall.'"

The intro to "Redondo Beach" came through the speakers, tapping hi-hat, bouncy piano lick, chicken scratches on guitar. It was Badge's favorite song on the album, but he'd never been crazy about *Horses* as a whole. Why Smith had gotten all the attention and Television, his favorite band as a teenager, had never caught on was a tragedy for the ages. It must've been timing, and politics, and all the heroin Television had done. "That's what you want?" Badge said, meaning the guitar.

"You know the way 'Breakfall' kind of has that reggae feel?"

"Yeah." It was quieter than the stuff he'd been playing, but she was the boss. "I grew up listening to Television. Have you ever heard of them?"

Betty shook her head. "Never liked the singer."

"Tom Verlaine? Patti Smith loved him."

"No way."

"She used to hang out at their shows hoping he'd notice her."

"Good lord."

"He's one of the most influential singers in punk history. The Sex Pistols, the Ramones, they all loved Verlaine."

"And you?"

Badge smiled. "I preferred their other guitar player Richard Lloyd. He always complimented the song, didn't have to be the star."

They cruised along winding Mulholland. Betty's legs eased against each other as she worked the pedals.

"Okay," he said, clapping his hands. "Chicken scratches on 'Breakfall.' Anything else?"

Betty looked hurt. Badge wondered if her charms had ever failed her. "Tell me about Albuquerque."

"What do you want to know?"

"What's it like?"

"It's like living on an island, except instead of ocean you're surrounded by desert."

"What else?"

"I read somewhere it's the place you're most likely to see kids riding in cars without car seats."

Betty laughed.

"It doesn't change much. The state's unofficial motto is, 'It might be new, but it's still Mexico.'"

"Then why do you stay?"

"Malcolm's there. My home is where Malcolm is."

Betty seemed to hesitate, her legs stiffening. "You love your kid."

"He's ten—kind of at that age—but I'm learning every age is kind of at that age."

"When I first moved here," Betty said, "I used to park on Mulholland and just watch the city go by. I was so happy to be out of Orange County."

"You still happy?"

She glanced at him, her green eyes conspiratorial. "Promise not to laugh?"

"Sure."

"Or call me spoiled?"

"I promise."

Her lips slid against each other. "This is turning out to be a lot tougher than I thought. It seemed like, back when I was fourteen or whatever, the music world was a lot different. Now it's all these *people*, with all these *opinions*, trying to steer me this way or that. It's not what I wanted at all."

"No one said it was a cakewalk."

"I'm not out to make a million bucks. I swear to God I'm

not. I just want to realize this thing that's inside of me." Her brow arched, her eyes widened and sloped, a smitten woman, if only with herself. "I want to get it out of me, you know? I want to see if it's as beautiful as it feels."

"There's nothing wrong with that."

"But I can't do it by myself. I need someone to help me, someone I trust."

Badge looked at her, but Betty, perhaps afraid her offer was too unveiled, didn't look back.

"Listen," he said. "Being some kind of partner with you would probably be the best thing that could happen to me, but I'm not sure it's what you need."

"I'll pay you double what you're making now."

"That's not it."

"Then what?"

"For one thing, I'd have to be in L.A., and my kid's in Albuquerque. I'd be bagging out on you all the time, and you'd be pissed."

Betty's mouth got small, and a layer of tears, smooth and thin as lacquer, emerged over her eyes. "Forget it," she said.

"Of course I'll help you when I can."

"The offer's rescinded. You had your chance."

"I want to say yes, but it would help if you understood a few things."

Betty steered around a curve, said nothing.

Badge adjusted himself in his seat. This might be the last time she had to listen to him. "First, you gotta give the business side some leeway. Glen, the label, you can't hate them so openly."

"Hey, *I'm* the one who has to—"

Badge held up his hand. "See? That's where you need to stop going. When you feel that come on, just hear people out. It won't kill you."

Betty exhaled through her nose, seemingly doing her best to hear him out.

"But just because you're civil, that doesn't mean a thing when it comes to your art. Your job is to realize yourself through music. When it comes to that, we listen to the business side, then do what we want."

Betty half-smiled, watched the road.

"That's it," Badge said. "That's the key to making this work. You make the music, they do the business. If you can handle that, I'll help you in any way I can."

Betty's jawline tightened, like something sweet had just hit the back of her tongue.

"What?"

She leered at him, then back at the road. "You kind of look like Kurt Russell when you get all serious like that."

"And stop it with that stuff."

"What stuff?"

"You know what stuff."

Betty grinned. "You should be flattered."

"I am, but we're in a band together, so stop pulling my chimes."

"Is it working that well?"

Badge watched L.A. drift by below them. It looked smoggy, as it always did, but he remembered there were better and worse days for the smog. You could feel the difference in your lungs. "No comment."

"Wow, you don't let on at all."

Badge said nothing.

"Then I guess the last thing you'd want is for me to pull over here and–" She started to slow down.

"Knock it off, Betty."

"Okay. Jesus, you're uptight."

5

Darcy, their producer, sat in the papasan chair in the rehearsal room and listened while the band played "Emboldened." His blond mop showed the hints of age that weren't so much a change in color as a general lack of luster. A smile crept across his face, as slowly as if it had grown there. "That works."

"We chopped the intro," Badge said, "and changed the chords in the bridge."

"*Who* changed the chords in the bridge?" Betty said.

Darcy laughed a little. "Whoever did it, they did right. I'm trying to figure out how I'm going to take any credit for it."

Eight years ago, around the time he gave up drinking, Badge changed his approach to guitar playing. He quit scouring his instrument for the most potent four-note hook he could find, the kind that could decapitate with its sharpness. Now he liked to meander through a song as long as possible, feeling out ideas, turning over every rock, like a scuba diver searching the ocean floor. The right parts were out there. He'd get to them eventually.

But once he found them, his licks and solos planned to the last note, he was finished, and he'd play the song exactly the same way every time. It was a process that better suited his sober life, a change from out of control to in control, from seat of the pants to driver's seat. Once they got into the studio, Darcy would have none of it.

"That's the way you played it last time," he said after the second pass through "Revolt." Darcy stood behind the thick-paned glass of the control room, staring at Badge, his body bent over to push the talk button. Badge, Les and Flip were set up in separate corners in the gymnasium-sized main room, with Betty in an isolation booth, guitar over her shoulder, headphones on.

"What?" Badge yelled. He had no microphone.

"You're going to play it that way every time?" Darcy said. "That's the solo."

"Is that the way Richard Lloyd does it?" Betty chimed in.

So Badge let 'er rip, and it was fun. It reminded him of his early days, a deadly axe-slinger trying to play his way out of Albuquerque, his licks shining brighter than the chrome accents of his Stratocaster. It was un-distilled recklessness, the kind you tried to harness while tape rolled and hopefully could get away from afterwards. Once Darcy hit record, Badge lost himself in his takes, even forgot which song he was playing. He stopped only when the music disappeared from his headphones.

All of these free-flowing chemicals—the music, the energy—kindled passions in all of them. Badge couldn't help but notice something simmering between Darcy and Betty. It wasn't overt—the way they agreed on tones, lingered together in the control room, the timbre of Betty's laugh when Darcy cracked a joke—but it was there, like an individual bee hinting at a swarm coming over the horizon.

And despite having no right to it, Badge felt jealous. He and Betty were nothing to each other ... but then again they were more than that. She asked his opinions, told him—or tried to tell him—how to play. They made music together. What could be more intimate?

The tension was exactly what the album needed. The struggle between voice and guitar—for attention, for respect—seeped onto every track. At times it was a game of one-upsmanship, Betty's vocals pushed forward by what Badge played, forcing her to new heights. At other times it was more complimentary, Betty's subtle changes evoking Badge's responses in kind. Even the rhythm section picked up on it. Les played with an aggressiveness that surpassed anything he'd done in the practice room, and Flip pounded his snare, keeping them all just ahead of the beat. Badge had the feeling every take would either blast them off into the stratosphere or explode them into a million pieces. He couldn't quit smiling when, at the beginning of each day, Darcy played him the tracks from the night before.

"Amazing," Badge said.

Darcy smiled, cat-like.

And that was all before "Calypso."

Late one night, while Darcy changed tape, the three sidemen corralled at Flip's drums.

"It all comes down to the ass," Les said. Betty was cloistered in her isolation booth, noodling her guitar. "I've backed up every female artist in the book, and you'd be surprised how often their success corresponds to how shapely they look from behind."

"The ass does speak volumes," Flip said.

"Take Madonna," Les said. They all still had their headphones on, except Flip, who'd wrapped his around his knee. "Talented woman, good singer, nothing to write home about. But get a look at her rear and you start to sense what's ahead for her. I played six months with the Material Girl, watched her shake it night in and night out. That was when I knew, this one's going somewhere."

"What about Aretha Franklin?" Flip said.

Les looked confused. "What about her?"

"Very successful lady. Very large—"

"I'm not talking R&B," Les said. "You're talking a whole different criteria."

"So, it's a pop thing," Badge said.

"Exactly," Les said.

"What about Alanis Morrisette?" Flip said.

That made all three of them pause. Les ran his fingers down his beard, a philosopher pondering the meaning of life. "I don't know if I have a strong sense of her ass."

"I don't either," Flip said.

"All those records sold," Les said, "it must be good."

That was when Badge heard through his headphones the song Betty was playing. He thought he recognized it from somewhere but couldn't place it. The hummed melody, dark and ominous, raised goosebumps. He went to her booth, opened the door. "What's that?"

"This thing I'm working on."

"Play it again," he said. Again, the recognition. He sensed he knew it from somewhere deep, elusive. He had a strange feeling it had come from inside of him, a gem Betty had mined from his soul and was displaying in the world for the first time.

"Go to D there," he said.

She tried it.

Badge turned up the volume on his Strat, played a lick over the top, a simple arpeggio that was poignant without being overwhelming. Betty stepped to the microphone.

> And if I never seem to go with the flow
> It's all I know
> Calypso
>
> And if you're pulling everything from the past
> You're always last to know
> Calypso

The words came light and breathy into Badge's headphones. He added a soft, spacious lick in a minor key, leaving plenty of room for the words to happen. Betty hummed her way through the verse, and the melody sucked him in, warm, addictive. She had no words for the verse yet, but he knew what she was after, what she would eventually get out of it. Les joined in with an eighth-note pump, and Flip followed, propelling the rhythm forward with extra pounds of his floor tom. Thirty-eight years old or not, if Badge heard this song on the radio he would've stopped whatever he was doing, driven to the record store and bought the CD. Betty sang the chorus again.

> And if I never seem to go with the flow
> It's all I know
> Calypso
>
> And if you're pulling everything from the past
> You're always last to know
> Calypso

The foursome rode out the verse chords, letting the progression build to a fine crescendo. A song was born, their best yet. Hell, it was *the* song, the reason Badge was in L.A., maybe the reason he'd learned guitar in the first place. Even back when he'd talked a good game about being done with music, he'd never given up searching for this territory where no one had ever been but everyone immediately recognized. He was right not to give up on it. Here it was.

After they finished, Badge shot a look into the control room. "Darcy, did you get that?"

While Les overdubbed bass lines, Betty dragged Badge to a beauty salon on Wilshire.

"I want you to cut your hair," she said.

"What's wrong with my hair?"

"You look like you've been playing Beatles songs in your bedroom."

"I *have* been playing Beatles songs in my bedroom."

"You're not exploiting your plus features. You've got great bone structure. A snip here, a clip there, and you could look like Nick Drake."

"The dead guy."

"If we're touring together, you need to get with the twenty-first century."

Marzipan, a beauty salon off Wilshire, could've been pulled from a fifties copy of *The Saturday Evening Post*. Red patent-leather barber chairs dotted the room, and an arch of round bulbs outlined each mirror. The floor was tiled with red and white squares, checkerboard-like, and the place smelled of hair dye. Badge remembered the smell from his mom. She'd sat on the edge of the bathtub, worked the dye through her bangs with a little plastic comb. "What do you do that for?" he'd asked. "Because I can't get old yet." "You're not old." "Aren't you the charmer."

From around the corner came the only midget hairstylist Badge had ever seen.

She strode into the room, all three or so feet of her, a blond bouffant wig on her head. She wore a red, knee-length dress that featured a floral design, and her smile was punched up with lipstick. Her manner suggested grace and poise. Badge would've guessed she'd been an actress, maybe starring in a little-people version of *Hairspray*. "Say, Bette," she said.

"Rosalie," Betty said, and the women embraced.

"Girl," Rosalie said. Her voice, thin as tissue paper, was nonetheless heavy with a New Orleans accent. She looked Badge up and down. "He's as good lookin' as you say he is."

"Isn't he?" Betty said.

The two women eyed him spookily.

"Not good enough apparently," Badge said.

"Oh, we can always use a little more," the stylist said. "I'm Rosalie." She took Badge's hand with nothing but her fingertips.

"Give him the works," Betty said, flopping onto a divan.

Rosalie motioned Badge to a chair, which he now noticed had a stepped, U-shaped apparatus that would serve as her boost. "Hop on up. I won't bite."

Badge sat as Rosalie mounted behind him. Her fingers worked through his hair, like a child's but more nimble, business-like. "So, what kind of haircut do you see in my future?"

"I could tell you, but just trust me. You're gonna leave here happy."

When she finished, Badge couldn't help but like it.

The new style retained his length—Jeff Beck had modeled the same cut for years—but Badge's had a swoop, everything breaking in one direction. He inspected himself in the mirror. "Not bad," he said.

"I think he likes it," Betty said.

"I might."

"Don't worry, hon," Rosalie said. She whipped the drop cloth off him, sending locks to the floor. "If you liked it too much, *we* wouldn't like *you*."

The record tracked, nothing left to do but listen to the mixes as they came down the pipe, Les drove the four of them to Silver Lake.

"My favorite place," Les said. "Little bar called Sweet Release. Got drunk with Muddy Waters there a long time ago. I held his coat while he threw up."

They walked into a crowded room, boxy, with a thin hallway leading back. People cavorted in groups, the noise of conversation loud enough to drown out the music. A wide-screen TV, taking up all of one wall, soundlessly played a metal video. The crampedness of the place was magnified by a pool table, which took up at least half the room. People had to shift to accommodate players angling shots.

"I'm glad we got here before it got crowded," Les said.

"This isn't crowded?" Badge said.

Les shook his head. "Karaoke hasn't even started."

An Asian girl, as lanky and beautiful as a heron, approached them. "What are we having tonight, swine?"

"Hey, Phong Lee," Les said. "Me and the gang are lookin' to get lit. Flaming shots all around."

"Minus one," Badge said. "Club soda."

Out of nowhere, Badge felt a rough push on his ass, scarily close to his rectum. "Two drink minimum," someone said.

He turned to see an Asian woman, seventy years old at least, with white, geisha-style makeup and red lipstick. "You drink two drinks, or I fuck you up the ass."

Everyone laughed.

"Okay," Badge said. "A club soda."

The lady looked askance at him, like he might try to pay with pesos or chickens or a song and dance number. "You drink *two* club soda."

"Let's start with one."

"Eight-dollar club soda."

"Eight dollars?"

"*Eight-dollar club soda!*"

Badge shrugged, reached for his wallet, handed her a ten. "Keep the change."

"Damn right, keep the change." And she walked off.

"Wow," Les said. "I haven't seen her take to someone like that in a long time."

"I think she likes you," Betty said.

"I'm flattered," Badge said.

"You should be," Les said.

The waitress returned with a tray of drinks. Flames hovered

like little ghosts above the shot glasses, and Badge's club soda sat in the middle, a child's drink mixed in with grown-up ones. For the first time in he didn't know how long, he wanted a drink.

"Here's to Betty," Les said. He hoisted his shot into the air. "Little lady, I've played with everyone, and I ain't never, ever felt as good about a project as I do about this one."

"Hear, hear," Badge said.

"And thank you for not firing us," Flip said.

"You guys are the best," Betty said. They all clinked glasses. "How am I supposed to drink this?"

"Easy," Les said. "Blow." He puckered his lips like he might to kiss a grandchild and blew out the flame. "And slam." With a quick backward flick the shot went down.

Flip did the same, grimacing like a pipefitter when the booze hit his mouth.

Betty looked at Les, Flip. Then with a puff she blew out the flame and threw the drink down. They all watched her wrestle with the booze, using the power of her squint to give it a final push. "Oh yeah," she said.

"You like?" Les said.

"I need another. Phong Lee, set us up over here."

"You sure you're ready?"

"The record's done," she said. "We're getting hammered."

When the madame rolled out the karaoke machine, Badge took it as his chance to duck out.

"Nooo," Betty said. She grabbed him by the collar, pulled him close. "You have to watch me sing 'Like a Virgin.'" After her third shot, she'd claimed to anyone who would listen that she had first dibs on the karaoke machine.

"Not tonight," Badge said.

"What do I have to do?" And to Badge's surprise, she kissed him, seductively, on the mouth. He tasted the booze on her, as if the two were spies and the booze was a message she had to pass him without anyone else seeing. He got the message.

"Get a room," Flip said.

Betty broke away, wiped her lips, looked embarrassed.

Badge grabbed her by both forearms. "I gotta go."

Betty turned in a huff. "Phong Lee," she yelled.

"Leaving now might be a good idea," Les said. "Of course that doesn't mean I'm gonna do it."

Badge walked into the Los Angeles night. The atmosphere of the club, the flames above the drinks, the taste of booze on her lips, he wanted it all, which meant he had to leave.

6
Spring 1992

Badge lost Part I of his adult life to Reina's hips.

The arch of Reina's back, with all the subtle contour of a Stratocaster body, never would've brought him so low all by itself. The gap between her thighs, two curves forming something sleek and frank between, made him do a double take, but they never could've broken him on their own. Her lips, which always looked ready to taste something wet and sweet and tropical, kept his mind aware of the myriad possibilities, but alone they never would've allowed him to bridge the chasm he'd dug between himself and any woman not Holly, not his wife.

Reina's hips, however, that subtle, swinging foot or so of flesh and blood and bone, set off an alarm in Badge no amount of booze could temper, each sway another tick of the pendulum bringing him closer to his own sweet oblivion.

Montrose, twenty years her senior, introduced Reina to the Famous Dead backstage after their first L.A. showcase. "Boys," he said. Montrose always looked the businessman—white sport shirt, pressed pants, bright teeth—even though his business was rock. "Not only is this woman my wife, she's also the best scout at the label. Meet Reina."

Reina glided over, parting them like a boat through reeds. She had straight long black hair and bangs that framed her cherub face, and her black dress accented a figure that would've forced any model in the room to restrain her sneer. On first glance, Badge was already sick with her, Reina's presence an elixir both intoxicating and toxic. The band was stunned silent.

"Yes," Montrose said. "She's that hot."

Everyone laughed but Badge.

"So," Reina said, her eyes sliding this way and that. "Are you boys gonna quit screwing around and sign with Municipal or what?"

"There are a couple of other opportunities we'd like to fully explore–" Glen started. Glen, their freshly-minted and slightly soused manager, had stood just offstage during their set, a smile on his face, reveling in his latest find.

Reina raised one graceful hand. "I have a sense for these things, and my sense is always right."

"You guys familiar with Boycott?" Montrose asked.

They nodded. Boycott, a political hard rock band from the East Coast, had spent all of the previous summer on MTV, not to mention on the covers of any music magazine you could name.

Montrose nodded in Reina's direction. *That was her.*

Reina scanned all of them, like she looked for something in their eyes. She stopped on Badge. "Boys," she said. "Let's have a drink."

When he got back to Albuquerque, a few minutes past midnight on a Monday morning, Badge found Holly in the dining room changing Malcolm. They lived in a house in a new subdivision just off I-40. The area had once been cotton fields and now was filled with rows and rows of tract homes. They'd bought the house with every penny they could scavenge after the wedding, plus a little extra from Holly's parents for the down payment. Badge thought it was too much, but they were both high on their future at the time. The realtor kept telling them that stretching their finances would make sure they didn't sell themselves short.

Malcolm squirmed on the dining room table, his two-year-old body trying to escape Holly's powdering. It was hot for a spring night. A box fan, wedged in the window, spun on a low setting, but Badge couldn't feel the breeze. Holly's belief was that a fan put backwards in a window "sucked the hot air out." He had almost a decade on her, but his experience didn't seem to matter. Taking care of the home and baby while he played rock star, her opinions somehow trumped his.

"How'd it go?" Holly said, not taking her eyes off Malcolm. She wore the long blue T-shirt she slept in, and her hair was tied back into an impromptu bun.

"No deal yet." Badge was hung over, wanted sleep. Holly used to party as much as Badge, but she hadn't picked the booze card back up after having Malcolm. Badge suspected she'd dropped it on purpose, to make him feel guilty for using it as his wild card.

"Why not?"

"Glen wants to get some other labels interested."

Holly sighed, grabbed a diaper from a giant box.

"What's that about?" he said.

"What?"

Badge mimicked her sigh.

"I don't know why you don't tell Glen to get on with it." This sounded like her dad, who'd never liked Badge, his silver eyebrows going crooked every time the two shook hands.

"Because it doesn't work like that."

"He's your employee. It works exactly like that."

Badge set his guitar case on the floor. He hated feeling like the Famous Dead was something she had to patronize him in, like she had all the answers and was simply waiting for him to catch up. "Holly," he said. "This is who I am. I play guitar in a band, we play gigs, I'm in and out of town. Are you okay with that?"

She squinted at him. She needed glasses, but she was probably forgoing them because they couldn't afford them. "And I'm the mother of your kid, who needs food. Are you okay with that?"

"I can't tell Glen to hurry up with the deal because we need cash."

"Well, maybe you could take a few shifts at the canning plant."

It was exactly what he didn't want to hear. That place had killed his dad. It would kill him too if he let it. "It's that bad?"

Holly lifted both of Malcolm's legs, scooted a diaper underneath. "I don't know where the mortgage is coming from next month."

Badge shook his head. They'd been married in a rushed ceremony two summers prior. Holly was pregnant. It seemed the best option. "I'm going to bed."

"We have to deal with this."

What does my beauty get me? What does all this power bring as an endgame? Those seemed to be the questions Reina asked herself as she glided through life. Badge came to think of her existence as one long perusal of a dessert bar, dragging her finger along the glass case, deciding what she would devour. Being married to Montrose didn't seem to matter. If at any point during their affair Badge had confronted her about it, Reina would've said, "Why should it?"

Badge knew which dessert he wanted.

A few weeks later, while the Famous Dead toured the West Coast for the first time, a short swing funded by Glen to make the band "look hungry," Montrose and Reina met them in San Francisco. The couple was in town for Reina's twenty-fifth birthday, out deep-sea fishing on a yacht, and they made a point to stop by the club to see their "number one priority."

"I can't wait to get you guys in the studio," Montrose said. His face, pink from too much sun, radiated bliss, like a CEO remembering his best round of golf ever. "I know a producer who's going to die when he hears you."

"We like you too," Badge said. "If it were up to us we'd sign now, but Glen wants to—"

Montrose shook his head. "You're right to explore your options. That way, when you sign with us, you'll know how good you got it."

It was a cool San Francisco night, the Famous Dead's fourth and last show of the tour. Badge had submerged himself in vodka all week, away from Holly, needing the booze to completely put her out of his mind. He was tuning his guitar in the back of the bus when Reina popped in. Her eyes looked glassy, pinched slightly towards closing, and she held a plastic cup. When she saw him, a bemused smile eased across her face, the product of too much alcohol. Badge knew the expression well; he saw it every time he looked in a mirror. The rest of the band and Montrose were in the venue. Cliff, their drummer, soundchecked. You could hear the thuds of the kick drum through the walls.

Badge sat back on the couch. "Reina," he said.

"Badge," Reina answered. She wore black leather pants that sat low on her waist, and her white top looked made for a pirate, only lighter, more billowy. She set her drink down, strolled right up to him, her knees inter-weaved with his. "Do you know what I want for my birthday?"

Badge leaned back, a tightrope walker straddling an invisible line, careful not to slip one way or the other.

She bent over, leaned into his ear. "I want you to see me naked."

He set his guitar aside. Her pelvic bone protruded just above the waistline of her pants, and Badge kissed it, tasting sea water. Reina's breath grew deeper, and her fingers meandered through his hair. Badge pulled her closer, unzipped her pants, took her in.

That first kiss of her pelvis, the feel of his lips tasting her, was almost worth everything that came after, all the pain they would cause. In its own way, it *was* pain, a desperate groping for the top of the mountain, if only to find the sky unattainable. Her pants slid off, and they moved quickly, furtively. By the time the rest came looking, she was dressed and hidden in his bunk.

A month later, Glen somehow got them on the bill of the Cinco de Mayo Festival in El Paso, and the band dropped everything to play it. Reina arrived in town unannounced, called Badge in his hotel room.

"Hey, lover boy," she said.

"Holly," Badge said, checking to see if Cliff looked up from the television.

"Someone right there?"

"Yeah."

"I'm at a pay phone across the street. Want some lunch?"

They met at the diner next to the hotel, formica countertops, red swivel chairs. The pair took a booth, ordered coffee. Reina was all smiles. It was like she could only see her presence as a gift, one that offered no complications. "How's life?" she asked.

"Same as yours, I bet." Badge tilted his vodka flask into his coffee cup. He was on his second refill of the day. Glen had been razzing him by phone.

How much are you drinking?

Why?

People talk, Badge. They talk to me.

Yeah? What do they say?

They say you're acting like a guitar player.

Cliff.

Do me a favor. Don't go from being one in a million to one in ten. Can you do that for me?

"How's Holly?" Reina asked.

Badge took a tug of his coffee, looked out the window. Cars drove by, their drivers on their way to the places where lives happened, where they didn't have to hide. "Distracted," Badge said. "How's Montrose?"

"Don't worry about Monty."

"As simple as that," Badge said. "'Don't worry about Monty.' What's taking so long with the contract?"

"Contracts take time. Lawyers, managers, they all have to have their say. Monty loves you guys."

"Not if he finds out you're here."

Reina touched Badge's hand. Something shined in her cheeks like very small flecks of wayward paint. "If it's worth doing, it's worth getting caught at."

The Marriott was booked solid, so they wound up in the fire escape stairwell, on the side of the hotel no one seemed to use. They went all the way to the top, ten floors up, where they were least likely to be happened upon. Reina came prepared—miniskirt, no underwear. They had trouble finding a way until Reina grabbed the railing with both hands. When Badge slid into her, she must've been able to see right down the stairwell, all the way to the bottom. They'd barely started when Montrose came through the fire escape door.

Montrose always looked in control, but he looked strangely so then, framed by the open door, his eyes un-startled. He held a pack of cigarettes, and he slid one out, leaned against the door jamb, lit it. It was as if, instead of catching his wife having sex with another man, he'd walked in on them studying for exams or doing their taxes or talking real estate.

Badge pulled away from Reina, started dressing.

"Don't bother," Montrose said. He exhaled smoke. "It's too late. I've already got what I need." He reached into his shirt pocket, revealed a small camera.

Reina adjusted her clothes. "What the fuck are you doing here?"

"What am *I* doing here," Montrose said. He laughed, hard, like he might at a college buddy's sick joke. "That's great. And you? Did you get lost on the way to your parents'? By the way, I didn't know Bob and June lived in El Paso."

"I'm not going to dignify that."

"You might want to put on underwear before using a word like dignify." Montrose sucked his cigarette, exhaled. He seemed to be taking pleasure in keeping them there, suspended in their guilt, a detective savoring a smoking-gun moment. "There will be some papers waiting for you when you get home. I suggest you sign them before you get out."

"I'm not going anywhere."

"Yes, you are," Montrose said. He dropped the cigarette on the floor, mashed it with his toe. "Badge, watch your step on the way down. It's a long way."

"I'm sorry," Badge said.

For the first time, signs of hatred crossed Montrose's brow. His face stiffened, and as he spoke his teeth looked ready to gnarl. "What are you sorry for? You think you're the first? Claris of Boycott's been fucking her for over a year. Did she tell you that?"

Badge shifted his weight. He was bleary from booze, from sex. Every possible response seemed hollow, like a gourd that had been dried out, seeds rattling inside. "I'm sorry for everything."

Montrose's demeanor cracked, and his eyes wavered ever-so-briefly toward tears. Then he shook his head, turned away. "I called Holly, told her of our mutual problem."

"You what?"

"I called your wife. Your world is shit too, my friend."

7

The record in the can and their tour a couple of months away, Badge flew home. The last time he'd been back to Albuquerque, weeks ago, Holly had let him have Malcolm for the night. Father and son watched a basketball game, listened to rough takes from the album.

"That's the singer?" Malcolm said, hearing Betty's voice for the first time.

"That's Betty," Badge said.

Malcolm wrinkled his nose. "Sounds like Mom."

Badge couldn't help but smile. Something in Betty's voice did, vaguely, after Malcolm pointed it out, remind him of Holly. Two gale force winds not afraid to blow, one predictable as the jet stream, the other chaotic as a hurricane.

On his first night home, Badge didn't hope to get Malcolm for the night. He'd bum-rush Holly if he showed up at her door asking for the kid. He went to his apartment first, emptied his mailbox, got some laundry going, before making the call.

"Hey," he said when Holly picked up the phone. "How you doing?"

"Fine," she said. "Are you home?"

"Yep. Record's done, and I don't have to leave again until June. I don't suppose you'd let a wayward father have his son for a while."

"I would, but he's at baseball camp."

"What?"

"He told you on the phone."

Badge smacked his forehead. The week in Santa Fe, unlimited time in the batting cages, Wally Joyner stopping by to show the kids how to field.

"Doesn't get home until tomorrow night," Holly said, "but if you've got nothing to do, I'm making lasagna."

He had to shower first, wash the styling gel out of his hair, change out of the leather jacket Betty had bought him. He didn't want Holly to see him all gussied up. To his ex-wife, Badge was a no-nonsense musician in a T-shirt and jeans. After all his years bitching about it, he'd have to eat his words to walk into her place looking like Tom Cruise.

Badge had been invited to dinner before by Holly, but never when Malcolm wasn't there. He couldn't help but feel some line was being crossed, some change revealing itself to him for the first time.

When Holly answered the door, she looked pleasantly surprised to see him. She wore a blouse and a pair of beige shorts, and her hair seemed at the end of a long day of being styled, giving way here and there. The years had done nothing to tarnish the pretty girl Badge had first seen at the Pixie, spinning as the Famous Dead played.

That first night Badge couldn't help but think of her as a church, one of those tall, skinny ones he imagined peppered throughout the Northeast. That was how he noticed her on the dance floor, taller if younger than the rest, in a skirt and bleached jean jacket. He saw his chance when Holly and her friend Megan struggled to work the cigarette machine. At the end of the night the three of them—with Browning making a fourth—wound up at Megan's apartment.

On the living room couch, Holly showed Badge her fake I.D.

"I bought it from these guys in a dorm room. You have to sit in front of this board, which has all your information on it. Then they take a picture, and that's your I.D. It's not hard to tell. There's my shadow."

Badge looked. In the picture, her head—a different, more sober Holly—shaded into the wrong part of the I.D. He loved having this beautiful-if-somewhat-awkward girl next to him, her legs as convivial as her manner shy. "Ever get caught?"

"The guy at the door barely looks."

"I don't doubt it."

"Why?"

"It's not every day a club can have a girl like you on the dance floor."

Holly scoped the room, seemingly avoiding the compliment, the tone of it speaking too directly to what had brought them there, what they wanted. "I was a pole vaulter in high school."

"Really."

"Finished fourth in State junior year."

"What happened senior year?"

"Missed the pit twice. Almost broke my ankle."

"Ouch."

"I've got trophies."

"Do you still?"

"Have trophies?"

"No, pole vault."

Her brow wrinkled. "Why would I still?"

"Drive toward excellence, college scholarship."

"It was just something I did for fun."

Badge moved to kiss her and she backed away, a lighter-than-air rise and fall from the couch.

"How many times have you done this?" she said.

"Done what?"

"Brought a girl— You know what."

Badge sat back. He'd actually had a fairly chilly year with the ladies. One of Megan's cats paraded through the room, jumped onto the TV. "I don't count."

"Twice?" Holly said.

"I don't know."

"Twenty? Thirty?"

"Less than thirty."

"That's reassuring."

"Listen," Badge said. "I'm very glad to be here with you tonight."

"Did that line work on number twenty-nine?"

"I had to get on my knees and beg for number twenty-nine."

She caught a giggle. "Well, I'd be a fool to settle for less."

Taking her cue, Badge hopped to his feet, got down on one knee, looked up at her, took her hand, and knew it wouldn't be the last time he'd be on one knee in front of her.

"Come in," Holly said.

The house smelled of lasagna. She'd been working at it all day, he knew, her sojourns into lasagna-making as involved as a Shuttle mission. Still, the kitchen was immaculate, all the dishes put away, plates set on the table. A bottle of wine—its contents half-gone—sat on the counter. Badge put his jean jacket over the back of a chair, the same chair he'd used when he lived here. "No work today?"

"Herb wanted to go to Mexico." Herb, Holly's boss, was famous for sliding off at the drop of a hat, leaving the rest of the office to do as they wanted. It seemed she hardly ever *had* to be at work. She kept waiting for the day it would come tumbling down on them but it never did.

"So, how's Malcolm?" Badge said. "Does he know he still has a dad?"

"You know him," Holly said. She pulled a spatula from the drawer, eased it into the lasagna, releasing steam. "He's too busy to notice. I sometimes wonder if we're raising some kind of genius. He gets so locked into what he does. Reminds me of you that way."

Badge remembered when he first got his Stratocaster, with money he'd made one summer clearing a dried river bed. Once he learned the main lick of Jimi Hendrix's "Foxy Lady," there was no stopping him. You couldn't get his attention for the next decade or two, until Holly came along. "Maybe we should buy him a guitar."

"No way." Holly grabbed the plates off the table. "One of you is enough." She crouched to scoop the lasagna, like she might to pick up a baby bird. He loved watching her, the smell in the air. He'd been given many gifts by women this past month. He had to remember it wasn't a one-way street.

"Can I help with something?" he said.

"Don't sweat it."

Badge grabbed the salad bowl and with a clumsy grappling of tongs doled out salad for each of them. Holly stopped in transit, letting him finish.

The food looked great, especially after all the pizza he'd eaten in L.A., not tasting it, too focused on the music to care. "With no kid around I wouldn't expect you to cook."

"Malcolm wants fast food most of the time. This is for me."

"And for me, apparently." Badge took a forkful of lasagna, found it too hot, went to work on the salad.

"So, how's it going in L.A.?" she said.

"Good. The record'll be out in June."

"Are you and Betty sleeping together?"

She'd developed a directness since their divorce—cut to the chase, don't waste my time—but this went beyond anything he'd ever heard from her. He wondered how much she'd drunk. "Why do you ask?"

"I don't know." She picked at her salad. "I opened that door tonight and thought, 'Now there's a guy who's getting some.'"

"Well, it's no one's business."

"At least *someone's* getting some. I haven't so much as had a guy in here in I don't know how long."

"And why not? You're young, a free agent, completely put together. Christ, you look like a college girl in that outfit."

Holly's brow unwrinkled, and her lips curled into a smile. "You like?"

Badge smiled too, set his napkin on the table. "That was never a problem."

"No, it wasn't, was it?" To his surprise, Holly got up, eased over to his side of the table. The effect was like that of a favorite song coming on the radio, one from his high school days, filling him with current. He remembered a similar time just after they'd bought this house. Holly had cooked mushroom stroganoff and treated him to dessert right there in the kitchen. She hovered next to him now, her pole-vaulter legs close enough to touch.

Badge sat back in his seat, looked up at her. "Is this what you want?" His eyes said the rest. *Because if it is, you'll get it.*

Holly's hips teetered close to him, like they drifted in the wind. Then she meandered back to her seat. "The food's getting cold."

Conversation was stilted after that. She talked of Malcolm, how he was doing in school, how excited he was about making catcher, what he'd said the other night that made her laugh. Badge ate and nodded. After they finished, he stood up. "I guess this is where a gentleman would say goodnight."

Holly scratched her head, wouldn't look at him. "Guess so."

"Thanks for the meal."

"You're welcome."

"Gotta use the bathroom."

When he came out, she stood in the hallway, blocking his path.

"What's this?" he said.

"You're not going anywhere."

"Is that right?"

She grabbed onto opposite door jambs, leaned back, her body arching inwards, a cup to pour himself into. "That's right."

"This is a surprise."

She came closer to him, a playfulness in her step, like she'd just accepted a dare she'd made with herself. Badge remembered this girl, the fun Holly. He was glad she wasn't gone forever, that he hadn't ruined her. "Why are you surprised?"

"I'm surprised I haven't been waiting for it all night."

She leaned in, kissed him, and the kiss brought back nothing of the girl Badge once knew. This was someone else, someone who'd made the decision to let this evening happen, to accept him into her home, to her table, her lips.

She escorted him to the bedroom, what used to be their bedroom, which Badge hadn't seen in years. It was larger than he remembered, and the color had been changed from beige to light blue, with curtains–drawn against the night–to match. Badge remembered a flurry of remodeling right after the divorce, moments when he wanted to know what was going on. It was so long ago he'd almost forgotten about it. The bed, large enough for one person, ran along the wall.

"That's not our bed," Badge said.

Holly smiled. "Our bed made me miss you."

Badge eased his hands over her, felt the rise of her breath, the slant of her hips. "Do you still miss me?"

She smiled. "Not tonight."

Afterwards, crickets filed away outside, sounding so close Badge thought some might be in the room.

"Holy shit," Holly whispered.

Badge pulled her closer. "Holy shit."

"Badge, you gotta go."

The warmth of their passion had dissipated, escaping through the sheets, creating a window where such possibilities could arise. "The bed's not that small."

"It's not right if you stay."

"It's not right if I leave."

"Badge, please."

"Wait. This is real, isn't it?"

"I'm not sure," she said.

"You're not sure?"

"I know it happened."

"It more than just happened."

"We're moving too quickly. I don't want to wake up next to you and not know what it means."

"I know what it means."

"No, you don't."

As he walked to his car, the crickets louder, more annoying, she stuck her head out the front door. "But don't stay away long. Malcolm will be jealous I got to see you and he didn't."

As soon as he got home, he called Holly.

"Hello," she said groggily.

"I called because I can't stop thinking about you."

"Badge?" she said. She clearly hadn't been thinking about him.

"I know it's late, but I want to take you and Malcolm to a movie tomorrow night."

"Mmmhn."

"You don't have to say anything. Just be ready at seven."

"Badge, I–"

"It's a date."

"Don't call it that."

"See you then."

8

Badge could've floated back to Holly's the next night. After eight years, why was she finally breaking for him again? It could've been the presence of another woman, Betty's crush on Badge like a halo following him around, making his ex-wife notice. But there had been other women over the years, girlfriends Malcolm no doubt told her about. No, it wasn't Betty, it was *music*. Holly had originally fallen for Badge as a rock musician. His immersion in this new L.A. band had reignited her, like a matchstick that had forgotten how to burn until a quick strike across the pavement.

"I come bearing gifts," Badge said upon entering. He laid the wrapped presents on the kitchen table.

"Cool," Malcolm said, picking up the one in baseball wrapping paper. His face was bronze from all his time on the field.

"I don't get a hug first?"

Malcolm rolled his eyes, wrapped his arms around his dad, and Badge felt love for his kid stir in his chest, winged, threatening to force out tears. "I hear you were quite the phenom in Santa Fe."

"Sho' nuf," Malcolm said. *Sho' nuf?* A new phrase, probably something the kids at baseball camp were saying.

Despite her miffed exhale when she'd let Badge in, Holly did all the right things when opening her scarf. She stretched her eyes wide, ran it through her hands. "Pretty," she said and put it back in the box.

Malcolm looked baffled by the Wally Joyner rookie card. "That's not him."

"Yes, it is. He was younger then."

"He was a lot bigger at camp."

"It happens to the best of us," Badge said.

Holly snatched her purse off the counter. "So, what are we going to see?"

"*High Fidelity*," Malcolm yelled.

"What's *High Fidelity*?" Badge asked.

"It's a movie about these guys who work at a record store. It's supposed to be *totally* funny."

"Sounds good to me," Badge said. "Hol?" But she was already out the door.

Malcolm sat between his parents at the theater, and the kid split himself laughing every time the short, fat music zealot came onscreen. The guy would dance behind the record store counter, embarrass customers for the albums they wanted to buy. Everyone knew this guy growing up, the one who'd memorized everything there was to know about music and wasn't afraid to use it against you. Hell, Badge may have been this guy a few times.

The main character, the actor who plays the same lovelorn slacker in every movie he's ever been in, created funny categories and classified his favorite records one through five in each. The movie hit on something essential about rock fans, their striving to put order to the music, to create a hierarchy, to make sense of the power it had over them. That was what Badge wanted now. He wanted to make sense of his life, to give it order. From here on out, Holly and Malcolm would be One and Two.

As they strolled from the Cineplex, Malcolm dodged

between parked cars. Badge reached for Holly's hand but she pulled it away.

After sending Malcolm to bed, Holly escorted Badge to the door.

"So, what's the deal with—" Badge said.

Holly slapped him.

"Hey."

"What the hell do you think you're doing?" She was whispering, but the whisper had bite.

"Huh?"

"Don't pull this shit."

"What am I pulling?"

"You knew I didn't like this movie idea from the get-go."

"Jesus, who would've guessed that?"

"*Sshhh*," she hissed, glanced up the hallway. Malcolm. "We can fuck with each other as much as we want, but we will not mess with his head."

"I'm not messing with anyone's head. I'm ready to start over."

"You're making assumptions."

"Not for me."

Holly put her hand on her forehead, wouldn't look at him. "I know," she said. "I know you're not. I'm sorry. Please, could you just leave?"

The next Saturday, Badge picked Malcolm up for a planned day together. Malcolm climbed into the cab of Badge's pickup, baseball gloves in tow. "Are we going to Reggie's?"

Badge had mentioned the possibility of a Reggie trip the week before. Reggie was Badge's one remaining friend from high school, the only one who asked after Malcolm, sent him birthday cards, even made it to his games sometimes. Malcolm loved Reggie's stand-up video game collection, which he had full access to during their visits. "We'll see if he's home. First, I want you to show me what you learned at baseball camp."

They stopped at the old diamond next to Lincoln Elementary. The school had been permanently closed, and grass grew in random patches around the infield, islands of green in a sea of brown. The pair headed for the outfield.

"Throw one in the dirt," Malcolm said.

"Huh?" The kid had his catcher's mitt on, but he wasn't wearing a face mask or chest protector.

"Throw it in the dirt."

Badge wound up and let one go half speed, which landed well in front of Malcolm.

"No," Malcolm said. "You need to really throw it or it doesn't work." He grabbed the ball and let it rip back to his dad. His throw featured the new "arm slot" he'd been talking about, the one he'd learned at camp. The kid looked good, his motions quick and automatic. The ball landed with a *thwack* in Badge's glove.

"You mean you want me to throw it like I'm pitching?"

"Yeah."

Badge got into a pitcher's stance, which prompted Malcolm to crouch down. Badge started his windup but stopped. "You're sure you want this?"

"Yes," Malcolm said. "We did it all week."

Badge looked into his son's target. It seemed like a great way to ruin the day, but it was what the kid wanted. Badge checked a pretend runner at second, wound up and let it fly.

Malcolm brought his knees to the ground and lowered his glove between his legs. The pitch dropped obligingly a few feet in front of him and bounced up, catching him on the collarbone. Without missing a beat he bounded to the ball and launched it back to Badge, who had to jump to grab it.

"Hey," Badge said. "You look good." He threw the ball and

Malcolm caught it, stumbling as the force of the throw tried to pull him over. "When's your first game?"

"Not until June," Malcolm said.

Badge caught the ball, squeezed it in his mitt. *June*. The tour would start by then, all summer on the road, every city you could name. He'd barely be involved in Holly and Malcolm's lives. Badge looked at the ball, turned it over in his hand.

At his apartment, Badge spent the next day restringing his guitars. In six weeks he'd be on tour, and where would he and Holly be then? He knew the wildcard the road brought to their lives. No doubt visions of the Famous Dead would dance in her head. Before he left, he'd make it clear to her where he stood, how he felt.

The day before his flight back to L.A., Badge made reservations for two at Andre's. He had his truck detailed, his suit dry-cleaned, and he bought a new pair of shoes. At five o'clock, he drove to Holly's office and waited for her in the parking lot.

"Hey," Holly said when she emerged. She looked him up and down in his suit, her expression incredulous, a little scared. "What are you doing?"

He pulled open the passenger's side door. "You'll just have to wait and see."

He drove them north up Sandia Peak Tramway to Andre's, which had famously tender steaks and a panoramic view of the city. From up there, Albuquerque looked like a thriving metropolis, especially at rush hour. Cars eased up and down the roads like blood cells in the veins of the city, keeping it healthy. Badge promised himself long ago he'd take Holly to Andre's for some special occasion. The occasion had arrived.

He'd reserved the best table in the house, right next to the window. A deck wrapped around the front of the restaurant, where later they could take in the last moments of spring.

"I'm not entirely on board with this," Holly said as the *maitre d'* slid out her chair. She wore a casual Friday ensemble of blue jeans and short-sleeved T-shirt. The restaurant was chillier than Badge had expected.

"Do you need my coat?"

"It's okay." She seemed nervous, like the way she got when she had a doctor visit coming up. "I'll order wine."

Their waiter, a kid with puckered lips, approached with a lit candle and menus. "Thank you for joining us." He set the candle between them. The unbuttoned cuff of his shirt brushed the table. "What can I get you to drink?"

After they ordered—he the filet, she the mahi—Badge reached into his pocket and felt the small, velvet box. He'd bought the ring earlier that day, the saleslady pushing him to buy the bigger diamond. He didn't know if he could wait until dessert to unveil it.

Holly looked at him suspiciously. "What's this about?"

Badge brought out the box, opened it with a creak, set it on the table. "Marry me," he said. He took her hand. "Again."

Holly stared at the ring like it hypnotized her. He loved the way this grand gesture had shattered everything else about the night, her discomfort, the temperature in the room, the emptiness of the place. This little ring was a game changer. "Badge—"

"I love you. I've always loved you. You know I've always loved you."

"I know that."

"You must've seen it coming."

"That's not true."

"Our night together—"

"It was great."

"It *was* great. I want it back, Holly. I want us back."

Holly looked down at the box. This time she seemed to refuse to take in its significance, like instead of holding the ring it contained the pushy saleswoman herself. The light from the candle flickered, bringing out the dilemma in her eyes.

"You're not answering," he said.

"I know."

"Why not?"

"Because this is infuriating."

"Huh?"

"Why are you bringing this up now? We're finally– We've settled into something."

"We can be more than this."

"I don't know if that's true." She looked at her hand as she fiddled with her napkin. The candle flickered, causing vague ghosts to dance on her face. "Badge, you wanted out."

"What?"

"I know you don't think you did, but back then you wanted out, and I don't think you really want back in now."

"That's not true." He was furious now too. This wasn't his past, these weren't these feelings. "I made a mistake."

"It's not that."

"I don't know how long I have to pay for–"

"Badge, it's not that."

"Then what?"

"I know it's hard for you to go on the road," she said, not looking at him. "But I swear it's easier to leave than it is to be left behind."

"*We love each other.*" His voice was louder than he expected. An older couple–at the only other occupied table–looked over. Badge lowered his voice. "Isn't that what's most important? Can't everything else work around that?"

"*Voila,*" the waiter said, appearing out of nowhere. He set Badge's plate in front of him, then moved the ring box to set down Holly's. The juice from Badge's steak ran around the base of his potato, an aluminum foil ark in a sea of red. "Can I get you anything else?"

When Badge didn't answer, Holly said, "I think that's it."

Badge dropped Holly off at her car, gave her some money for the sitter.

"Are you mad?" she said. She stood at the curb, speaking to him through the open passenger's side window. She may as well have been on the other side of the world.

"How can I not be mad?"

"I know, but you still love me, right?"

Badge looked at her. Wind blew from behind her, making her hair a kind of nest in which the egg of her head rested. "Loving you was never a problem."

He drove to his apartment, tried to sleep but couldn't. At three in the morning he packed his things, called a cab.

"I need a ride to the airport."

"Sure. What time's your flight?"

"I need a ride now."

Part II

The Triangle

9

Badge watched Albuquerque disappear beneath the clouds. Next stop L.A., and Betty, and their first tour as a foursome. He didn't speak to anyone on the plane, feigned sleep, avoided eye contact.

When he got to the venue, the Pie Shack—a little black-painted club on Sunset Boulevard—a tour bus sat out front. Their tour bus. It was chrome with big square portions painted yellow.

Inside, Les, Flip and others lounged. A guy in flip-flops got up from the couch. "Massey." He shook Badge's hand. "Road manager. You can store your stuff underneath."

In the little kitchen area, Les made margaritas. "Special blender," he said, patting the machine's chrome matte finish. He poured the tequila over the ice—just the right amount, you trusted—and flicked in margarita mix. He pushed one of the blender's buttons—three quick bursts—*whrr, whrr, WWHRRRRR*—until the ice ground to a lime mulch, then poured the mulch into the first in a line of plastic cups. "Who wants it?"

"Me," Badge said.

Les stopped pouring. Everyone went silent. Even the new guys seemed to pick up on it. Tad, their heavyset, buzz-headed roadie, pushed himself off the couch. "Well, I'm not just gonna let it sit there."

"There's more where that came from," Les said, and he poured the remaining contents into the cups.

"Then I'll take one of those," Badge said.

Tour buses hadn't changed much. A couch, a TV, a little kitchenette. Funny, but since climbing aboard, Holly hadn't been on Badge's mind at all. Good. He'd keep it that way. There was plenty to do—new crew to bond with, booze to drink.

Betty flounced up from the back, aglow with the excitement of her first tour. She had her acoustic guitar, which tugged on her V-neck T-shirt, revealing ample cleavage. When she saw Badge with his drink, she seemed to hesitate, the color briefly leaving her cheeks. "I wanna sing a song together, to commemorate our tour. What do you guys know the words to?"

"'Highway Star,'" Tad yelled.

"'On the Road Again?'" Les volunteered.

Betty looked like they'd suggested "Row, Row, Row Your Boat."

"'From This Moment On,'" Flip said. Flip had a notorious weak spot for Ella Fitzgerald.

"'Yellow Submarine,'" Cosmo, their soundman, said, presumably a nod to the yellow of their bus. Skinny as a kite support, Cosmo's boyish good looks—long hair, easy grin—must have served him well during his high school years. But pushing thirty, he now looked like someone who didn't bathe enough, and probably smoked too much pot.

"Anyone know anything from this century?" Betty said.

Everyone was quiet.

"'Margaritaville,'" Badge said.

"Yes," Tad said.

"This century?" Betty said.

"Everyone knows 'Margaritaville,'" Badge said.

Betty rolled her eyes, figured out the chords quickly. "Okay, you old fucks," she said and broke into the beginning of the song.

"Woo hoo," Tad said.

They mumbled through the verses. No one knew which lines went where, but once Betty got to the chorus, they were ready. The men bellowed like sailors, matching up almost too perfectly, and Betty's voice cut through them all, a Jet Ski slicing the wake of motorboats. The second time through the chorus they sang louder, Tad all but yelling, Flip nailing a harmony. After the third chorus, they held the last note, letting it get louder and louder until Betty conducted them to a stop.

"To the tour," Les said. He extended his cup. Everyone did the same, and as they all hoisted their glasses to their lips, Badge took his first drink of alcohol in eight years.

When Badge gave up drinking, he didn't learn how by reading books or by going to church or Alcoholics Anonymous. So much of what he'd heard about "recovery" didn't resonate with him. "Admit you have a problem," "Talk about yourself at your worst," "Give yourself over to God." It sounded too dramatic, like he was the star of the TV show of his life instead of the guy living his life. The real answer was simply to quit doing it, and that's what he did. He swore off liquor, threw all of his booze into the Dumpster out back, stayed away from clubs, and like a bird that learns the toxicity of certain berries, switched his attention to things that might prove more nourishing.

One margarita didn't turn Badge back into an alcohol-craving, unprincipled lunatic. It was more like he'd slipped into an old consciousness, an old version of himself, one who wasn't going to worry about everything that passed through his head. He didn't relish the sensation, or resent it, or care much about it one way or the other. He simply accepted it, in the same way he accepted the bus, the company, the traffic outside. The rush of alcohol was part of the moment, and the moment was good. Why would he deny himself this life, this drink? He wouldn't.

Not anymore. If nothing else, Holly's rejection of him had taught him that.

During soundcheck, an older couple, maybe in their late forties, came in through the side door. Betty's parents.

In from Orange County, Alex and Gloria Koenig looked the part of senior professionals. Gloria wore a smartly tailored black blouse and an almost-to-the-knee skirt that accented her no doubt yoga-induced figure. She was so tan her face looked copper, and her smile—porcelain white—announced SoCal to anyone who caught a glimpse of it. Alex looked like he'd come straight from the office, the top button of his button-down shirt undone, the wrinkles around his collar suggesting a tie had been there earlier that day. He'd somehow managed to rustle a drink, even though the bar wasn't open. The pair looked like proud suburban parents, not entirely out of place in this setting but no doubt heading for the exit right after the last song.

"I tried to keep them from coming," Betty said as Badge shook Alex's, then Gloria's, hand.

"I'm glad you didn't," Badge said.

"Betty tells us you just arrived from Albuquerque," Gloria said. She looked nothing like her daughter. Maybe something around the eyes, an inquisitiveness waiting for a reason to flip toward irony.

"Born and raised."

"That's quite a commute," Alex said.

"It's worth it to play with your daughter."

"He's such a liar," Betty said. She was oddly comfortable pretending to be uncomfortable around her parents. It had to feel good to have them there supporting her. Badge remembered his own mom showing up to Famous Dead shows, sitting by herself at a table with her scarf tied to her purse as people twenty years younger than her danced. "I pay him way too much. He wouldn't give me the time of day otherwise."

"Feisty," Badge said. "I can tell you're ready to play."

"Ready?" Betty said. "You haven't even seen my outfit."

"What outfit?" Alex asked.

"You don't want to know," Gloria said.

"You're gonna love it," Betty said. "It'll remind you of Betty Page."

"It better not," Alex said.

Right before the show, in the six-sided afterthought of a backstage room, Betty waltzed in wearing first-night-of-the-tour attire: sleeveless black bustier, red leather mini, polished knee-high Doc Martins.

"*Whhtttz*," Les whistled.

"Hel-lo," Flip said.

"Going for subtle?" Badge said.

Betty scoffed, strutted through the room like a model on a runway. "Go for subtle in L.A. and you don't exist."

At showtime, when Badge hopped onstage, he sensed a familiar connection. He remembered it from the Famous Dead. Bands are like gangs, and a gang's existence within the throng—in this case the L.A. types who occupied the room, faces angled up like fish waiting to be fed—depends on an unspoken commitment to one another. At the first note of the first song, the four of them meshed in the primitive bond of Us versus Them. It was the bond that led to all great rock and roll.

Their songs, perfected in the studio, were finally unleashed, the pent-up energy unwinding like kite string. None of them would've chosen to make a record without playing live together first, but with these three it didn't matter. Badge could barely breathe in the midst of it all, Betty's strumming, Les's pulsing, Flip's snare hitting him squarely in the chest. Everyone onstage knew the power of the spell, they'd waited to cast it, and now they spared nothing. The music traveled to the audience at the speed of electricity, invading everyone with its shock.

By walking onstage, Betty transformed into something otherworldly. She sucked the attention of the room like she was on fire, her bustier-ed figure outmatching the older, boring men surrounding her. She sang with more aggression than she had in the studio, her highs full-throated, her screams accented with growls. One song she played guitar, the next she brandished the microphone stand like a weapon, the next she sauntered back and forth like a stripper. Every time Badge looked up she was doing something sexy or clever or provocative. Once, in between songs, she tripped over a cable, and her recovery actually looked elegant.

The band ended with "Calypso," and the audience, stunned for most of the set, wouldn't let them leave. Fresh out of material, they were forced to jam "Heartbreaker" by Pat Benatar—a cover they'd half learned—and the crowd whooped it up as Betty cavorted in front of them. She smiled coyly, used her hips to accent the beat, pulled a fedora off an audience member's head and flung it to the back of the room. When they finished, the band bounded like happy children off the stage. Les wrapped his arm around Badge. "Hope you don't have any plans for the next couple of years."

"I'll cancel them."

Backstage, Flip hugged Badge between vodka hits. "I love this man," he shouted.

"Who needs the Gentlemen's Septet, right?" Badge said.

Flip's eyes lit up, a slot machine hitting jackpot. "*Who needs the Gentlemen's fucking Septet?*" He hugged Badge again.

Les shoved peanuts into his mouth and talked to a blond "actress" who kept touching his chest with the tips of her fingers. Les didn't seem to understand he was being hit on. Peanut shavings dangled like snowflakes from his beard.

Betty, of course, was the center of it all. She sat elevated from the rest in a chair on a slight riser. She'd thrown on a Dodgers cap and a T-shirt, and she looked anxious, a college softball player both pining for and fearing the next pitch would be hit to her. Glen introduced her to industry folks.

"This is a hit if I've ever heard one," Joe Buck, the goateed promotions guy, said. "I can get it on the radio without ever taking out my checkbook."

"You're going to start with college radio, right?" Betty said.

"Of course," Joe said, "but I can also hear 'Calypso' on three big stations in Sacramento alone."

Betty rolled her eyes, took a hit of her drink.

"That's where you sell records, my dear," Joe said. "You should count yourself lucky. We've got bands playing nothing but casinos from here to Wendover because no radio station will touch them."

"Betty would love to be on the radio in Sacramento," Glen said.

Joe took a hit of his cigarette, blew out smoke. "Good thing, because if this is going to work, we need Betty on board." He watched her.

Betty seemed to want something else to focus on, something to keep her from having to respond. Finding nothing, she hopped down from her seat, looked at Joe squarely. "Of course I'm on board. Now if you'll excuse me, it's been a long night." And she headed for the door.

Badge followed her outside. Despite their transcendent gig, the real world kept spinning out here. Traffic buzzed by on Sunset, people strolled along the sidewalk, one guy begged for bus fare.

"Hey," Badge said.

Betty pivoted. Her T-shirt was way too big for her, and she'd tied a knot at its waist to keep it from hanging to her knees.

"What'd you think of the show?"

"It was fine. Whatever."

"You were spectacular. I've played for these L.A. crowds before. I've never seen one act like that."

"A little too good, apparently. Joe Buck wants to turn me into the suburban rock queen of Sacramento."

"I heard that. Probably not what you had in mind."

"Yep."

"Listen," Badge said. "I'm feeling really grateful tonight, so I better take advantage of it to thank you."

Betty's forehead wrinkled, her expression somewhere between confusion and bemusement, how the Queen of England might look if someone asked her to jitterbug. "For what?"

"For letting me come along on this ride with you. It's a dream come true."

"Oh," she said. "No problem."

"Where're you off to?"

She pointed up the road. "Old boyfriend's gonna get lucky."

"Gotcha," Badge said. "Have a good time. I'll see you tomorrow."

Betty turned to leave, then flipped back around. "You aren't by chance so grateful you'd like to start sleeping with me?"

Badge laughed, shook his head. "I'm a crazy man."

Betty shrugged her shoulders, strolled away, her shadow long and tall in the streetlight. "You are a crazy man."

10

At noon the next morning, the bus pulled away from the curb and lurched onto Vine Street. The transmission ground as the driver, Gaston, shifted gears. Gaston was a huge mass, his sleeveless T-shirt barely covering his chest and belly. The blond, curly locks of his head matched those of his arms, and when he spoke he resembled nothing so much as a fisherman at the end of a long day, smiling even though he'd caught nothing.

Tad had claimed Badge's sleeping compartment before Badge had come aboard, a middle bunk, one usually reserved for a musician. That was okay. Badge would save his favors for later, when he might need them.

Their next gig was three hours north up I-5 in Bakersfield, where McDonald's, Chevron and Home Depot signs battled for attention in the hazy afternoon. "What do you think?" Les asked as they climbed off the Yellow Submarine.

The heat felt otherworldly, kicking an Albuquerque summer day's ass in the first seconds of the first round. "Why are we starting in Bakersfield?" Badge said.

Les shook his head. "I quit asking those questions a long time ago. Bakersfield's not a bad town though. Got drunk with Waylon Jennings here. I remember Waylon took off his boots in the cab and *whew* did his feet stink."

Their venue for the night, Smiley's, in a strip mall between an Ace Hardware and a vacuum cleaner repair shop, was a small, square room with rickety tables, un-level chairs and wooden barstools. The floor hadn't been swept from the night before, and broken glass mingled with their boots and tennis shoes. A pool table had three balls sitting on its surface. The little stage, a few inches off the ground, looked like it slanted in one direction. All of Badge's years of wondering what a real tour would be like, and here it was. *You've come a long way, baby.*

If Betty was depressed by this, she didn't let on. She took in Smiley's with deep, soul-affirming breaths, bounced through the room, kicked a random cup on the floor.

"You like?" Badge said.

"Perfect."

"You're an easy gal to please."

"Who would've thought you'd be saying that?"

The best way to load in was through a trap door in back, which wasn't quite tall enough for someone to walk through. Massey almost fell backwards carrying an amp. Tad bumped his head twice.

At soundcheck, Betty instructed Tad to tape down her cords, tested her guitar like she was a scientist with NASA, worked intently with Cosmo on her monitor mix. "More," she said, pumping her thumb in the air.

Cosmo turned the knobs of the soundboard. "Any more and it'll–"

Feedback. Everyone winced.

"Good," Betty said.

Badge didn't see her again until right before the gig, when she showed up in a new outfit: a nurse's uniform, collared dress, white cap, white combat boots. The rest of the band was scattered about the backstage room drinking Coronas. Badge had missed the taste of beer, its cool bitterness, and he let it sit on his tongue before swallowing. Les had just cracked the tequila bottle.

"You look adorable," Les said.

"Anyone know when we go on?"

"Soon," Les said. "People are starting to show up. Grab a seat."

Betty didn't sit down. She opened a bottle of water and spent the next half hour pacing the little room, opening new bottles of water and jumping whenever someone walked by. After Massey gave them the five-minute warning, she flopped into her seat, bent her head over her knees, sucked in air. Any casual onlooker would've thought she was going to throw up.

"Just do it the same as last night," Les said, patting her on the shoulder.

"Don't touch me," Betty said.

But when Massey finally ushered them down the hallway to the main room, Betty transformed into something else entirely. She hopped onto the stage with the confidence of a veteran, threw the strap of her Gretsch over her shoulder, strummed her guitar once, twice. Badge couldn't help but think of her as a baby bird, scared of flight but soaring the instant it leaves the nest. She cast her cord behind her, meandered to the microphone, adjusted the stand. "What's up, people?" she said to the audience of forty or fifty, nothing but vague forms moving around in the darkness. A few came up from the pool table in back. Betty strummed another chord, this one dark, dissonant, the first chord of "Breakfall." "What ails you tonight?"

The stage didn't hold the band that night so much as conduct it. The four members created a cauldron of energy that bubbled from the first song. For as small and wobbly as the stage was—Badge flailing this way and that, Les not so much playing as riding his bass, Flip finding freedom in the full volume of a rock show—Badge would've thought they'd be bumping into each other at every turn. But it never happened. They played in a sublime zone that protected them from everything, like a god had granted them immunity so long as they played for his pleasure. If Badge would've stopped once to think about it—and he didn't—he would've thought that nothing trumped this feeling, the four of them volleying licks and rhythms around like a game of badminton, their instruments infallible rackets, the birdie never quite hitting the ground.

The tequila worked its magic as the band threw themselves into "Yellowtail," then "Pinhole," then "Recon," then "You'll Never Know if I'm Lonely." Each song brought a new mood, a new way to take a chance none of them had thought of before. If there was a top to this mountain, they'd reach it, a depth to this pit, they'd plumb it, a gem to be mined from this fervent digging, they'd discover it. When they finished "Calypso"—the rapid-fire hits of Flip's snare at the end stacking like a pyramid of pennies—the people down front, tired from slam dancing, could do nothing but raise their arms in salute.

After the show, the band congregated in the backstage room while Betty signed autographs out front.

"Did you see that crowd surfer fall on his head?" Flip said. He grabbed the almost drained tequila bottle.

"How the fuck did he get back up?" Les said.

"He just shook it off," Flip said. "Dove right back in."

"They'd've carted me off on a gurney," Les said. He took a sip of tequila, his upper lip curling over the edge of the glass. His flannel shirt, wet from sweat, clung to his back. "Most of what we play isn't slam-dance appropriate."

"They see it on MTV," Flip said, "and they have to do it. You know what some record company gal once told me? 'Kids are the best because they do whatever you tell them to do.'"

"That's depressing," Badge said. He took a drink of his shot. He liked tequila more than he remembered liking it back in the day. Someone once told him, if you fight tequila, it'll fight back. His face heated up, and his brain floated in what felt like a thick, healing liquid.

"These companies," Les said, "they control the game. We all survive on the scraps they throw from the table."

"Here's to the scraps," Flip said, and they clinked glasses.

Betty stuck her head into the room. "Badge," she said. "Got a minute?"

She led him out back, through the trap door and into the alley. A streetlamp hung from the back of the club. Dumpsters sat on uneven pavement. "We're an American Band" played from inside.

"Fun crowd," Badge said.

Betty, arms crossed, looked ready to scold him. "You have a new hobby?" She pointed with her eyes to the empty shot glass in his hand.

"What, *this*?" He had to laugh. He hadn't been hassled about his drinking since his mom was alive. Even Holly had spared him most of the time. "Don't tell me you've taken up the charge against me having a drink."

"You're going straight for the tequila after the show?"

"Flip poured shots. I didn't want to say no. You should have one too, Betty. That was a great gig. Every person in there's gonna buy your record."

"Does this have something to do with your ex-wife?"

Badge turned away, watched the clouds edge towards the silhouette of mountains in the distance. The damage Holly'd done must show, like a car after a wreck. "How'd you know?"

"Just something I sensed. What happened?"

He flicked his shot glass in the air, caught it. "I proposed again, she said no."

Betty uncrossed her arms. A slight moisture clung to her throat, dew-like, and her nurse's cap sat askew on her head. "Sorry to hear that." She wasn't entirely sorry, he could tell, and looking at her there under the streetlamp, Badge wasn't either. The night expanded in all directions, in any direction they wanted. Betty grazed one combat boot over the cement. The song inside changed to "Jailbreak."

"So what's with the nurse's getup?" he said.

"You like?" She pirouetted in front of him, smiled over her shoulder, a wounded soldier's wet dream.

"Are you trying to drive every guy in the place crazy?"

"Yep."

Badge smiled, looked her up and down. "Then I'd say you succeeded."

The next morning, Badge slid out of his bunk, almost toppling over from what felt like wet sand adjusting in his head. His first hangover since falling off the wagon, and it was a doozy. His hands quivered just under his skin, and a headache gathered behind his eyes. Still, the feeling wasn't all bad. It brought him back to earth a little, a valley after ascending the heights of the gig and party the night before. On the bus ride from Bakersfield to Fresno, Les had introduced them to a dice game called Carolina, and everyone took part—even Flip, who allowed himself this one exception to his no-gambling policy. Once, when Tad tried to pocket some of his winnings, Flip grabbed his arm. "Keep 'em on the table," he said. "They're mine for later."

Les sat on the front couch, drying his hair with a towel. The bus was clean and neat; all of the beer bottles from the night before had been thrown away, the garbage, overflowing when Badge went to bed, emptied. Badge sat down, bent his head back. "Coffee," he said.

"Probably in the shower room." Les carefully wrung his beard with the towel. "We got a few hours yet before soundcheck."

Badge peaked out the curtain. Bright sun, Super 8, cattle field. "Fresno?"

"Yep," Les said.

"Ever play here?"

"A long time ago. Played a birthday party with a band called Hipstory. I was subbing for the normal guy, who had tonsillitis. I don't remember much of it."

"Must've been a good time."

Les smiled, flicked his hair back, ran the comb through it. "Might've been. I was shooting too much heroin at the time to notice."

That Les had once danced with the devil was hardly shocking, but his admission gave Badge a chill. He remembered one night, back before the Famous Dead, at his friend Devan's apartment. Devan's syringe reminded Badge of a chemist's beaker, the kind they'd used in high school to test compounds. Devan wrapped a belt around his arm, found a vein, angled the needle in. Badge would never forget the way his eyelashes fluttered as he drifted away.

"You ever use?" Les said.

"No. Too hardcore."

Les ran a comb through his beard, snapped it on his leg. "Of course that was twenty years ago. Seems like a different life."

It annoyed Badge, during his first hangover in eight years, Les wanted to talk about going straight. He got up, grabbed a room key from the table. "Anyone in the shower room?"

"Betty went in after me. It's 107."

The motel room was dark save a crack of light coming through the curtains. The shower hissed behind the bathroom door. A stack of towels sat crooked on one of the beds, and at the foot lay Betty's clothes—orange dragon T-shirt, miniskirt, underthings. It was almost like she'd dissipated and her clothes were all that was left.

The shower turned off.

"I'm out here," he said.

"Badge?"

"Yeah."

"What are you doing?"

"Looking for coffee."

"Oh." He heard footfalls. "Shit."

"What?"

"No towel," she said.

"No towel?"

"No towel."

"Lotsa towels out here."

"Come on." The bathroom door cracked open and out popped her hand, upturned.

"What's in it for me?"

"If you do it, I won't kick your ass."

"God, you're cute."

"Come on." Her hand gestured in emphasis, but he could tell she was enjoying it.

Badge picked up a towel, took his time strolling over. She'd opened the door just enough to slip out her arm, her hand hovering in the air, steam creeping. Badge touched the tip of one of her fingers, then again, bending it back, tracing the path of her palm to her wrist. What was this? It was whatever she wanted it to be.

The door eased open, and there she was—pink, curved, gleaming. Her breath eased every inch of her up and down, and her eyes looked as scared as he'd ever seen them.

Badge grabbed her, drank deeply from her lips, inhaling the smell of shampoo. Her legs wrapped around him, and he found pliant handfuls while he carried her to the bed. "We gotta keep this cool," he said. She was soft underneath him, a warmwater sea creature that could slither away at any moment. "Everyone's gonna get territorial."

"To hell with them," she said and kissed him again.

II

Later that day, at soundcheck at the Cotton Picker, Badge and Betty didn't acknowledge each other, didn't look at each other, avoided talking to each other. Nothing could've made their secret more apparent. Les rolled his eyes. Flip barely hid his grin. After a while the tension became too much and Betty blurted, "Okay, I'm screwing Badge now. Does anyone have a problem with that?"

The new couple started sharing a hotel room. "That'll be good for you," Glen said by phone from L.A. "Keep you both warm. Keep you out of the VD clinic."

"You're a hopeless romantic, Glen," Badge said.

"I've never envied anyone who had to spend ten minutes on the road. I did it once back in the eighties, a metal band called Traxxel. After three days, I was ready for Betty Ford. Got crabs too."

"It's not really like that anymore. I don't see a ton of sex and drugs out here."

"With your face buried between Betty's legs," Glen said, "how could you?"

Badge was consumed with her. The couple worked almost too well together, lubed fittings to a well-tuned machine. They spent their Sacramento afternoon in their room searching out spaces in each other, filling vacancies, finding new excuses to keep the train rolling. His brain was a mess of signals, all urging him forward in some vague attempt to devour and get beyond it. But there was no getting beyond it. At eight o'clock, sequestered by then for hours, the pair unhinged to play the gig.

"We got a whopping two pre-paid," Massey said. They were backstage at Indigo, their venue for the night. He dropped a file onto the coffee table, flopped onto the couch.

"What?" Betty said.

"Sunday night," Massey said by way of excuse. "Not to mention the fifteen-dollar ticket price."

"Fifteen dollars?" Betty said. "Who's idea was that?"

"Showmagnet, the promoter," Massey said.

"They can't do that," Betty said.

"They can and they will," Les said. "Everyone uses Showmagnet in Sacramento, and they don't know how to put on a show for less than fifteen bucks."

"So we play to no one," Betty said.

"Don't let it bug you," Les said. "In a few months fifteen bucks will be chicken feed to see you."

"I'm not playing to another empty club," Betty said and headed out the door.

She and Badge spent an hour canvasing the sidewalks, which stretched out among the buildings of downtown. Betty went after everyone, stopping bicyclists, bothering people at a bus stop, hitting up a group of college guys. Badge couldn't believe how quickly she'd changed gears. Gone was their coupling in their hotel room, replaced by this need to get an audience, to make the night as grand as it could be. That's a rock star for you. Badge, dazed and post-coital, was having a hard time caring.

All of their efforts led to a "crowd" of fourteen, most of them from an a cappella singing group that had just finished practice. Betty had Massey get everyone's name, which he passed on to the club as the guest list. The crowd milled around the too-cavernous room. The bartender scrambled to get everyone a drink. The smell of marijuana came from somewhere.

"Hey, folks," Betty said into the mic.

"'Free Bird,'" some yelled. A few laughed.

"'Free Bird,'" Betty said. She smiled, strapped on her Gretsch. "You want 'Free Bird?'"

Yeah said a few in the crowd.

She walked over to Badge, who'd just put on his Strat. "Do you know 'Free Bird?'"

"Sure, but do you really want to—"

"It's this or nothing." She went back to the mic. "Okay, everyone." She turned to Les, who nodded. "You want 'Free Bird?' You got it."

The three turned to Flip, who tapped out his best guess at a tempo, and the four broke into a shaky version of "Free Bird." After one rotation of the chords, they found the groove. Les relaxed into the changes. Flip stuck to a regular bass drum pattern. Betty sang the famous lines with a slight country lilt, which added a new, haunting level to the melody.

When they got to the chorus, the a cappella group, apparently waiting in ambush, joined in. All the voices sounded great together, the pristine noise of the band complemented by the choir-like din of the group, a merging as seamless as two rivers forming a waterfall. When they came to Badge's solo, he wanted to keep listening, but he dutifully slid up the neck and aped the famous slide lick from "Free Bird." Two college kids came forward, their lighters aloft. A transient in a dirty tie-dye danced by himself, his hands keeping time on his chest.

After the solo, the a cappella group came back in with Betty, and by the last chorus they all sang so loudly Badge could barely hear anything else. When they finished, everyone whooped.

The band took stabs at other covers, anything the crowd requested, "Black Magic Woman," "Refugee," "I Wanna Be

Sedated." After "China Grove" Betty announced, "Now we'd like to play a few of our own numbers," which sent most of the crowd heading for the door. "Just kidding," she said. "Here's another we hope you'll like."

"What happened to the indie rock queen?" Badge said to her.

"Shut up. Do you know 'Jack and Diane?'"

They finished with "Heartbreaker," which came together better than the rest since they actually knew it. The a cappella group again joined in on the chorus, and everyone clapped as the band bashed out the ending. Not one person had left save the bartender, who'd put two pitchers of water on the bar and disappeared.

After the show, the two paying guests, twins Mark and Tina Wang, were treated to a trip aboard the Yellow Submarine, where they promptly lost all their pocket money at Carolina. "Let us come to Oregon with you," Tina begged, the band's autographs scattered about her shoes.

"Sorry," Massey said as he ushered them to the door. "Good luck on finals."

In Eugene, Tad started overstepping his bounds. As the band waited to go onstage, he criticized the set list. "You've got too many slow songs." During the show, he stood just offstage, looking like a football coach as his team got ready to execute a crucial third-down play. He tried to take charge during load-out, making Massey and Cosmo roll their eyes in frustration. What bothered Badge most wasn't that Tad was taking his job seriously. He seemed to be *playing the role* of taking his job seriously. It was what Badge wanted to call posing.

"It's the sense you get that people are not being straight with themselves," he said.

Badge and Betty were holed up in their hotel room in Portland, getting ready for the gig. Out the window, fog hovered above Burnside, obscuring the topless joint across the street. The television played a figure-skating event, partners doing daring feats on ice. Badge lay on the bed as Betty primped.

"They're not living their true nature," Badge said.

Betty wore a short black skirt and a red strapless top that revealed a crescent of skin at her lower back. She bent over the sink to put on mascara, her eyes as big as ping-pong balls in the mirror. "Why would anyone not live their true nature?"

"It's not always that easy." Badge rolled onto his back, stared at the ceiling. He'd taken up smoking again, something to do during the waiting game, and he took a drag of his cigarette. He'd always been able to start and quit whenever he wanted. "You have reasons for doing or not doing something or other. You can't always do what you want."

Betty stared directly into her own eye as she put on mascara.

Badge took a drag of his cigarette.

Betty blinked into the mirror. "Why not?"

"Because there are people in the world you don't want to hurt."

"Who do you hurt by doing what you want to do?"

Badge snuffed out his cigarette. Betty looked delicious, one leg cheating up damsel-like as she leaned closer to the mirror. He climbed off the bed. "For instance." He slid his hands around her. "If I were to fuck you right now, that would be very inconsiderate."

Her eyes flickered, sparks from an anvil. "And who would that be hurting?"

Badge touched his lips to her neck. "We'd be late for the gig, for one."

She turned, accepted his lips. There was a lightness to her body, a buoyancy. He felt he could pick her up and put her over his head like the skaters on TV. "Everyone would be wondering where we were."

He eased up her skirt, found the giving place that sent air into her lungs. "And you'd have to get ready all over again."

"Very inconsiderate," she said as Badge carried her to bed.

Somehow, in Seattle, for reasons no one could explain, they had a packed house.

The Verve, an all-ages club just off the interstate, was the kind of place any touring band hoped to avoid. It was a grey cinder-blocked box, capacity 400, so close to I-405 as to be underneath it. The shadow of the off-ramp made it darker and danker than it would've been otherwise, and with no other businesses around, the chances for a walk-in crowd were nil. Inside there were no seats, and the cement floor would've been more suitable for storing utility vehicles. The bar, which looked like a concession stand at a Little League game, was tucked around the corner, far away. The stage was so high horny kids would spend the night looking up Betty's skirt.

Band and crew watched from the bus as people piled in. They were students mostly, high school age or a little older, wearing slacker clothes and sporting hairstyles meant to piss off parents. They parked their cars in no discernible pattern in the lot, and when the lot was full they parked across the street. They poured onto the grounds in groups of twos and threes, giving off an energy Badge associated with the last day of school. Some went into the venue, others hung around smoking cigarettes. Betty watched out the window like a kid watches a snowfall, visions of Christmas and sledding and snowball fights dancing in her head.

"Where do you think they heard about it?" Tad said.

"Word of mouth," Les said. "News of No Fun Intended has traveled up the coast."

"The record isn't even out yet," Betty said.

"The best way it could happen," Les said.

Betty watched, the same kid seeing life after the snow,

freezing cold, ten-feet drifts, not wanting to get lost in it. "Grab your acoustic," she said to Badge. "We gotta warm up."

A pop musician writes, plays, records and waits for a signal. Most of the time he plods along, does his all-too-mortal best, reaches for the stars but winds up with something closer to home. Anyone who struggles in the pop world knows the drill: keep at it long enough, and maybe one day you'll wake up with that gnawing question, *when*, finally answered.

And then it's answered, and all of a sudden, on a day you thought you'd rake the lawn or visit your parents or renew the tags on your car, you're on a surfboard riding the zeitgeist, hunched over in the tube of popular sentiment, realizing too late you'd forgotten to learn to surf. Most people don't like this mad rush to the rocks. The ones who do might also like the trenches of war, ducking sniper fire, dodging bayonets, avoiding land mines, and always with one eye trained on victory. In short, it's something you'd kill to get to and can't wait to be over. When you're dead a hundred years from now and everyone who knows you is dead too, if anybody bothers to remember you, it will be from this moment. That night in Seattle, Badge realized this was his moment. He would play these songs, with these musicians, for these people, for as long as they'd let him.

Onstage at the Verve, Badge felt taller, stronger. The packed room rose and fell ocean-like, and Badge and band were above it all, the stage a moored dock. The swirling action of people reminded Badge of a colony of ants, each doing its own thing while somehow staying in synch with the whole. None of Badge's moments in the Famous Dead could compare to this. All these folks in this room saw him as elevated, and hell, maybe he was.

Betty commanded the Verve stage more with her aura than herself. She sang with abandon, wielded her Gretsch against boredom and ennui and uncertainty. The crowd couldn't help but be entranced. Kids looked up at her from the floor, shining faces asking for benediction, for a message. The message was simple: watch, love, slam dance, but more than that feel the pulse of the music around you. If anything more real existed in the world, you wouldn't have been able to convince anyone who was at the Verve that night.

The band closed with "Calypso," and the crowd wouldn't leave, screaming for an encore well after the band had left the stage. The four re-emerged to wow them with "Heartbreaker" and, out of material, scurried off for the night.

Backstage, Flip tried to open the Patron bottle on a chair's metal armrest, cracking its lip. No one could find shot glasses so they used plastic cups.

"These kids up front said they heard about it online," Les said. He took a drink from his cup, swished the tequila around in his mouth, making sure he didn't swallow glass. "Some blog called *Neil Diamond Must Die* or some shit."

"Aw," Flip said. "I love Neil Diamond."

Badge looked out at the crowd. The tops of heads peeked over the stage gopher-like, wondering if a second encore was coming. "They're not going anywhere."

"We need more material," Flip said.

"Leave 'em wanting more," Les said. "It'll make sure they come back next time."

Betty had disappeared, so Badge went looking for her. He found her in a fenced-off area behind the club. Stacks of liquor boxes leaned this way and that. The freeway above kept things dark and cool. On the other side of the fence the crowd dispersed. A few hummed the melody of "Calypso," Gregorian chant-like. They hadn't even heard the album, and they already had a favorite song. Betty sat on an overturned milk crate, her head in her hands. She was crying.

"Hey," Badge said. He crouched next to her. A mascaraed tear ran over her fingers. A mist sprinkled down from somewhere above: the off-ramp, the heavens. "This isn't how a rock star is supposed to act."

"I know," she said. Her voice was scratchy from the night's singing. "I was just listening to them and I—" She choked on her words.

"Come on," Badge said. He hugged her, both of them squatting, two dance contestants trying an impossible, low-to-the-ground move.

Betty wiped her eyes. Her cheeks were flush with the heat of the gig. "I know I should be happy, but I can't help but think of all I've given up to—"

"What did you give up?"

She wiped her face, harder this time. Mascara found safe havens in the creases around her eyes. "Never mind. I'm just being a baby."

Badge angled her head up, wiped mascara away with his thumbs. "You're going to be bigger than Jesus."

Betty cracked a smile. "I am, aren't I?"

Badge picked her up, pulled her close to him. "You did it, girl." He hugged her, inhaling some combination of sweat and skin and the Seattle night.

She sobbed again, hugged him, her arms around his neck. "*We* did it."

Badge sighed. They had done it, but instead of reveling in it, Badge's mind flashed to Malcolm, Holly, his life in Albuquerque, which seemed less his life than ever. He squeezed her tightly. "We did do it."

12

On the day *No Fun Intended* hit the streets, Badge and Betty flew to L.A. for the record release party. The event, at Tower Records on Sunset, netted only seventy-five people, but they were the right seventy-five people.

One was Clay, a heavy, balding autograph collector, the kind who only showed up to these things if he thought the signature would yield income. He bought five copies of the CD, had Betty sign each cover—"only on the white part"—and took pictures for verification.

There was Berri, a leggy single mom from Orange County who'd somehow gotten her hands on a pre-release copy and was so hooked she took the day off "just to say I was here." Her kids waited in the car.

There was Jorge, the quiet, skinny janitor from the recording studio who'd taken extra time emptying the trash whenever Betty was around. As he waited in line, Jorge stared at Betty. He could've been a starstruck fan or a cold-blooded killer; only time would tell. When it was his turn, Betty said, "Hey, Jorge," and his face broke into a smile, relieving everyone.

There were three college guys from Evergreen State who'd skipped class to make the trip. The tall one in John Lennon glasses asked Betty to pose for a picture with him, and the rest leaned in, one flashing a gang sign as the shutter snapped.

The air was palpable with ... *what*? Badge didn't know. This was much bigger than anything he'd experienced, a potential boon that felt strangely foreboding. "What if it's real?" was only slightly less traumatic than "What if it's not?"

Shelei, the record company presence, her T-shirt not quite covering her navel, said afterward, "That was not a normal L.A. signing. Those people were *fans*. We sold a hundred-sixty units. Badge, tell me. How did we sell a hundred-sixty units when we didn't have half that many people come through the turnstile?"

"Because we've got a major industry occurrence on our hands," Badge said.

Shelei laughed, clapped once. "That's right. I see what I saw in there today and I start thinking, 'Look out, world.'"

"As long as they like the album," Betty said.

On the ride back to Betty's place, where she and Badge would crash before catching up with the Yellow Submarine the next day, Betty said nothing, stared out the window. Maybe it was all weighing on her, a tsunami getting closer but still not visible from shore.

Her apartment, in a brick building above a dry cleaning business in East Hollywood, looked like some combination of musician's pad and squatter's flophouse. The only furniture—mattress on the floor, couch, swivel chair—would've quickly found its way into the trash at Badge's place. Clothes were strewn about. A jam box, used to prop open a window, looked ready to fall to the ground. Badge had seen dozens of apartments like it in his day. They now made him feel old. The centerpiece, a giant stuffed orange cat, stood eight feet high in one corner, its head bent to accommodate the ceiling.

"You been to the state fair?" Badge said, pointing to the cat.

Betty giggled, betraying a hint of nervousness at having him here. She'd changed into grey spandex pants that must've been made for a dancer, and a sweatshirt that crept up her spine. "My signing bonus. The label wanted to buy me something. I found it in a catalog, and they thought it was hilarious."

"What's it's name?"

"Darby."

"Terence Trent?"

"Crash."

"Of course."

Betty stepped over some junk—a four-track recorder, cassette tapes, a scattered deck of cards—to get to the couch. It appeared to be half of a sectional. "Do you wanna smoke a joint?"

"Sure." Badge wanted a gin and tonic, but he'd take what he could get. He sat on the couch, which gave deeply underneath him.

Betty grabbed a cigar box, flipped it open. "I just need to zone out for a while." She took out a joint and a lighter. "How long's it been since you smoked?"

"A while."

She held the joint in front of her, how one might hold a firecracker, then touched the flame to it. "How come?"

"I don't want to encourage my kid."

She put the joint to her mouth, dragged. "Well," she said, handing him the joint. "Time to get stoned, Daddy-o."

The pot tasted harsh. He exhaled to keep from choking. "Good Christ," he said, handing the joint back. "I thought rock stars were supposed to get good weed."

"I don't smoke it fast enough." She took another drag, held it in like a painful secret, blew it out. "What kind of guitar player complains about free weed?"

"The good kind." He took the joint from her, inhaled, a slighter hit this time.

"I had one too," Betty said as she took the joint from him.

"One what?"

She tugged on the joint, softer this time. "One kid."

Badge looked at her as she held in smoke. Something about what she'd said seemed too random. "Are you kidding?"

"I was seventeen." She exhaled smoke. "I had it without my parents knowing."

Her words swam in triplicate in his head. He couldn't believe it.

"I ran off to this place in Utah where they take care of you," she said. "They paid for everything, found a home for my baby, gave me as long as I wanted to recover. In six months, I had the kid and came home."

"What did your parents say?"

"I told them I was following the Tragically Hip."

"No way."

"They weren't even on tour at the time," Betty said, laughing a little.

"So you gave your kid up for adoption?"

"Yep."

"You were seventeen?"

She nodded, how a child might nod, her chin touching her chest. "I had to sign a form saying I had no claim to the kid–it was a boy, by the way; I found out that much–but right after I had him, I so wanted him. I knew that he was out there and breathing and mine, but the nurse took him away. I never even saw him."

The room buzzed with what passed for silence in an East Hollywood apartment. Car noise rose from Sunset, old utilities hummed. The pot made everything sound important, like their conversation slanted inevitably toward the truth.

"Why'd you give him up?"

Betty shrugged. She looked unsteady, like if he nudged her she might tip over. "I heard about Patti Smith giving up her kid. I kind of liked the idea of having someone out there who might come find me someday. He'd be four years old today, by the way."

"Really?"

She hit the joint again, handed it back. "That's why I wanted today to be the release date."

Badge remembered when Holly had Malcolm. His heart pounded as he paced the waiting room. He felt the best thing about him was being brought forth that day, the cream of his essence leaving behind the chafe of his baser needs. When he held Malcolm for the first time, he felt like a Greek god. He wouldn't simply make himself a better person, the world a better world. He'd launch a lightning bolt at anything less than pure, less than devout. "Well," Badge said. He had no drink to toast with, so he extended the joint in the air. "Happy birthday to your kid."

Betty smiled, took the joint from Badge's fingers. "That's why No Fun Intended has to be great. I gave up too much for it not to be."

Badge and Betty lay on the mattress, their bodies taking the rays of the lone night-light. Their lovemaking had been surreal, the haze of Badge's buzz distorting everything, making her feel far away. The night-light hue was like the one in Badge's grandparents' dining room, frosted glass giving everything an old-fashioned photograph look.

"I used to watch *Days of Our Lives* when I was a kid," Betty said. She stared at the ceiling. The light cast a single rectangle into each of her eyes. "God, did I have a thing for Bo."

"All girls had a thing for Bo."

"And all boys had a thing for Hope."

"Wait," Badge said. "How does a girl go from watching *Days of Our Lives* to Patti Smith?"

She smiled coyly. "There was a guy."

"Does this guy have a name?"

"Yeah, but I'm not going to tell you."

"Why not?"

"Because I don't have to."

Badge looked at Betty. "You know, you kind of remind me of Hope."

"What?"

"You kind of have a little Hope thing going on."

"No, I don't."

"You'd fit right in on *Days of Our Lives*."

Before Badge could react, Betty was on top of him. She gathered his arms, pinned them under her knees, straddling him. "What the hell are you doing here?" she said.

"Um, you have me pinned."

"No. What are you doing in this band with me?"

"I need the work."

"Bullshit. You play guitar like your life depended on it. What are you trying to– Where are you trying to get when you play?"

Badge remembered one day when he was nine or so. His dad had picked him up in his car, and the two sang along to Steve Miller's "Jet Airliner" on the stereo, his dad's voice low and raspy, his own too high but somehow belonging there with his dad's. He didn't even like the song, but the memory stuck.

Badge made an attempt at shrugging his shoulders. "Make some good music, play on a good record. What else is there?"

Betty smirked. "You know what I think?"

"What?"

"I think you're trying to get into the pants of the hottest girl in the room."

"Well, it worked in this case."

"Either that, or you're a has-been rocker groping for one last chance at–"

Badge made a quick move with his waist that shook her foundation. "Hey!" One more and she was off, falling to the mattress. He tried to trap her but she was too quick, scampering colt-like into the other room. She screamed when he came after her, their bodies flickering in and out of the light. He corralled her in the corner in the kitchen. No escape.

"You know what I think?" he said.

Betty stood hunched over, panting, looking for daylight.

"I think you need a spanking."

"Nooo," Betty yelled, but it was too late. Badge grabbed her, put her over his shoulder, thumped away.

13

The next morning, before Badge and Betty flew to Idaho, they stopped by an Internet cafe to see what was being said about the band online.

The anonymous blog *Neil Diamond Must Die*—no doubt written by one of the kids they'd had on the bus in Sacramento—was overzealous in its praise, calling Betty "A new kind of rock queen for the twenty-first century," but the comments were mixed. Among the compliments, people attacked Betty for the way she looked, the way she sang. One implied Betty hadn't written any of her songs.

"That's bullshit," Betty said, her forehead going pink. "They don't know what they're talking about."

"Then don't read it."

"They're making me sound like a tool."

"They're going to say whatever they want to say."

"*They're my fucking songs.*"

"And the people who matter know that."

"I'm gonna respond." Betty punched some keys on the keyboard.

"Don't," Badge said.

"Fuck them. This is my honor we're talking about."

"Never argue with an idiot."

"Why not?"

"Because from the outside it's hard to tell the difference. Let's go. We'll miss our flight."

In Boise, KNRG's annual The Freaks Come out at Night Show awaited. An early add of "Calypso" had gotten them invited to lead off the "Freakshow," and band and crew had been talking about it all week. A Friday night in June, an outdoor setting, seven bands playing for thousands of people. It would be No Fun Intended's coming-out party.

But Badge and Betty's flight arrived late, and for some reason Massey had the bus wait for them at the hotel. The end result was that the Yellow Submarine competed with rush hour *and* concert traffic to get to the show, and they arrived just fifteen minutes before they were supposed to play. Betty watched out the window as volunteers got their equipment onstage. "We're not gonna soundcheck?"

"No time," Massey said. He snapped and unsnapped the lid of a bottled water. He'd been anxious ever since Badge and Betty had shown up, fumbling with receipts, getting snippy with the hotel people.

Outside, someone dropped one of Flip's rack toms and scurried to pick it up.

"It's gonna sound like shit," Betty said.

"Cosmo will take care of you," Massey said, but watching the scene outside, he didn't seem to believe his own words.

"Bullshit," Betty said.

Massey laughed nervously, slunk out the door.

"Take it easy on him," Badge said.

Betty shot him a look. It was just the two of them. Les and Flip warmed up backstage. Gaston napped in his bunk, getting ready to drive later that night.

"He's still learning the ropes."

People milled about the grounds, a minor league baseball

park converted for the show. A giant tarp covered the infield, and many fans poured in past the outfield fences, forming clusters. A few kids stood up front, wearing garbage bags in case it rained.

"He annoys me," Betty said and disappeared into the back.

In Aspen, as the tour began a three-city ski-town leg, Holly called.

"I'm going to be in Breckenridge when you're there," she said.

He'd given her the band's itinerary before he'd left, all of the hotels they'd be in, phone numbers. Betty sat on the bed, wiping down her Gretsch.

Badge didn't want to see her. He'd managed to keep her out of his thoughts most of the time. "Why are you going to be in Breckenridge?" he said.

"Insurance seminar. No one else wanted to go."

"What about Malcolm?"

"Staying with Jack and Maureen. It's only two days."

There was a pause. He felt it was her job to fill the pause.

"I just thought you should know," she said.

"So what's it supposed to mean?"

"What do you mean?"

"Do you want to meet up? Should we avoid each other? Send me a smoke signal."

"I almost didn't tell you at all."

"Why did you?"

"It's a small town ... and it would just be weird. We're not enemies."

Badge thought about whether they were enemies or not.

"So, maybe we should meet up for coffee, if you have time."

"Sure. Call me when you get in town."

When he got off the phone, Betty looked at him.

"Ex-wife," he said. "I have to meet her in Breckenridge."

"Oh boy."

"Do you want to meet her?"

Betty wrinkled her forehead. "Why?"

"It might be nice to know her."

"No thanks."

In Breckenridge, while the rest of the band and crew took advantage of some free mountain bike rentals, Badge met Holly at a burger place downtown.

She waited at a patio table. Behind her, three boys in bike gear ate french fries. There were a lot of BMXers all around. Apparently the insurance seminar wasn't the only event in Breckenridge that week. Badge sat across from her. "How's the seminar going?"

"Don't know," she said. She was dressed in a flouncy white blouse that came off the shoulder, tight jeans and heels, new clothes for the trip, no doubt. "I haven't made it there yet. I'm putting it off as long as I can."

"What happens at those things?"

"Presentations, new products, actuarial stuff I might need to know when I get home. I just wanted to get away."

Their waitress approached, a girl with stud earrings at the corners of her mouth. "What can I get you?" It all reminded Badge of their last meal together. The young waiter, the wedding ring, the blood on his plate.

Holly looked at the menu. "I'll have an Everything Burger, fries and a Coke."

"The same."

"You got it," the waitress said and disappeared.

He looked at Holly as she continued studying the menu. He couldn't believe it was his job to sit across from her now. He got up. "Why are we doing this?"

"Huh?"

Badge motioned around him. "What is this?"

"It's lunch."

"It can't be that simple."

"Badge, sit down."

"Not until you tell me what this is about."

Holly sighed. "Sit down and I'll tell you."

Badge sat down.

"We have a son, and for his sake we have to learn how to be civil together. I thought this meeting, away from it all, might be a good start."

"Civil," Badge said.

"Yes. It's what people do."

He leaned over the table. "I see you sitting there, I feel a lot of things, not one of them civil."

Holly picked up the menu, wouldn't look at him.

Badge leaned back in his chair. "This was about you wanting to see me."

"I see the road hasn't hurt your ego any."

After they ate, Badge offered to walk her back to her hotel.

"I need to get to the convention center," Holly said.

"Then I'll walk you to there."

"Don't you have soundcheck or something?"

"Not for an hour."

"Badge, don't."

"Don't what?"

"If you act like this, you'll make me feel this wasn't a good idea."

"What's not a good idea? I was just—"

Her eyes slanted ever so slightly toward sadness. She patted his chest once, twice. "It was good to see you. I'll see you when you get home."

"The tour stops in Albuquerque next week."

"Great."

In Colorado Springs, the four band members sat "backstage" at the Catylyst, a club/restaurant in the heart of downtown. The backstage room was normally a storage room for the restaurant. Canned tomatoes and boxes of dry goods lined the shelves, and a milk machine sat cold and stoic above them. A couch, card table and tub of beer had been brought in to satisfy the bare minimum of the rider. A plexiglass window, normally used by the kitchen crew to view the dining area, extended along one wall. The band watched aghast as their support band, the One-Trick Peonies, crashed and burned.

The Peonies' gaunt, grinning lead singer stumbled naked about the stage, his skinny ass on full display. The gung-ho bass player wore his pants on his head, pharaoh-like. His fingers worked his bass, warbling notes coming from his amp. The heavyset lead player—who'd mercifully kept his clothes on—hadn't played a note in five minutes. His arms outstretched, his guitar dangled from his neck, and the feedback caused a headache in two distinct places behind Badge's eyes. Ten minutes over their set time, the band showed no signs of quitting. Massey had gone out a few minutes earlier to put a stop to it. The audience waited for it to be over.

"They already turned the P.A. off," Flip said.

Betty paced the room, her fury seeming to grow with every step. "The P.A. went off two songs ago."

"If you can call them songs," Les moaned.

Badge watched as the drummer stood on his stool, turned his back to the crowd and dropped his pants. "Come on, Massey," he said.

Then the drummer fell.

The crash jarred everyone, the adjoining wall shaking like a boulder had slammed into it. Badge came onto the stage and there was the drummer, pants down to his knees, lying in the area that used to hold No Fun Intended's guitars. The headstock of Badge's Stratocaster peeked out from beneath him. Betty's Gretsch was on the floor, upside down.

Badge rushed the guy, picked him up by the hair. He swung twice before he knew what he was doing, landing punches on his face. The drummer, stunned like a caught dog, broke away, struggled to pull up his pants.

The other three Peonies stared at Badge. The lead singer, puffy-lipped, looked confused. The bass player's pants drooped on his head. The guitar player stood with his hands at his sides, ashamed. They were kids. They thought they were impressing everyone.

The next morning, Betty tossed their hotel room key onto the front counter as Massey checked out. "Nice job last night," she said.

Despite the fisticuffs, or maybe because of them, the show had gone great. The crowd, relieved to move on, gave No Fun Intended a huge ovation. Betty's Gretsch had been banged up but was playable. Badge's Stratocaster was cracked at the neck; he had to play the gig with his back-up Tele. At first, the pain in his knuckles screamed with every picked note, but it was nothing a little tequila didn't cure.

Massey looked down at the key lying between his hands. He looked nervous, something in the way his eyes bounced this way and that. He finished checking out and found Badge and Betty waiting for him in the lobby. The morning sun came harshly through the plateglass window. Dust particles eased towards the carpet at the speed of little hot air balloons. "Are you calling last night my fault?"

"You better believe it," Betty said. Badge, drunk and exhausted after the gig, had avoided bringing up the incident. He was done defending Massey. It was Betty's call.

"What was I supposed to do?" Massey said. "Jump onstage? They had no manager."

"They didn't know the rules," Badge said. "All they needed was someone to tell them to stop and they would have."

Massey ran a hand through his hair, shifted his weight. "I had to chase the club owner into the alley."

"You have to anticipate this stuff," Badge said.

Massey looked down. Badge could almost see the friction grinding in his head. He sighed, rested his hands on his hips. "It was me," he said. "I screwed up, all right? I should've gotten the band off."

"You got that right," Betty said, and as though that were the end of it, turned to leave. The bus, its idle louder than a purr through the window, sat waiting for them. She stopped at the door. "Are we all checked out?"

"Yeah," Massey said.

"Well, check yourself back in. You're not coming to Vegas."

"What?" Massey said. "You mean I'm fired?"

"Glen hired you," Betty said. "He can fire you." And she left.

Badge and Massey stood there. Massey's face edged toward despair. He'd been so proud of this job, finally getting off the christian rock circuit, bragging on calls home to his friends. "Dude," Badge said. "I'm—"

"It's okay," Massey said. "At least now I can quit trying— Whatever."

As the bus pulled away from Colorado Springs, Badge found Betty in back. "Wow," he said.

"What?" Betty said.

"That sucked."

She looked out the window. "Men are pussies."

"Maybe, but that still sucked."

"Notice I didn't ask your opinion."

14

In Las Vegas, No Fun Intended would play the Hard Rock Hotel, but they'd stay at the Luxor.

"Gratis from the record company," Glen told Badge over the phone as the bus careened towards Sin City. "Travis is thrilled with the early sales, and he wants everyone to have a good time."

"Cool," Badge said. He spoke on Betty's cell phone. He didn't like the thing. It was too light, and the line kept flickering in and out. "When are we getting a new road manager?"

"I'll probably have someone for you by Albuquerque, but until then I need you to do a few things for me."

"What?"

"Road manager-type things. It'll be easy."

"A day off in Vegas and you're making me den mother?"

"I'm handling everything I can from here."

Badge sighed. At least he could sober up before the trip to Albuquerque. Maybe his son wouldn't notice the smell of alcohol coming from his every pore. "What do I have to do?"

When Badge hung up, Betty and Flip came up from the back.

"I get to check everyone in at the Luxor," Badge said.

"We're staying at the Luxor?" Betty said.

"Compliments of the record company."

"That place is nice," Flip said.

"You been there?" Badge said.

"Never inside."

"Does someone want to tell me where I'm going?" Gaston said from the driver's seat.

"It's on the new strip," Flip said. He looked out the windshield. "There it is."

Sure enough, in the distance, mixed in with the lights of the city, stood the giant pyramid of the Luxor. The site of it made Badge's heart flutter. The perfect black triangle against the night sky was beautiful; he didn't care what anyone said. It was a signal to whatever else was out there that something was going on down here, wants were being pursued, even satisfied at times.

"I'll follow the signs," Gaston said.

Badge and Betty's suite became No Fun Intended's headquarters for the night. A wall-length window looked out over the scores of people playing the tables and slots. A statue of an entombed pharaoh stuck up from the center of the casino, at least fifty feet tall, its arms crossed over its chest, one of its giant eyes staring through the window at them. Their courtesy bar contained booze, an invitation to break seals, consume, worry about it later. The granite bathroom begged to be sullied.

Badge bent over and picked up the cup of dice on the bed. He'd lost a hundred right away at the craps table and came back to his room before he lost more. Les and Cosmo hadn't been far behind, slouching in after taking their lumps, and the three settled for a game of Carolina. Les sat on the bed's edge, singles interlaced with his fingers. Cosmo sat on the floor wearing a red floppy jester's cap, undeniable evidence that they were indeed partying, having a good time. The rest of the band and crew came in and out, the deadbolt twisted so the door never shut. Badge tried to keep his attention on the game and away from the eight-dollar lagers in the courtesy bar.

Betty sauntered in, her acoustic strapped over her shoulder. Something about Vegas didn't quite mesh with her. She seemed outmatched by it, a diamond lost in a sea of cheap—if brilliant—facsimiles. She wore a UNLV sweatshirt and ate a hot dog. "Flip's up four hundred at blackjack," she said.

"Go, Flip," Les said.

"Isn't he supposed to be a gamble-holic or something?" Cosmo said.

"He says he's got it licked," Betty said. "He says he going to buy us all hookers with the winnings."

"Gotta love a guy who buys his friends hookers," Les said.

"Give me a bite of that dog," Badge said. It had something wrapped around it, a strip of bacon maybe, and Badge's stomach growled.

"No way," Betty said.

"Where did you find a hot dog at a casino?"

"They sell *everything* down there," Betty said. "Oh my God, did you see the sushi bar?"

"Sushi in the desert?" Les said, wrinkling his nose.

"Beats the hell out of truckstop food," Betty said.

"There's Flip," Cosmo said, looking out the window.

They all gathered. Flip sat with his elbows on a blackjack table, chewing a straw, chatting up an older, bejeweled woman next to him. The stacks of chips in front of him were dark green, distinct from the red and orange chips Badge had lost earlier. "Look at that pile," Cosmo said.

"With that luck," Les said, "you can be as addicted as you want."

"Where's Gaston?" Badge said.

"He and Tad went to some girly review," Betty said, rolling her eyes. "I don't know why they didn't ask us."

"You wanna go to a strip club?" Badge said, incredulous.

"I wanna do *something*." Betty banged out a chord on her guitar. "Better than being stuck in a hotel room all night."

"Did you gamble?" Les said.

"Yeah, but it was *boring*. There's got to be more to Vegas than sex and booze and gambling."

Les chewed his gum, smiled. "Nope, that's pretty much it."

"We could play some music," Cosmo said.

Betty's eyes grew to the size of slot tokens, and just as shiny. They had the opposite effect of the pharaoh's eyes out the window; Betty's eyes asked and answered everything.

Getting the equipment to the room was the only obstacle, but it was nothing a couple of overloaded luggage carts couldn't handle. With Flip playing blackjack, Cosmo brought up the case that held tambourines and shakers. All of the beer they'd managed to save on the bus was brought up too, clankily, and Badge grabbed a flyer for a local pizza joint. Beer, pizza, guitars, the four would be as content as dolphins. As they pushed the luggage carts through the hallway, Cosmo jumped to touch the lowest hanging jewel of a chandelier, the bells of his jester's cap ringing as he landed.

An hour of jamming and drinking yielded a new song, "All, all the Time," the lyrics to which Betty wrote off the cuff. The chorus went:

> All sex, all booze
> All margarita attitude
> It's all me, and it's all you
> All, all the time

Cosmo, as keyed up as a teenybopper, dropped his shaker and scurried out of the room. He came back with his briefcase, which held his recording gear. "I gotta get a copy of this," he said, taking out his four-track, unraveling cords. "It's my *percussion debut.*" He set up a microphone, repositioned Betty in front of it, made Les turn down so he wouldn't drown everything out.

When they finished, they listened to the take with the lights out, the curtains drawn. The four sat on the bed, their backs against the head rest. Besides the music, the only sound was an occasional flick of a lighter as they passed around Cosmo's pipe.

"Amazing."

"Yeah, it is."

"Cosmo, do you hear—"

"Yeah."

"You hear your hat?"

"Yeah ... *ha!*"

"It's like another—"

"Like a bell or something."

"Yeah."

The light around the door disappeared and reappeared, people walking by.

"Think they can smell it?"

"Who cares?"

"What happens in Vegas—"

"Cosmo, you're burning—"

"Is that your—"

"Yeah."

"Sorry ... *ha!*"

"Stays in Vegas."

"It sounds beautiful. Badge, isn't it beautiful?"

The four-track clicked to a stop, and they all sat there, stunned to silence. The song had just finished, but Badge could barely remember it. He remembered the lighter being flicked, the sound of the pot crackling in the bowl. He was about to get up and play it again when Flip burst in, the light from the hallway flooding them.

"I'm up fifteen hundred bucks," Flip said, "and you know what that means."

"I've got it licked," Flip said to Badge as they waited for the hookers to arrive. Cosmo had run to the bus to get the jam box. Les had opened the tequila bottle from the courtesy bar, and now, one seal broken, everyone helped themselves. Even Badge cracked a beer, the roaring tiger on its label calling out to him. "In rehab they said gamble-holics don't know when to quit, they can't quit when they're ahead. Well, I just walked away from the table with fifteen hundred bucks. How's that for quitting when you're ahead?"

The ladies arrived with a knock so dainty anyone would've known who it was.

The four women strolled in, single file, each representing her own spot on the hooker spectrum of color and flavor. One was a tall redhead in a nurse's uniform with Spice Girl-worthy legs and a stethoscope around her neck. Another, Asian, straight hair, was wrapped in a pencil-thin burgundy skirt and business jacket. A third, short and blond, wore a green slip-like dress and matching feather boa. The fourth, a powdered brunette in black leather, held a horsewhip. They stood there as though in a police lineup, doing their best to look appetizing. Tad, who'd just gotten back with Gaston, rubbed his eyes, astonished. Les grinned, chewed his gum. Everyone seemed to wait for a signal. Finally, Flip approached the nurse, took her hand. "Gentlemen," he said. "Enjoy."

Cosmo put on an R&B CD, and everyone danced. Flip twisted with his nurse, her stethoscope around his neck. The Asian slow-danced with Tad, cradling his bald head against her chest. The feather boa-ed one sat on the arm of Les's chair while Les cut out lines of coke. Badge didn't know where the coke had come from; one minute they were dancing, the next the mirror was out, a dollar bill being twisted into a cylinder. The blond sat cross-legged, listening to Les or pretending to. The horsewhip one had left with Cosmo, promising "a full fireworks display, with a state-of-the-art grand finale."

The curtains had been opened, and the pharaoh stared in, offering no opinion.

Badge danced with a hopelessly drunk Betty. She rocked back and forth in his arms, her eyes half-closed, her smile so relaxed it threatened to slide off her face. The raspy singer crooned, "*Who's the best if the best ain't me?*"

"So, this is it," she said.

"This is what?" Badge said.

"Rock 'n' roll debauchery."

"Maybe a modern version of it."

"It wasn't like this back in the day?"

"I was younger and stupider then, which made it seem crazier somehow."

"Guess we're not young and stupid enough anymore."

"Young and stupid probably isn't enough these days." The jam box broke into a boogie-woogie tune, and Flip and his date started swing dancing. "It's different now. I'm not sure what went on ten or twenty years ago is even possible anymore."

"What?" Betty looked at him, her nose wrinkled. "Bullshit."

"I'm serious. This is like Disneyland compared to what it used to be."

"Disneyland?" Betty stopped swaying, pulled away from him. Her face looked disgusted, like she'd just walked into an orgy at an old folks' home. "You think this is fucking Disneyland?"

"Betty." He reached for her, but she stumbled away, almost tripping over the heel of Tad's hooker.

"You wanna see Disneyland? I'll show you fucking Disneyland." And she disappeared out the door.

No one much noticed the incident save Gaston, who mixed drinks at the courtesy bar. "Don't chase her," he said.

"She's hammered," Badge said.

"She'll never respect you again." But Badge was already out the door.

The hallway, curving in both directions, looked more golden than it had earlier. Betty was nowhere to be seen, but in the middle of the hallway lay her UNLV sweatshirt. *Shit*. Badge snatched it up, hurried towards the elevator. There he found the rest—bra, miniskirt, underwear.

When the elevator hit the ground floor, the doors took so long to open Badge almost pushed the emergency alarm. The bright red carpet of the lobby stretched out before him. To his left, people milled about the casino. If he knew Betty, she'd go for the largest crowd. He hustled to the casino entrance, scanned the room for a drunk, naked rock star. People gambled. Slot machines bleated, tokens clanging in troughs. A more dressed-up element leaned over the craps table. Then Badge spotted her.

Later, he couldn't believe he hadn't seen her instantly, her pink skin contrasting with the gold and turquoise of the statue. Scaling the foundation of the pharaoh, Betty's naked body looked like a hairless monkey's, the statue an old growth banana tree with its best fruit at the top. She'd made it about ten or so feet up, and with her combat boots finding ready footholds, clearly had her mind set on more.

Miraculously, no one had seen her yet, the gamblers in their daze, the croupiers manning their tables, the stationmasters asleep at the wheel. But that changed when, getting to the top of the pharaoh's foundation, Betty stood full up, her feet spread, her hands at her hips. "Hey, everybody," she yelled. Her auburn bush looked like a little heart that had slipped down from her chest. "Who says rock 'n' roll is dead?"

A few tourists laughed. Some guys at a blackjack table

pointed and gawked. One fumbled for his camera. The room went from a buzz to a spasm to a frenzy. Betty pumped her fists, gyrated her pelvis. "How fuckin' rock 'n' roll is this?" She did a funny bump-and-grind dance against the statue, and people whistled and cheered. A flood of security poured in from three different directions, all wearing yellow shirts. By the time Badge got to her, they'd gotten to her first.

Badge and Betty were led to a "holding tank," a little room just off the casino: table, telephone, four chairs, nothing on the walls. An air duct blew up from beneath Badge's seat. Betty dozed in a chair, her sweatshirt on backwards and inside-out, a towel wrapped around her waist. She held her underwear in her hand.

Three other men were in the room, none of whom smiled. Two yellow-shirted guys stood with their arms crossed behind Joe, who sat across from Badge. Joe had a calm, business-like demeanor and a full crown of greying black hair. "Badge," he said. "By the way, is that your real name?"

"Funny story." He needed this guy. "My dad was in the air force when I was born, and he was big on decorations."

"Decorations?"

"You know, medals, epaulets. Badge somehow came from that."

Joe smiled again, but this time with no mirth. "What you need to understand, Badge, is Betty's not in jail right now because of the overwhelming kindness of the Luxor Resort and Casino."

"The girl got drunk."

"Yep."

"And lost it."

Joe said nothing.

"And she's gotta play for six hundred people at the Hard Rock tomorrow night."

"Is that my problem?" Joe said.

Betty dropped her underwear, which fell like a small cloth bomb to the floor.

"This is a complete fuck-up on our part," Badge said. "We'd be grateful if you let us go upstairs and go to bed like it never happened."

Joe leaned back in his chair, folded his hands on top of his head. "That's not how it works."

"How does it work?"

"We can't just let you go without ... something from your end."

How bad did Badge need a road manager right now? He'd left Glen a message, telling him to call right away. "If you'd like to wait until morning, I'm sure we can make this right by you."

"Badge, I don't want to wait until morning. I'm here, you're here. It's either deal with me, or I call the cops."

"Okay, let's deal."

"So, we're negotiating."

"Sure."

"Good." Joe sat up. "I don't know if you noticed, but the Luxor Resort and Casino also has a concert venue."

Badge had seen a sign earlier in the night, Tut's Tomb, Capacity 675. He'd tried the doors but they were locked.

"This may surprise you," Joe said, "but we haven't had much luck getting the concert element to the casino."

"Really."

"The young crowd prefers other places." Joe folded his hands over his belly. "Betty's playing the Hard Rock tomorrow. Good for her, good for the Hard Rock. But the next time you come through town, how would you feel about playing Tut's Tomb?"

Everything was quiet save the slot machines paying off on the other side of the wall.

"So you won't have Betty thrown in jail if we agree—"

Joe waved his hands in front of him. "Let's not talk about jail.

Let's talk about–What is it? No Fun Intended?–let's talk about No Fun Intended playing Tut's Tomb."

Badge sensed that, before everything else, his first priority was to keep Betty out of jail. "I don't see why that would be a problem."

"So I can tell my boss we got you guys?"

"Sure."

"Sometime soon."

"Sounds good to me."

"Great," Joe said.

Badge looked this way and that. "So we can go now?"

"Of course," Joe said, and he waved Badge towards the door. "You two get some sleep. We'll contact you tomorrow about the show. And Badge."

"Yeah?"

"Just so you know, we've got cameras everywhere in this place."

"Huh?"

"We got cameras ... film ... of everything that happens here."

"Oh," Badge said. Nothing like a little extortion before bedtime. "Yeah. No problem. G'night."

Badge escorted a bleary Betty through the casino–where she received a hero's welcome–up five floors and back to their suite. The party had cleared out, but its remnants littered the room. Bottles and glasses covered every surface. Ashtrays overflowed with butts. Half a pizza sat upside down in the bathroom sink. Someone had vomited, if not entirely in, very near the toilet.

"*Mmnbbr*," Betty said.

"You are *fucked up*," Badge said. He took her towel off, sat her on the edge of the bed. She looked weak, vulnerable, like when Malcolm used to fall asleep on the living room couch and Badge had to carry him to bed. With a little maneuvering, Badge managed to get her underwear on.

"We rock," Betty mumbled.

"Yeah," Badge said.

"We rock out." She coughed.

"We rock out." Badge eased her down onto the bed. "And now we go to bed."

Betty rolled onto her belly, her face squished like a baby's against the pillow. "*Luvou*," Betty said. "*Luvou*, Badgie."

"Love you too."

Amid the wreckage, Badge found a pack of Viceroys. He slid one out, sat in a chair. He smoked and looked out at the pharaoh, black pits for eyes, no smile. That's right, pharaoh. Nothing for you. No happiness or sadness or trouble of any kind. But no tomorrow either, or the day after that, or the day after that.

The phone rang and Badge answered it.

"She okay?" Glen said.

"Nothing twelve hours of sleep won't cure."

Glen let out a sigh.

"I had to make a deal to keep her out of jail. We're playing here the next time we come through town."

"Well, there are worse things." Glen was whispering, too early in his world for business talk. "How'd it happen?"

Badge remembered the party, their dance, the way he'd popped off about Disneyland. He had no idea he had that much power over her. "We were having what I thought was a pretty innocuous conversation, and she flew out the door."

"You need to keep an eye on her."

"That's what road managers are for."

"Let me tell you what I'm worried about," Glen said. "Betty pulls something like this a month from now, and she's on the cover of the *National* fucking *Enquirer*, which for some second-rate act I'd love, but—"

"I know," Badge said. "We don't need it. The single's on fire."

"*On fire*," Glen said. "We got something going here, Badge. We could *all* retire after this."

Badge exhaled smoke. All of his buzz was gone, magically disappearing once he'd picked up the sweatshirt in the hallway. "I'll try," Badge said. "I mean, she's her own person, Glen."

"Try is all I'm asking."

After he hung up, Badge finished his cigarette, looked out the window. I'm surviving, pharaoh. That's what I'm doing out here. That's all any of us can do. He pulled the curtains closed.

15

Badge jumped out of his bunk as soon as he woke up, knowing the bus had arrived in Albuquerque and his day with Malcolm was just beginning.

In the kitchen area, an older man counted out cash on the table. He wore wire-rimmed glasses that made his bald head look doll-like, and what was left of his grey hair was pulled back into a ponytail. He stood up when he saw Badge. "Philly," he said. "New road manager."

Badge shook his hand. "We could've used you a couple nights ago."

"I hear Vegas was none too good to you."

"You got that right."

"Well, know that dealing with that crap is my specialty. I've road managed for thirty years—10cc, the Alarm, Third Eye Blind—and I've never had a rock star go to jail on my watch."

"Ours is quite a handful."

"I don't pretend I can control anyone," Philly said, "but I can give you structure, which if nothing else will keep you too busy to go to jail."

"Great. Listen, I'm off to see my son. We got a shower room?"

Philly handed him a hotel key. "226."

"What time's soundcheck?"

"Five p.m., which of course means five-thirty."

Albuquerque.

Badge rented a car, a new Chevy, and cruised up Central Avenue. Banks, gas stations, jewelry stores, he knew all these places, but he hadn't been in any of them in years. He lived south of here, where everything was quick and convenient. Still, he wanted to reconvene with his city, enjoy it like he and his dad used to.

And then the gig at the Revolution, New Mexico's best live music venue. The 800-seat hall slanted up beautifully from stage to balcony, a curve as smooth as a dove's back. Art Deco features accented the walls, and each velvet chair felt like a throne. Badge had seen Thin Lizzy there, the Pretenders, Los Lobos. It had been a goal to play that stage someday. He just wished his mom were around to see it. He'd think of her tonight while he played.

As Badge pulled into Holly's driveway, Malcolm ran out of the house.

"Whoa," Malcolm said. Badge had ponied up for the more sporty model Chevy, candy apple red. Anything for the kid. "When'd you get *this*?"

"It's a rental." Badge climbed out of the car. Coming back to Albuquerque made him feel taller than he was, like he hovered above his hometown. He outstretched his arms. "Come here."

Malcolm felt young to Badge, and he smelled of bubble gum. It's a good thing kids don't know how much they're loved by their parents, how every cell in Badge's body urged him to protect Malcolm, please him, provide for him. That knowledge would make any childhood too burdensome. The only dignity was in keeping it to yourself, which was what Badge was good at anyway. "Where's your mom?"

"Glassblowing," Malcolm said.

"Glassblowing?"

Malcolm ran his hand over the car's fender. "She said she wants to come to the show."

Badge didn't want to hear this. Holly offstage, watching him. It sounded like a new, diabolical form of ex-husband torture. Maybe he could call in sick. "We'll put her on the guest list."

"She said she wants to be on 'plus one.' What does that mean?"

It means whoever got her into this glassblowing thing is coming with. Great. Maybe they could all go to dinner afterwards. "It means your mom's bringing a friend."

"Larry," Malcolm said, and Badge didn't miss the note of distaste.

They climbed in, and the car's engine engaged with the slightest turn of the key. Once they'd turned the corner Badge said, "Who's Larry?"

"Mom's boyfriend."

Badge's stomach curled. "When did this start?"

Malcolm squirmed in his seat, fiddled with the stereo. "Do you have the CD?"

"Do I have the CD." Badge reached into his bag, handed Malcolm a sealed copy of *No Fun Intended*. Malcolm unwrapped it, slid the disc into the player. The intro for the first song, "Margarine," played, and Malcolm kicked up the volume.

"This rocks," he said.

Badge smiled, both because it did rock and because his son knew the difference.

"This is her?" Malcolm said. He pointed to a headshot of Betty from the inner sleeve, a black-and-white, her eyes doctored to look more menacing than they were.

"Yep," Badge said. He didn't know how he felt about introducing Malcolm to Betty. They'd both be at the show. Badge would treat it as naturally as the sunrise and, God willing, it would be. "Let's swing by Reggie's. He hasn't seen you in months."

Malcolm flailed his arms, mimicking the rhythm of the song. "Mm, mmm, mama, mama-nama, mm, mmm."

"What's this?"

"I'm wanna be a drummer when I grow up."

"No, you don't."

"Why not?"

"Too much equipment, and it's tough to get songwriting credits."

"Who cares?" Malcolm said. "I just wanna—" And he flung himself into a solo, his arms thrashing, his head bobbing.

"Keep working on your defense," Badge said. "Next year we'll teach you how to switch hit."

Reggie answered the door on the first ring, smiling broadly. Single, over 300 pounds, Reggie ran a computer chip business and seemed resigned to give up on his decades-long search to marry and have kids. "Gentlemen," he said and hugged them both.

His front room was lined with stand-up video games—Galaga, Pac Man, Asteroids—as many as could fit. A New Mexico State baseball pennant, old and tattered, hung from the wall. "I've never seen that before," Badge said, pointing to the pennant. Malcolm had already hijacked Front Line. He'd be dead to the world until Badge pried him away.

"My weak spot for my alma mater," Reggie said. "I couldn't say no."

"How much?"

"One-fifty."

"Good God."

Reggie's face turned red. "I couldn't let it fall into the wrong hands."

"Well, I'm glad it found you."

"And what about you?" Reggie motioned Badge towards the living room. He'd had the place remodeled last year, cutting out a giant, window-like vacancy in the living room that looked into the game room. Reg was always entertaining, throwing Super Bowl parties, waiting for an excuse to have a barbeque. "I see from this CD I bought that you are once again on top of the rock and roll heap."

"Betty's unreal."

"Wait," Reggie said. "Can I get either of you something to drink?"

"Coke," Malcolm said.

"A Coke, *please*," Badge said.

"A Coke, please," Malcolm said.

"Right," Reggie said.

Badge watched Malcolm play the game. A digital soldier occupied a war zone. Tanks, grenades. The frenzy reminded Badge of life on the road, except the assaults came from within, your passions coming at you from all directions, exploding on impact. Being away from it these few hours, Badge remembered how tame the rest of the world felt. Part of him already looked forward to tomorrow, when he'd be barreling down the interstate to the next gig, civilian life left behind. Hell, if Malcolm wanted to be a drummer, let him. On the scale of genuine fulfillment, he could do worse.

Reggie came back with a bottle of Coke and two cups. He handed Badge a cup and poured from the bottle. "So," he said. "I hear you've managed to screw things up with Holly again."

Badge looked at Reggie as he finished pouring. "What's that supposed to mean?"

"You know what it means."

Badge motioned to the kid. "You think we could take this outside?"

In Reggie's backyard, a squat Palo Verde tree took up most of the space. A gravel path led to nowhere but the back wall.

Beyond, a golf green, a black number six on the flag, was surrounded by teenagers, each carrying a putter and a pitching wedge. "What's on your mind, Reg?"

Reggie glared at him. Badge could imagine how opposing linemen must've felt when Reggie, after the ball was hiked, sprang into action. "You had her back," he said, "and that boy. And you gave it up for what?"

"I didn't give it up. *She* gave *me* up."

"What?"

"I asked her to marry me."

Reggie looked startled. The plot of this movie had taken an unexpected turn. Wherever he was getting his information, it was incomplete. "And she refused you?"

"Yes."

"*She loves you*," Reggie said. "Why would she refuse you?"

Badge turned away, walked down the gravel path. One of the teenagers got down on his knees and, using his putter as a pool cue, thumped the ball towards the hole. "She refused me because she doesn't want to be married to a musician."

"Someone on the road."

"Someone on the road."

"And you'd rather go on the road than—"

"Stop," Badge said. He felt his face heat up. He wouldn't be spoken to this way, not by Reggie or anyone.

"What is wrong with you that you would choose a life in a rock band over—"

"And who are you to pass judgment? You just spent a hundred and fifty dollars on a baseball pennant."

"*She's your wife*," Reggie said. "That is your life, and she is your wife."

"She doesn't agree."

"*She loves you*." You could hear the mythical tone the word held for Reggie—like "Zeus" or "Hera" must've held for the Greeks back in the day. "Holly and Malcolm love you. That's the beginning and the end of it. You know what I'd do if I had people like Holly and Malcolm love *me*? Do you know what I'd give up? No baseball pennant would mean a thing."

Badge had never seen Reggie like this, not even in high school when that kid from Wesleyan took a cheap shot and nearly shattered his knee. These passions were new, urgent. They were getting older. Their decisions carried more consequence. Where had Reggie been that this was news?

Badge grabbed both of Reggie's shoulders, looked at him. "This is my life. I won't have you look down on it."

Reggie looked, if not mad, somewhere between confused and resigned.

"Malcolm and I have to go. You're on the list for tonight. Come if you want."

16

Soundcheck at the Revolution seemed the perfect time to introduce Malcolm to Betty. The band's soundchecks had become routine. No fans, booze or drugs. Badge could make the introduction and see what happened.

"Tell me about how you can't do your job," Betty yelled from the stage. She smacked a stack of CDs from a woman's hand, sending them clattering to the floor.

The woman, young, Asian, her bangs cut like Uma Thurman's in *Pulp Fiction*, stood with her mouth agape, her hand frozen where it had held the discs. Betty stalked back and forth, the thump of her combat boots the only sound. The rest of the band and crew, ready for soundcheck, watched on.

"Grab a seat," Badge told Malcolm and hopped onto the stage. "What's the problem?"

"'Calypso' got added at KTGS," Les said.

KTGS, "the Grand Salami," a radio station out of L.A., the most influential station in the world. Getting the nod from KTGS meant your single was automatically added to most of the pop stations across the country. It meant mothers of four in Des Moines would hear "Calypso" on their way to pick up their kids from soccer practice. It meant eight-year-olds in Wichita would sing the words to the song without knowing what they meant. It meant *American Top 40* would make room for "Calypso" in between R&B hits and Disney movie theme songs. To Badge's knowledge, KTGS hadn't played anything left-of-center since Nirvana. For a girl who loved Patti Smith, Betty's career had just taken a turn toward Patty Duke.

"You should be thrilled," the woman said. "Ricky hasn't ever gotten a song on KTGS. You're the first crossover in label history."

"You can take your crossover and shove it up your ass," Betty said.

"Hey," Badge said to Betty. "This is not the end of the world."

"They play Mariah fucking Carey."

"And they play you too, so they can't be that bad."

Betty glared at him, a dictator who'd just uncovered a traitor. "Whose side are you on?"

"Yours," Badge said, "but I'm not going to have a heart attack because you got added to the best station—"

Betty's eyes doubled in size.

"The *most popular* station in the world. Betty, there's no point in playing this game if that's not a win."

Betty paced the stage, her hands behind her back. "They said they'd work Alternative first."

"KTGS heard it and loved it," the woman said. "There's no saying no to them. You don't get a second chance."

"I didn't ask for a first chance."

"Betty," Badge said. "Do you know how many bands get no radio play? Hey, there's someone here I want you to meet." Badge motioned for Malcolm to come onstage. "This is Malcolm."

Betty's eyes got big again, this time full of wonder. "Holy fuckin' shit," she said. "He looks just like you."

Malcolm snickered.

"Um," Badge said. "That's holy cow."

"Right," Betty said. She scanned Malcolm, crossed her arms. "So, what do you think, kid? Do we let KTGS push us around?"

Malcolm shrugged. "I don't know. It's cool, I guess."

A smile crept across Betty's face. "All right. We'll roll with it, but only because this kid says so."

After soundcheck, Betty let Malcolm play her Gretsch, and the two disappeared for a while, giggling as they ran out the door. Badge knew better than to ask.

Betty had interviews to do, so Badge and Malcolm would go to dinner without her. As Malcolm climbed into the car, Betty pulled Badge back into the entryway of the Revolution. She kissed him, her lips warm, a baked apple just out of the oven.

"I want one," Betty said. She kissed him again.

"One what?"

"A Malcolm."

"Huh?"

"Yeah."

"Holy fuckin' shit," Badge said.

"Um, that's holy cow," Betty said.

"You want a kid?"

"Yeah."

"Because of Malcolm?"

"I've always wanted one. Give me one." She kissed him, pulled him closer. Badge's knees buckled.

"I'll give you a kid," Badge said.

"I want your kid," she said. "I want to have your baby."

"I want you to have my baby."

"Betty," Philly called from inside. "*Billboard*'s on the line."

"You should go," Badge said.

"I'll go," she said, "as long as you want one too."

"I want one too." He kissed her. "If you don't get going, you'll get one right here."

Badge and Malcolm went to Badge's favorite restaurant, Esposito's, just up Central Avenue from the Revolution. It reminded Badge of his youth. He'd come here many times with his dad, ate at booths together, chatted up the waitresses.

The place had remained unchanged. Dusty Mexican curios lined the shelves. Two plateglass windows looked out at traffic. The vinyl booth seats, most of them torn up the middle, were held together by duct tape. At Esposito's, Badge could believe he was in a different, better era, as long as no one's cell phone rang.

Malcolm leaped into the only free booth, right next to the kitchen. For Malcolm, everyday acts needed to be embellished by leaps or kicks or imaginary slam dunks. Some things never changed. At least Badge hoped they wouldn't.

"You still like this place?" Badge said.

"Yeah." Malcolm shoved an oversized tortilla chip into his mouth.

"You should try the salsa."

"No way."

"Since when don't you like salsa?"

"I never did."

"Come on," Badge said. "You used to go through the Old El Paso like it was water."

"That stuff's hot."

Badge pulled the cup towards him, dipped in a chip, took a bite and fully tasted it—his old life in his town with his parents, his wife, his son. Waitresses darted in and out, customers worked at their plates, the kitchen smoked, and Badge savored it. He was home, if only for a day.

"So," Badge said. "You like Betty okay?"

"I think I love her," Malcolm said.

"What?"

"Yeah." Malcolm shoved another chip into his mouth. "I think I'm in love with her."

Badge couldn't help but smile. "Malcolm, Betty's *my* girl."

"Nooo."

"I told you about her on the phone."

"I didn't know you meant *her*."

"That's her."

Malcolm rolled his eyes, dove back into the chips. "Lucky bastard."

"Yes," Badge said. He remembered the look in Betty's eyes when she pulled him close in the entryway, the feel of her lips. *I want to have your baby*. "Daddy is a lucky bastard."

The power of KTGS. That was what Badge thought when he saw the cobra-like line in front of the Revolution. It was unfair for one station to hold so much power, but it seemed a little less unfair now that Badge's band was on its playlist.

The lot attendant tried to wave him off. "I'm in the band," Badge said, and he waved him in.

To his surprise, Holly was waiting for them in the backstage room.

"Hey, kid," Holly said. She wore a short black dress Badge had never seen before, and Badge felt a renewed pang for her. A man, a big man, a mountain of a man with a grey ponytail, stood next to her. "What have you been up to?"

"Went to Reggie's," Malcolm said. He went straight to the table that held the backstage fare, eyed the bowl of fun-size candy bars. "Met Betty."

Holly looked at Badge, who looked away. The moment felt surreal. He could handle about one-tenth of what was happening in this room. That guy's ponytail was more than he could handle.

"I'm Larry," the mountain man said, and he made two quick steps towards Badge.

"Good to meet you," Badge said, shaking his hand. Larry's hand felt rough, calloused, older than his. His blue shirt had light blue flowers on it, how they might look if they were underwater.

"I've heard a lot about you from, well, these two," he said, laughing a little.

"All good I hope," Badge said. He could barely mask his disapproval of him. He could steal Holly from this guy in an instant. Somehow, he felt it was his *job* to steal her from him.

"Of course," Larry said.

"Thanks for getting us on the list," Holly said. "And backstage passes. Were you expecting this kind of crowd?"

"Yeah," Badge said. Her eyes cut right through him. She belonged with him. Anything else was unthinkable.

"Well," Larry said. "Malcolm, what do you say we check out that pinball machine?"

Good move, Mountain Man. The two shuffled out of the dressing room.

Holly edged towards the couch, not looking at Badge. "So," she said.

"So marry me," Badge said.

She flipped around. "What?"

Badge grabbed her hand, knelt in front of her, felt the curl of her fingers in his, just like he had on their first night together. "Marry me, Holly."

Holly blushed. A moment passed when she seemed to love him as much as ever, her eyes radiant, playing tricks with the light. Then she covered her face. "What are you doing?"

"I'm asking you to marry me."

"It doesn't work like that."

"Two people love each other, they spend their lives together. It works exactly like that."

She started crying, placed a hand over her eyes. "If you only knew how boring glassblowing is."

"It could be good again," Badge said. "Like when we started. Do you remember?"

"I do."

"Then say yes."

The backstage door squeaked open, and Badge stood up quickly. He exhaled when he saw Flip carrying a stack of merch—CDs, T-shirts, magazines. "You seen Betty?" he said.

"Giving interviews," Badge said.

"A bunch of girls out front want their stuff signed."

"I'd better go," Holly said.

"You don't have to. Flip, this is Holly, my ex-wife."

"Nice to meet you," Flip said.

"I'm going to catch up with the others," Holly said. She looked at Badge, her eyes hopeful. "Will we see you afterward?"

"You bet," Badge said.

Betty burst through the door. She marched right through the drinking, smoking band and crew to the backstage spread. "*A fucking limousine*," she yelled and launched a bottle of water against the wall.

Philly came in behind her, shaking his head.

"What about a limousine?" Badge said.

"The record company picked her up—" Philly said.

"*In a fucking limousine*," Betty yelled. She grabbed a can of chips and launched them against the wall.

"Betty," Badge said. "If the record company wants to treat you—"

"Then they can shove their limousine right up their ass." She paced the room. Then she stopped, her brow wrinkling like she might cry. "They drove right through the line of fans."

"And what did the fans do?"

"They screamed like I was Sheryl Crow."

"They screamed because they love you."

"They didn't scream for me," Betty said. "They screamed for the *fucking limousine*." She whipped her arm across the table, sending a bowl of pretzels to the floor.

Les picked up a pretzel, examined it, plunked it into his mouth.

Badge strolled across the room, crunching pretzels under his feet. Fruit plate, cheese plate, chips and salsa. So many choices. He picked up the relish tray. "We just got added to KTGS," he said and launched the tray into the air.

Flip hustled over. "We've got a line of people around the block," he said and dumped the fruit plate onto the floor.

Les watched with raised eyebrows. Everyone seemed to wait for him to react, to get his approval—or otherwise—of their rock and roll mayhem. With a grunt, he pushed himself up, ambled around the table. "And tonight," he said, putting his hands on the tabletop's edge, "we're gonna rock the fuck out of Albuquerque." And with one quick motion the table was sent to the floor.

Betty laughed, flopped onto the couch. "Okay, I get it. Badge, crack that tequila bottle."

17

One shot for Badge became two, which became four, which became another bottle from the bar. They were all drunk by the time they hit the stage, which made it easier to mingle with the vibe coming from the audience. The four knew, even before they touched their instruments, something more powerful than themselves ruled the night, and they would get to occupy the center of it.

The place erupted when the lights went down, but more than a sound, it was a rumbling under Badge's feet, a vibrating that felt like it could break the stage open and eat him. He would never get sick of this. In those few seconds—walking onstage, strapping on his guitar, hearing the crowd—he felt he'd been given many gifts, split seconds of split seconds of time, each one a flower blooming in its own fertile soil. Badge didn't need to choose which moment was *the* moment, in the same way he didn't need to choose between Holly and Betty, or Albuquerque and life on the road, or the verse and chorus of a song. It's all one chain, one reality, each its own truth.

Betty circled the dark stage, her Gretsch slung low, a skip in her step that said she recognized the magnitude of the night. Some guy from the radio station stood at the mic, barking on about upcoming shows. How could he not know there would be no other show like this one? Finally the guy announced, "And now ... what all you crazies down front have been waiting for ... all the way from Los Angeles ... NO, FUN, INTENDED."

The lights of the hall went up, and the rumble from the crowd took on an earthquake-like shake. Betty kept circling, not acknowledging the spotlight on her, the rumble of the crowd. She stirred something with her motion, her romp taking the energy of the room and whipping it into something more potent, more pure. The crowd quieted and Betty kept circling, her head down, the thumps of her combat boots audible to Badge and maybe everyone in the place. Then, like a sound conjured by her motion—like from the lip of a wineglass traced with a finger—Betty played the intro chords of "Calypso." The place exploded, the band joined in, and all of the heads in the audience bobbed, buoys on the ocean of the song.

Holly watched from stageright, the light and heat enveloping her. She looked like Badge had just pulled up to her house in a Learjet. *Yes, Hol. It's amazing, this thing I do. It's part of the reason you love me.*

Malcolm stood in front of her, completely focused on what was happening onstage. He'd seen his dad play many times in cover bands, but that didn't compare. *Can you believe it, kid, that life has so many gifts to offer?*

Larry danced awkwardly behind both of them.

Betty sang the verse.

> It was Friday, it was my day
> My sit around get high day
> My don't ask why day

Flip and Les doubled each other on a little trill, and Badge had to smile. Rhythm sections could save the world if we just let them. Betty sang the rest of the verse.

And where'd you go to steal that careless smile?
I haven't seen one like it
In quite a while

A bouncer hoisted a girl out of the crowd down front. She wore a white top and had smeared red lipstick, a disheveled version of the Betty picture from the back of the CD. When the girl saw Badge, she uncorked the sign of the goat in his direction. Betty sang the chorus.

And if I never seem to go with the flow
It's all I know
Calypso

And if you're pulling everything from the past
You're always last to know
Calypso

The crowd sang along, the loudest points coming on the word "Calypso."

Betty strolled over to Badge as the crowd churned. She stood right next to him, bumped him with her hip. Her face acted as a mirror, reflecting Badge's own bliss back at him. *I know. I love it too, Bette.*

The second verse brought a flannel-shirted kid onstage. He pogo-ed around the band, evading a bouncer, and managed a pirouette as he fell back into the crowd. Another guy, this one with pink hair, climbed onstage right in front of Betty. He got down on one knee, Romeo-like, and blew her a kiss. Betty smiled, pushed him back into the crowd with the toe of her combat boot.

By the second chorus, the crowd was ready. Badge strolled to the front of the stage, cupped his hand around his ear, the international gesture for *I can't hear you.*

> And if I never seem to go with the flow
> It's all I know
> Calypso
>
> And if you're pulling everything from the past
> You're always last to know
> Calypso

The band careened into Badge's solo, which he started with a blues lick, which became a climb up the neck, which became a screaming high note. The spotlight shined on him, and he played a dark lick low on the neck, the notes shimmering with false harmonics, rainbows reflecting off a waterfall. A rock and roll *chug-chug* brought his solo back to earth, and he ended it with a fun, fast heavy metal-tinged climb that took him all the way back up the neck. Betty glanced at him, incredulous. *Sorry, hon. It happens.*

Badge strolled back to his amp and saw Malcolm, who grinned ear to ear. Holly was dancing—actually dancing, just like when they'd met—and Larry waddled behind her, trying to keep up. *No one can blame you for loving her, Mountain Man. Even I can't blame you.*

Betty belted out the chorus.

> And if I never seem to go with the flow
> It's all I know
> Calypso
>
> And if you're pulling everything from the past
> You're always last to know
> Calypso

Les howled with joy, shaking his head, his beard whipping like a kite tail. Flip popped his snare double-time, a new thing he'd started doing that made "Calypso" more rambunctious at the end. Everyone joined in, and Betty went back to her circle routine, a skip in her step, a crazed punk girl hurrying home from school, her Ramones records waiting for her once she got there.

Another kid, this one with the most impressive mohawk Badge had ever seen, as tall and evenly spaced as a peacock's feathers, had climbed the P.A. stacks to Badge's right. The kid stood at the top, some twenty feet above the floor, ignoring the bouncers screaming for him to get down. The kid pointed to the throng down front, which had turned into a mosh pit. *That's where I'm going.* As the band ended the song, Flip smashing the cymbals and the rest slamming down on the tonic, the kid sent himself tumbling, his flailing arms and legs disappearing into the crowd. Somehow, Badge knew he was all right. On this night, everything would be all right.

"Thank you," Betty said into the microphone, and the crowd whooped. Her eyes thinned in a way Badge couldn't quite follow, like something dangerous, caustic flashed through her mind. "Everyone. That's Badge on guitar. I'm going to have his baby."

Badge froze. All of the feelings he'd had to that point ran off him and scurried into cracks he didn't know existed. He looked offstage, and there were Holly and Malcolm. Malcolm looked confused, and he glanced up at his mom, whose mouth was agape. When Holly saw Badge's own fear, saw the shame in his eyes, her expression mutated into hurt.

Larry waddled back and forth, seeming not to get that the music had stopped. He gave Badge a thumbs up.

Badge wanted to shrug, an *aw shucks* moment, but he wouldn't let himself. They should know how he felt about Betty. Holly should know Betty was in him, just like Holly and

Malcolm were in him, and music and concerts and the roar of
the crowd. He wouldn't be ashamed. *I love you all. Kill me for it.*

Flip popped the snare four times, signaling the beginning
of "Recon." Badge turned to the crowd, coming in late. By the
time they reached the chorus, Holly and Malcolm were gone.

18

After No Fun Intended's last song, Badge ran to his car. The effects of the tequila had burnt off during the set, and he was left with an anxiety, all of his muscles tight, his clothes wet. He thought briefly of driving to Mexico, saying *hasta luego* to all of it, but this feeling would haunt him. Dealing with Holly, with Betty, that was what the night had in store for him. Now he remembered—too late—why one woman was enough.

At Holly's, the shadow of a telephone pole angled across the driveway. Badge glided to a stop along the curb. A few lights were on, no cars. If Mountain Man was out of the picture, that was probably the only favor Badge could ask for.

Before he had time to knock, Holly whipped open the front door. She was in her bathrobe, all of her makeup removed, her hair tied back. Her eyes looked frazzled. He could tell she'd been crying. "No," she hissed.

"Let me explain."

"Malcolm is sleeping."

"I love you."

Holly's face twisted with irony. He'd seen this expression on her before. It was never good news. "Badge, if you weren't his dad, I'd call the police."

"I proposed last spring," Badge hissed. He could hiss too.

"You said no. Are you going to hold it against me because I lived my life afterward?"

"You live your life no matter what I do."

"I still love you."

"Thanks, I've got enough problems."

Holly went to close the door, but Badge, an instinct borne from rage, put his boot in the doorway.

"Stop it," she said, furious. She pushed the door closed, pinching his boot. "Get out."

"Not until you hear me out."

"Like hell I will."

Malcolm, messy-headed from sleep, came around the corner. He wore last year's baseball jersey, and he looked startled, like he'd just stumbled across two drunks wrestling in a supermarket.

"Hey, kid," Badge said. His heart dropped. Holly released the door. Badge felt his smile grow large and fake across his face. "We keeping you up?"

"Am I gonna have a brother?"

"What?"

"Betty said she's gonna have—"

Badge glanced at Holly, who, he could tell, wanted to know too. "No, Betty's not having a baby."

"Why'd she say it?"

"Because grown-ups say stupid things," Holly said, going to her son. "Let's go back to bed. Your dad and I will keep it down."

"See you next time," Badge called down the hallway, missing his son already.

Holly came back, her arms crossed, head down.

"We need to talk," Badge said.

"Great," she said. "I'll start. You are not welcome in this house anymore. You're Malcolm's father, and that's all you are to me. Furthermore, if I ever hear you're drunk around

Malcolm again, I'll contact whoever I have to contact to keep you from seeing him. Finally, under *no* circumstances will that tramp have anything to do with our son."

Her words hung like zeppelins in the air. Badge was embarrassed; they'd never struggled like that before. He would leave, rack this up as a loss, see what could be done about it later. "I'm heading east tomorrow. I don't know when I'll be back."

"Well," Holly said. She grabbed the door handle, angled it open. "Have a good time."

When Badge got back, the backstage room was crammed with people. The bus jam box played the first Violent Femmes disc so loudly the speakers distorted. Everyone danced. Flip and Tad were in the middle, directing some sort of drinking game. A girl with straight blond hair bent down between them, crab-walk-style, and opened her mouth. Tad dumped beer, and the girl swallowed, letting the excess roll down her cheeks. *Yeah*, everyone yelled, and the girl climbed to her feet, wiped her face. A guy wearing no shirt—stomach muscles like an underwear model—got down in the same position, received the same treatment. Everyone yelled *yeah* and the guy hopped up, shook his head, dousing the crowd with beer from his hair. Badge grabbed Flip. "Do you know where Betty is?"

"No idea," Flip said. He was spectacularly drunk, his eyes looking at some point over Badge's shoulder. "Dude, why didn't you tell us Albuquerque was such a great town?"

Tad dumped beer on the next victim, a girl in a tube top, who took most of it on her forehead.

"Did you see her after the show?"

"I haven't seen much of anything since after the show."

"Tad," Badge yelled. "You seen Betty?" But Tad didn't hear him, so intent he was on dancing with the girl he'd just doused with beer.

Badge found Betty on the bus, talking on her cell phone. "Madonna?" she said, incredulous. "Madonna was fucking window dressing. Total eye cheese. That woman meant nothing to me. I still can't figure out what you people saw in her. Now Patti Smith. There's a woman with something going on. You wanna talk talent? You wanna talk sexy? Give me Patti in a garbage bag and she'd have Madonna pouting in the corner."

Gaston sat in the driver's seat, eating from a bag of chips. Les sat on the couch, reading what looked like a book from the library. Les pointed to Betty, mouthed *Rolling Stone*.

"I love the road," Betty said. "People to see, places to go, and I got this tall, sexy guitar player whose job it is to fill me with babies every night." She winked at Badge. Gaston blew chips out his nose. "Famous girl like me, you'd think I could get it anytime I wanted. But no, he makes me beg for it."

"I'll be in back," Badge said.

Betty came into the bus's back room, flopped onto the couch. "Where the hell did you disappear to?"

He'd been sitting there, alone, trying to figure out what to say to her. "I had to catch up with Malcolm. You got a second?"

Betty covered her face. "As long as you're not going to ask me what my influences are."

"*Rolling Stone*, huh?"

She dropped her hands to her sides. "This KTGS thing is going to ruin my sleep, I can already tell."

"*Rolling Stone* is huge."

"Whatever," Betty said. "It was better than talking to that bitch from the label. If you see her, tell her I'm dead."

"And you told *Rolling Stone* about—" The idea of getting pregnant had just come up six hours ago. He was surprised she hadn't forgotten about it. "About wanting to have a kid?"

"Sure."

"That might be something you want to keep to yourself."

"Listen," she said, sitting up. "I already heard it from Glen from here 'til next Tuesday about how I'm not supposed to say this or that. I'm not lying to the press. That's where people go wrong. You start lying now, and before you know it you're Michael Jackson."

"Well, I have an ex-wife and a son who took it pretty seriously."

Betty's eyes widened. "Your ex-wife was here?"

"Yeah," Badge said. He watched her closely. "You didn't know?"

"No," Betty said, an innocence so transparent it almost wasn't there. "How would I know?"

"She was standing just offstage, right behind Malcolm."

"*That* was your ex-wife?" Betty's eyes ballooned. "Wow, she's smokin'."

"Come on, Betty. You didn't know?"

"How the hell would I know? Seriously, that woman is a knockout."

"Well, thanks, I think."

"I looked at her and I was like, 'I'm gonna tap that after the show.'"

Badge couldn't help but laugh.

"Did they give you a hard time about the baby?" she said.

"I just had to explain to Malcolm he didn't have a little brother coming."

"I'm sorry." Betty eased over to him, ran her hand up his arm. "Would it help if he really did have a little brother coming?"

"What do you mean?"

"Of course, it could be a girl, which would totally suck, but there you have it."

Badge focused intently on her. A meteor could have crashed through the roof and he wouldn't have taken his eyes off her. "But you're not pregnant."

Betty turned to him, a poker player who held five aces. "I am."

Badge couldn't speak, couldn't understand. His brain felt like a spinning wheel, not knowing where to stop. "Betty, this came up two seconds ago."

"I was late," she said, "so after talking with you at soundcheck I bought a test."

"A pregnancy test."

"To see if I was—"

"And you're—"

She smiled.

She's going to have my kid. Badge loved this new information, this new start. Life kept rolling out opportunities for him, whether he deserved them or not.

"Are you still down with that?" Betty said.

Badge grabbed her, hugged her, lifted her off the ground. "I'm so down with that."

Part III

The Visitor

19

Betty lay on their hotel bed in Tulsa, Oklahoma, in nothing but her underwear. Badge, dutiful father-to-be, rubbed baby oil on her.

"Ooohh," Betty moaned.

"How can you have cramps already?"

"Don't argue. Get some over here."

"We've already used half the bottle."

"You can't use enough."

"I don't remember this with my first kid." Holly had had trouble with morning sickness. Badge remembered coming home once at three a.m. to find her in the bathroom, leaning over the toilet, her hair tucked into the back of her robe to keep from getting vomit on it.

"Ooohh," Betty moaned.

"And how's baby oil supposed to help?"

"I read it somewhere."

"You been hanging out at the library?"

"Ooohh."

With plow-like efficiency, Badge scooted oil down to her thighs. "This doesn't have anything to do with preventing stretch marks, does it?"

"What kind of vain person do you think I am? Get some under here ... Whoa, not there ... Yeah, that's it."

"So, what should we name it?" Badge said.

"I'm thinking Marmalade," Betty said.

"You're serious."

"Hell, yes."

"You want your kid to hate you?"

"Who would hate being Marmalade?"

"Anyone not last named Zappa."

"You got a better idea?"

Badge eased oil down to the backs of her knees. "How about after one of my parents."

"What were their names?"

"My dad's was Duke. After John Wayne."

"And your mom?"

"Alice."

"Sorry," Betty said. "Too cracker."

Badge grabbed her around the waist, shook her.

"I'm not naming my kid Duke or Alice."

"You know," Badge said. It had to be said at some point, if only so it didn't fester, a small leak in the roof of their relationship that could bring down the house. "All this could've been avoided if you'd taken your pills."

"Oh, so it's my fault."

"It's no one's fault. I'm just saying."

"Help," Betty yelled. "Pregnant woman being hassled by abusive father. Someone contact Child Services."

"Do you even know what Child Services are?"

"Heeelllp," Betty yelled.

Badge wiped his hands on a towel. "If you're going to scream, I'm done."

"Sure. Leave an ailing, pregnant woman to her own devices."

"Something tells me you'll be fine by showtime."

The band had been supportive enough about the news, but behind Les and Flip's "congrats" and "right on" was something more, something Badge, a working musician, could guess.

"I know you two are worried about your gig," he said.

"Naw," Les said.

"I know you're happy for us, but I also know you're wondering how long this can last."

Neither looked at him.

"Betty's got at least three months before she has to stop playing. And you know Betty's not going to stop until she has to."

"*Thank you, God*," Flip said under his breath.

"After she has the kid, she's going to need rest, but then she's going to want conquer the world again. We want both of you to be part of that."

Les crossed his legs, looked away. "That's fine, but if we should get another offer–"

"No promises," Badge said. "Just know we're going to keep going as-is for as long as we can, and then we're going to do it again as soon as we can."

"What about you?" Flip said.

"What about me?" Badge said.

"What's all this mean for ... you know ... What's it mean for you and Betty?"

Stations across the country hit "Calypso" with regularity, a few with vigor. Rock, Classic, College, almost every radio genre tried to lay some claim to it. With a little twang, some country stations might've picked it up.

The buzz was so great Glen jettisoned the band to Los Angeles to knock out a video. "Videos aren't that important anymore," Glen said as he and Badge waited in the green room. Betty was watching early takes, pointing out what she liked and didn't. "Too expensive. Record companies won't even consider them anymore, but this song is breaking all the rules."

"I've never been in a video before," Badge said.

"And you won't be in this one much. There's only one face people want to see, and it ain't yours."

Badge shook his head. "Les gets all the breaks."

The resulting video—stark, moody, dimly lit, featuring Betty up front with fake lightning strikes and silhouettes of the band behind—was hardly groundbreaking, but MTV and VH1 would add it to their rotations.

So much acceptance kept Betty on guard against anyone who thought she was selling out.

"These fucks," Betty said. They were in Minneapolis, a couple of hours before showtime. A giant mall extended out the window. Betty lay on their hotel bed wearing a hoodie and red underwear, reading something on her laptop, which Glen had given her as a gift when they were in L.A.

"What?" Badge said. He filed his pinky nail. He'd grown it long enough to use it for finger-picking during solos. His gin and tonic sweated on the table. Betty had quit drinking entirely for the baby and had yet to expect the same from him. Good thing. A drink was all but necessary these days. The Internet had become Betty's constant focus, searching crevices of it for anyone who dared write a negative word about her. Badge could've killed Glen for buying her that laptop.

"They're making it sound like Des Moines was some kind of bourgeois event where yuppies came to share golf tips," Betty said.

"So?"

"What do you mean, so?"

"So who cares what some asshole on the Internet thinks? Your single's on fire."

"Big deal."

"It is a big deal. Being on the radio everywhere is a big deal."

She typed. "Now every yahoo on the planet can totally not get it."

Badge set his file down. Betty's butt flexed, two mounds of red in a spasm of muscle, earthquakes decimating a hilly village. "If you keep this up, I'm going to have to spank you."

"No, you won't," Betty said, but her glance said she wasn't sure.

Badge stood up. He liked scaring her a bit, little chutes of angst giving the garden of their relationship spark. "You think you're the one who decides who gets spanked around here?"

"Spanking a pregnant woman? That'll look good on the police report."

After a disastrous trip to WBLU in rural Ohio ("That's quite a hairstyle, Betty," the DJ had said. "How can I make sure my daughter never gets one like it?"), Betty set up new rules for radio appearances.

"Any college or alternative station I'll go to with a smile on my face," she said. She spoke to Glen on her cell phone from the WBLU parking lot. The rented van idled next to them, waiting to go. "I'll give interviews, sign CDs, whatever. But if it's a pop station, they need to give a little ... I want to play DJ. I want to talk on the air, pick records, that kind of thing ... No, *I* get to pick the records, and I can pick whatever I want. That's the deal, or don't bother booking me into another one." And she hung up.

"You sure that's a good idea?" Badge said.

"Why not?"

"Things are a little different now." He motioned with his eyes to her stomach.

"You think I can't run this thing because I'm pregnant? Sorry, Tarzan. Get in the van."

The first and only station to go for it was WQFR in Erie, Pennsylvania, who only agreed to screw another local station out of an interview. Badge listened from the control room as Betty played "Holiday in Cambodia" by the Dead Kennedys ("Jello Biafra thinks he's an *artiste*, but I think he's more interested in pissing people off. Maybe it's the same thing."), "In my Eyes" by Minor Threat ("These guys were visionaries because they invented Straight Edge philosophy, which means they didn't drink, smoke or have sex. Noble enough. I could never do it.") and "Eight Miles High" by Hüsker Dü ("My favorite cover song ever. Every way the sixties failed, all that unfulfilled promise, is right there in Mould's voice."). The program director was thrilled with caller response, and he only had to hit the censor button twice during the interview.

In Buffalo, at the band's hotel, which sat along the Niagara River, Badge and Betty wound up in a honeymoon suite.

A heart-shaped bed took up most of the room, and a bottle of champagne chilled on the bar. Sinatra crooned from somewhere, and the air smelled of lavender. A giant heart of chocolate on the counter read "Congratulations."

"How'd this happen?" Betty said, eyeing Badge.

"Don't look at me."

"Don't tell me you had nothing to do with it."

"Must've been Glen." But Badge was thankful for it. Marriage had yet to come up between them. In this room, with all its overtones, it was impossible to avoid.

Betty inspected the wallpaper, which had a repeating pattern of little birds, ribbons in their beaks, tying bows. "All these men trying to tie me down."

"Who?"

"Glen. You."

"You feel like I'm trying to tie you down?"

Betty walked towards the sliding glass door, which led to the balcony. The Niagara was a broad river, and it stretched out in both directions. The falls were somewhere north, beyond the horizon. The guy at the front desk said you could hear them when it was quiet enough. "Maybe," she said.

"I'm not."

"Good thing, because I don't believe in marriage."

"Why not?"

"People can't stay in love."

"Where'd you hear that?"

Betty rolled her eyes. "Don't make me cite the obvious."

Badge and Holly. Despite his track record, he believed in marriage as much as ever. He liked its bold declaration, to himself and to the world. The need to declare it meant something. "So where does that leave us?"

"What do you mean?"

"What am I supposed to do after the tour?"

"We talked about this. I want you with me."

"Yeah, but how does that work? The three of us in your apartment?"

"We'll by a house."

"As simple as that."

"It's a detail. We pay people to take care of details for us."

"Just like you pay me."

Betty sighed, crossed her arms. She walked up to him. "Do you want me to say this will last forever?"

"If you think it will."

"Well, I won't."

"Great. I love you too, Betty."

"Christ," she said. "You're being a whiny-assed bitch about this."

"Just tell me the truth."

"The truth about what?"

"About how you feel about me."

She didn't hesitate. "The truth is I love you, but I'm not stupid enough to think it's gonna last forever."

20

In Philadelphia, Badge answered a knock at his hotel room door.

"Hey," Les said. "Betty around?"

"Doing interviews." She'd left an hour ago, crabby as a soldier on trash duty. ("If one more broad asks me what I think of Matchbox Twenty, I'm going to bite the head off something and spit it onto her lap.")

"You got time?" Les said. "I could use some help."

The hotel lobby bustled with people. Glen had started booking them into nicer places, and the Ramada was the nicest yet. Marble floors, Renaissance-style art on the walls. The bellhop opened the door for them as they emerged onto Commerce Street.

The neighborhood got groovier as Les led him south. Murals—some legal, some not—decorated retaining walls. Telephone poles were coated with fliers.

"What am I helping you with?" Badge said.

"I've got to meet some people."

"Who?"

"You'll see."

They went through the front door of an apartment building and up a long flight of stairs. A single bulb illuminated crayon strokes on the wainscoting. At the top, Les took out his comb, pulled it down his beard, straightened the collar of his flannel shirt. "Here we go," he said and rapped on the door, raising his eyebrows playfully. "Florida? It's Les, baby. You in there?"

"Les?" Badge heard from inside, a woman's voice.

The door opened and there she stood, forty or so by Badge's guess and plenty round, like she held the world in all its abundance underneath her terrycloth robe. She was brownish copper with freckles on her face and ears. Her eyes bounced from Les to Badge and back. "What the hell you doin' here?"

"Hey, Florida," Les said, and the two hugged.

"You know you got to call so I can put my face on."

"You always look good to me."

"And who's this with you?"

"Badge," Badge said, extending a hand.

Florida looked suspiciously at the hand, at him, at Les. "Is this the one supposed to keep me from chewin' you out for missing checks?" Despite her tone, her expression betrayed no anger. "Come on in. Y'all are musicians so you'll be wanting a meal."

Florida made fried chicken, collard greens, mashed potatoes. Her kid—*Les and Florida's kid*—Tyrone, all one year and two-and-a-half rambunctious feet of him, played with his dad on the carpeted floor.

"Come here, pork pie," Les said, swinging Tyrone, who screamed. Tyrone's skin was a dark chocolate, much darker than his mom's, and to be in the room with Tyrone's half-white mom and all-white dad, the science of skipped genes came into prominent relief.

Badge nursed a beer while Florida parsed shallots. It was nice to be in a home, food cooking, a child's voice. He remembered Saturday mornings with Malcolm and Holly, breakfast smells from the kitchen, *Sesame Street*. He doubted his life with Betty and their kid would be the same. Can you raise a kid with the

Butthole Surfers playing in the background? "How you two met must be quite a story," he said.

"Not as good as you'd think," Florida said. There was a hint of southern accent in her voice, like the flavor left behind in a mixing bowl that doesn't get washed before it's used again. "Six or seven years ago, Clotilda, my girlfriend, she wins tickets and backstage passes to go see Tony, Toni, Toné up the street. After the show, she made me wait with her until one of the Tonys came out of the dressing room—Les, don't do that to him."

Les had placed both of his hands over Tyrone's ears and, applying pressure, lifted him off the ground. "It don't hurt him."

"There's plenty of time for him to get brain damage."

"Am I giving you brain damage?" Les asked Tyrone, who coughed.

"So, we were hanging out backstage," Florida said, "looking like we don't belong, when this big, hairy guy from the opening act—" She tittered. "He comes strolling over and is like, 'Would either of you ladies like a some rum?'"

"Les, you sly dog."

"It worked," Les said. "We had some rum, didn't we?"

"I didn't know how to say no." Florida stirred the collard greens. "So, I've been hearing from this one off and on for years now, just when he's in town. Of course, he usually calls."

"We're real busy with the tour," Les said. Tyrone tried to shove a building block into Les's shirt pocket, and Les tried to prevent him. "We sold out the Condor tonight. You should see us."

"This is it for me tonight," Florida said. "You're lucky I answered the door."

They ate on the small cherrywood table in the dining room. Badge's plate wiggled as he cut his chicken. It had some red spice on it—paprika, he guessed—making his mouth water.

"You got family in L.A.?" Florida asked.

"A son, in Albuquerque."

"When's the last time you seen him?"

Badge remembered Malcolm coming around the corner the night he and Holly tussled, the fear in his eyes. "A while."

"I don't know how you do it." Florida stood up, stretched her arms. "I could never do it, I know that."

"It's what we do," Les said.

Florida snorted. "I know all about what *you* do."

After dinner, Badge left the family and emerged into the warm Philly night. On the street, a marimba band filled the air with its slack rhythms. The sun had migrated to just below the horizon, making everything golden. Lots of people were about, a nice summer weekend, the night young. A few were probably No Fun Intended fans killing time until the Condor opened. There was something Badge had to do, something he should've done weeks ago.

In front of the KFC, a pay phone sat unused. Badge picked up the receiver, dialed Holly's number.

"Hello," she said.

"Holly." He waited. He didn't want to sound too desperate, a traveler lunging for the departing train of her approval.

"Do you want to talk to your son?"

"Sure."

"Well, I'm sure he'd like to talk to you too, but he's not here. He staying the night at Wylie's."

"Do I know Wylie?"

"I don't know, Badge. Do you?"

Silence hovered between them. A kid in a basketball jersey walked past. "Listen," Badge said. "You gotta let me explain. Betty and I—"

"I don't want to hear that name. It's my night off from that name."

"What?"

"Ever since that concert, it's Betty-this and Betty-that. It's fucking Betty twenty-four-seven around here. I want to strangle the kid."

Badge looked at the sky, saw no stars. "I'm sorry."

"He can't quit talking about her. He brags to his friends about his rock and roll family with the rock and roll dad and the rock and roll stepmom he's gonna have."

"He's not gonna have a rock and roll stepmom."

"Well, you might want to talk to him first. He's got it all figured out. He wants to go on the road, play drums with you two."

"It'll pass."

"I'm afraid I've lost him. I think Malcolm's happier you're with Betty than he would be if—"

He wasn't used to hearing her like this, hysterical, filled with defeat. It was Friday night; maybe she was drunk. "You're his mom, and I'm his dad. Nothing's gonna change that."

"But how do you compete? A rock star for a dad and ... How am I supposed to compete with that?"

"No one has to compete with anyone." It was a horrible time to break the news to her, but there wouldn't be a good time. "But just so you know, Hol, he is going to have a little brother or sister."

The line went silent. A bus pulled up, people climbed out, a woman in business dress, a guy with grocery bags, an old lady taking one cautious step at a time.

"Well," Holly said, "that's sure to please him."

"It's not the end of the world."

"Who said it was the end of the world? I can't wait to see what you three cook up. I suppose you'll be on the covers of all those magazines."

"What?" Badge said. "No."

"Oh, really? You think the paparazzi gives you a choice? You think they gave Princess Diana a choice?"

Two overtly gay men, their shirts unbuttoned to the waist, danced to the marimba band, and people stopped to gawk.

"Listen," Badge said, "we have a day off coming up. I'll fly home, see both of you."

"*No.* Please don't come."

"I can talk to Malcolm. We can work this thing out together."

"I mean it, Badge. I really don't want to see you right now." And the line went dead.

21

Betty introduced Badge to Vince after their gig in New York.
"This is Goo," she said, smiling too grandly. "He's an old friend
from high school."

"Vince," the guy said, correcting her.

No more than twenty-five, he looked like a bad guy from
a Japanese cartoon. The angle of his jaw formed a V, and he
wore a black sport-coat-style leather jacket that looked slept
in. His eyes shot glances at everything, and one hand seemed
permanently jammed in his jeans pocket.

No Fun Intended had just finished a raucous, sold-out show
at Granderson Hall for 1,400 fans, and Badge stood there in
front of Betty and this guy, his hair dripping, needing a towel.
"So," he said. "Which is it, Goo or Vince?"

"Vince," the guy said. "Goo's a nickname from a long time
ago."

"You'll always be Goo to me," Betty said.

"How long's it been since you two have seen each other?"

"Seven years," Vince said. "Something like that."

"Has Betty changed?"

"You mean besides being a rock star now?"

"Is that how you found her?"

"She's hard to miss," Vince said. "Her song's on every radio station, and they play that video all the time."

"I'm gonna tell Glen to make them stop," Betty said. "They're gonna wear it out."

"No," Vince said. "Let it happen. The more fans you get now, the better. Then when the label slacks off, you can tell them to shove it and take your fans with you."

"That's what I've been trying to tell these guys all along." She motioned towards Badge.

Yeah, and you're welcome too. "You in the business?" Badge asked Vince.

Vince rubbed his hand around the back of his neck. His sandy blond buzz cut had a hint of unevenness to it, something around the ears. "I manage bands."

"Who do you manage?"

"Bands in Philly. You wouldn't know 'em."

"Give me a try."

"Naw. You wouldn't've heard of 'em."

Me and the rest of the world. Badge spotted a stack of towels by Les. "Well, you two probably have some catching up to do. Nice to meet you."

As Badge toweled himself off, he watched Vince and Betty. Vince spoke with his body as much as his mouth, his hands gesturing, his chin jabbing upwards. Betty listened, smiled, one foot flat against the wall behind her. They could've been teenagers at a sock hop, pretending that a casual conversation was all it was, all they craved. Badge poured a tequila shot, threw it back. *Sure. Old friends.*

No Fun Intended fans started searching Betty out—backstage, in parking lots, at their hotel—and the scope of where she could go got pinched. The worst was after their show in Baltimore. Gaston had pulled the bus off the Beltway to gas up, and Badge was late coming out of his bunk. Over by the truck stop, what must've been a high school kid–shaved head, wristbands–had grabbed Betty by the wrist and struggled to pull her away. The kid saw Badge and took off.

"What the–" Badge ran after him.

The kid hustled around the corner, where fluorescent lights shined on big rigs. Badge weaved in and out of the trucks, looking for him. When he got to the end, he scanned the lot. A semi hissed as it eased past. Gone.

When Badge got back on the bus, Betty popped up from the couch. "Did you get him?"

"No. Who was he?"

Tad sat in the driver's seat, rubbing his forehead. "Must've followed us out of town after the gig."

"That was a fan?"

"He came up to me outside the men's room," Tad said, "told me how much he loved you guys, asked if he could meet Betty."

"He wanted me to go to his car with him," Betty said, more incredulous than startled. "When I said no, he was all surprised."

"Good Christ," Badge said.

"Philly's calling the cops," Tad said.

"Good," Badge said. "From now on, if anyone asks to see Betty, just say no."

"What?" Betty said.

"You heard me."

"It was just one guy."

"One guy too many."

"Two more seconds and he'd've found a Doc Martin in his crotch."

"You almost got kidnapped."

"Oooooo," Betty said, mock fear in her eyes.

"This is not happening again."

Betty stared back at him. "What makes you think you make that decision?"

Badge said nothing, knew he didn't.

"I'm not cloistering myself," she said and stomped to the back.

In D.C., someone knocked at their hotel room door. Badge, fresh out of the shower, dried his hair with a towel. "Check to see who it is first," he said when Betty got up to answer it.

Betty rolled her eyes, made a big show of peeking out the window. "It's Flip. Should I let him in, or should I frisk him first?"

Badge ducked back into the bathroom but couldn't help overhearing their conversation.

"Hey," Flip said. "Got a minute?"

"Depends," Betty said.

"On what?"

The sound of someone, Betty, flopping onto the bed. "On whether this is about what Glen told me yesterday."

"The advance?"

"Yeah."

Flip sighed. "It's just a temporary thing. A couple of issues caught up with me that—"

"Atlantic City?"

They'd all played the tables after the gig. Flip had been on his own at a blackjack table. He didn't leave when everyone else did. "It's just a small thing."

"1,700 bucks?"

Something close to silence.

"Yeah," Flip said.

The sound of Betty adjusting on the bed. She'd been complaining of drowsiness all day.

"It's a one-time—" Flip said, but stopped himself. "I'm sorry. Can we just forget about it?"

"Sure," Betty said. "But what if—"

"It's not a problem," Flip said. "Really. My issue. Forget I said anything." *The sound of the door closing.*

When Badge came out, Betty had turned over in bed, her head deep in the pillow. He grabbed his shaving kit. "When did this happen?"

"Hm?"

"Flip needing money."

"Glen called last night."

"1,700 bucks?"

"That's what he said."

"Jesus."

Betty mumbled something into the pillow.

"Are you going to give it to him?"

Betty's head shot up. "I'm trying to sleep. Do you mind?"

Rounding the corner after soundcheck at the 9:30 Club, Badge almost ran over Reina.

"Whoa," he said.

"Hey," Reina said.

"Holy shit."

"Who knew I'd get that kind of reaction?"

"No one's supposed to be— How'd you get in here?"

"I scaled the wall," Reina said, rolling her eyes. "There's no security. I just strolled in."

Eight years had done nothing to tarnish her looks. Her hair was cut into a short bob, and she wore a business-type skirt and jacket that would've made it difficult for Badge to function in any meeting room she occupied. Her smile alone would've made him buy a dozen of whatever she sold.

Behind him, the crew was adjusting equipment so their new lead-off act, a band called Shoulder La Back, could set up in front of them. Betty was off to a local record distributor, where she'd meet employees, shake hands, sign autographs.

("I'm gonna stage a revolt," she'd said. "A revolt against what?" Les said. "How should I know? But it'll be funner than doing whatever they want me to do.")

"I was in town," Reina said, "and I thought I'd stop by to say hello."

"How'd you know I was–"

She held up a newspaper, which was folded in half. On the right side was a quarter-page ad announcing the gig. Betty stood at the center, and Badge and the rest were fanned out behind her. There he was, for all the world to see. Anyone could show up to these things, and probably would.

Reina smiled. "Come on. I bet you're happier to see me than that."

The streets of D.C. were loud, and cars rolled by, an almost depressing number of them. The Washington Monument stood in the distance, the sun giving it a shimmery quality. Badge's instinct was to stunt the growth of Reina before she spread, like a doctor working to contain an outbreak of cholera.

"Hey," Reina said. She trailed behind him as he walked, trying to keep up in heels. "What's your hurry?"

"There's a place over here we can talk."

"Do I frighten you that much?"

They stood at the corner, waited for the light to change. Badge half hoped she'd leave, hail a cab, not even say goodbye. But there she was. The daylight revealed the beginnings of wrinkles around her eyes, which somehow made them more seductive. If something like wrinkles didn't work on Reina, she'd get rid of them. "We didn't leave on the best of terms."

"Oh, you mean Monty."

Badge had to laugh. It was as though the events that had caused their divorces were as inconsequential as a flat tire on the way to a Pixies concert. "Yes, I mean Monty."

"It happened and it's over. I don't know what else to say to you."

"How about apologizing for getting me divorced?"

"*I* got *you* divorced. Listen, tiger. You may have had something to do with that."

Badge watched traffic ease by. She was right, of course. He grabbed her hand as the light turned green. "Let's go over here. I don't want to have to explain you to everyone."

They ducked into a pub with dark wood interior and only a few patrons. It was too early for happy hour, which the waitresses, filling salt and pepper shakers, were preparing for. Badge grabbed a booth away from the plateglass windows, protection against someone from their entourage walking by and seeing them. He ordered a gin and tonic, Reina a martini.

"Martini," Badge said. "That's new."

"When in Rome."

"Don't tell me you've gotten into politics."

"Not really. I consult for some Internet companies out of San Francisco. I come to D.C. a few times a year, drink with politicians, suggest how they might change this or that bill."

"You're a lobbyist," Badge said.

"More or less."

"Unbelievable."

"Why?"

"I bet you're good at it."

Reina smiled, shrugged. "I get results."

"You miss working with bands?"

"What? No."

"Why not?"

"Music's over," she said, as certainly as if she'd said the earth was round.

"How do you figure?"

"Many reasons." Her tone had authority, which she probably used in board rooms to quell dissent. "File sharing, Ritalin, the talent pool drying up. The world doesn't need its rock and roll anymore."

"Is that right."

"That's right. All the business side can do is circle the wagons and hope for the best."

"You don't think people care about music anymore?"

"There will always be exceptions, but rock's economic and political pull is dwindling. Don't believe me? In five years you'll be lucky to get anyone to listen to your music for free."

Badge tried to imagine a world without rock and roll. It seemed impossible. He'd been listening to it for as long as he'd been drinking, chasing women. Maybe those were disappearing too. "Well, you'd never know it by coming to our shows."

"I don't know how Betty happened. Where's she from?"

"Orange County. High school dropout. The girl's amazing."

"You sound smitten."

"She's one of the most vital people I've ever met."

The drinks came, brought by a T-shirted waitress who took Reina's cash without a word. Reina sipped her martini. "Is she good in bed?"

Badge tugged on his own drink, felt the booze slide down his throat. "We're seeing each other, yes."

"'Seeing each other,'" Reina said, mock shock in her eyes. "Sounds serious."

"They haven't come up with a good phrase for it."

"Fuck buddies?"

"More like lovers."

"Lovers," Reina said, a fake whimsy in her voice. "There's a word you don't hear much anymore."

"And guess what? *She's having my baby.*"

"Oh my."

"Yeah."

"You're full of surprises."

"Imagine how I feel."

"Your second?"

"Yep," Badge said. "Malcolm, with Holly."

"Two more Badges. How will the world survive?"

"Seems to be doing all right so far."

"Hey," someone said from behind them. Betty.

A split second of shock quickly melded into something closer to resignation. Here they were, Reina and Betty, occupying the same space, just like they occupied space in Badge. It felt purifying having them both there in front of him, being thrown into the bonfire of his own unconscious. Once the fire burned out, anything left would be impermeable. "What happened to the meet and greet?" Badge said.

"Canceled," Betty said. "Forklift accident. I'm supposed to dedicate a song to Dock Five." She eyed Reina. "Who's this?"

"This is Reina. She's—"

"A big fan," Reina said, extending her hand, "who's using her friendship with your guitar player to get a chance to meet you."

Betty shook her hand, a bit uncertainly. Reina still had the power to stun, her sales pitch like a boxer's jab. "So, what are—"

"I was just telling Badge here I need your input for some work I'm doing for some clients. You see, these folks are way, way up in the Internet music world. They're in the business of getting your music to the people who want it."

"Like Napster," Betty said.

"Not Napster, but like Napster, yes." Reina looked at Badge. "From the news you'd think Napster was the only one." She turned back to Betty, put her hands on the table. "You see, not everyone in the music world wants my boys to succeed. Some—big record companies, for example—are doing everything they can to shut them down."

"Then I think *your boys*," Betty said, "should tell the record companies to go screw themselves."

"See, that's why I wanted to talk to you," Reina said. "I read that *AP* profile and thought, 'Here's a woman with something to say,' and the companies I work for want to make sure you have a place to say it."

"Like a spokesman?"

"A talented, powerful artist telling it like it is," Reina said. "You say what you want into a few cameras, and you become the 21st century version of Fuck the Oligarchy. You'd be way ahead of the curve on this one, by the way. All the powder puffs—Spears, Stefani, that Lillith tripe—they're scared to death of this."

"Really?" Betty said. "Wussies."

"Exactly," Reina said. "All we need is an artist to come forward and say what she's really thinking about file sharing."

"Then what?" Betty said.

"Then we sit back and watch the walls come down," Reina said, one eyebrow raising. She'd used the same gesture years ago to sell Badge on infidelity. "All I need from you is to say yes, and we'll take care of the rest."

"It sounds cool," Betty said, "but I don't do that kind of work."

Reina looked confused. "What kind of work?"

"I'm a singer. If I wanna get paid, I write or play live."

"And I know that," Reina said, "and if this weren't more important than money I wouldn't even bother you with it. This is about one entity—record companies, big radio, big media, all coming together to form one gigantic Man—making sure people like your fans don't get the music they want the way they want it. It's about freedom, Betty. Where will we be if no one stands up for freedom? Not because it's profitable, but because it's right."

Betty looked worked up. Badge touched her hand. "You don't have to say anything now."

"Of course not," Reina said, as though everything she'd said *hadn't* been calculated to make Betty answer right then. Reina reached into her purse, slid her card towards Betty. "You think about it, and let me know if you'd like to have some fun fucking the world. For our end, we'd love to have you."

"Okay," Betty said. She took the card without taking her eyes off Reina. "Badge, is this the woman you were having sex with when you got divorced?"

Badge glanced at Reina, who, thankfully, looked bemused. "Um, yeah."

"Wow," Betty said. "I tell ya, Reina. You're the second hottie in a month to show up at a show who wound up being his old fuck buddy."

"Fuck buddy!" Reina said, looking at Badge, her eyes wide as poker chips.

These two together, Badge would either be the happiest he'd ever been, or the most miserable. He had no idea which.

"Don't worry, loverboy," Betty said. "I'm off to the hotel. You two can cavort a while longer if you want."

As she walked away, Badge called after her, "Could you at least *pretend* to be jealous?"

"That's quite a catch," Reina said.

"I told you." The booze was making its migration through his head, a syrup-y feeling.

Reina raised her drink. "To Badge and Betty," she said, and the two clinked glasses.

"So that's your new gig?" Badge said.

"What?"

"Finding artists to sing for the other side."

"For the moment."

"You like it?"

"Girl's gotta make a living."

"You used to be the best."

"Best at what?"

"Signing bands, making records, causing a general ruckus."

"My salad days," she said, whimsically.

"Why not get back into it?"

"No, thanks."

"You say the well's dry. Who better than you to fill it?"

Reina leaned back in her seat. The click of plastic darts came from behind them. "Monty took care of that. Funny, but when it came down to it, with our lawyers out and ready for war, he didn't care about the money or the house or the cars. He just wanted me out of the business." She smiled, but the smile held no mirth. "So now I'm surviving out on the fringe with the rest of the cast-offs."

"Well, there are plenty of us out here." Badge threw down the rest of his drink, got up.

"So," Reina said. "Are your words of wisdom and a watered-down martini all I'm gonna get for my ten bucks?"

"What do you want?"

"Come see me after the gig." Her eyes lit up, the dimmer switch pushed to the top. "I'm at the Watergate Hotel. We can look for secret rooms, dig up new evidence."

"Sorry. Can't."

"Betty wouldn't mind."

"I would."

"And you don't want to."

Badge smiled, said nothing.

"Then take my card," Reina said.

"That's not necessary."

She reached into her purse, slid a card across the table. "Loneliness has a way of making the rounds in this world. You never know when you might need it."

22

That night at the 9:30 Club, a sea of a thousand heads rocked as No Fun Intended played. Slam-dancers circled down front. Two kids stood just behind the mosh pit watching Badge's every move. Axe-slingers, or future axe-slingers, you could tell. The faces got more obscure as the crowd extended back, eventually becoming nothing but a blur.

But Badge spotted Vince.

He saw him just as he finished his solo for "Lucky Charm." Vince leaned against the wall, holding a longneck beer, wearing the same leather suit coat he'd worn in New York. A smirk, like he'd just beaten Badge at some game, stretched across his face. He stared at Badge, didn't blink, didn't turn away.

Backstage after the show, Betty was nowhere to be found. Badge was going to look for her when Philly stopped him, cell phone in hand. "You got a second? I got West Coast press on the line."

Badge looked towards the door, which led to the parking lot. "You want Betty. I'll check the bus."

"That's where I just came from." Philly pushed the phone at Badge.

Badge rolled his eyes, faked a smile, took the phone. "Hello?"

"Badge," said the interviewer. "This is Marcia Vollman of *Modern Baby* magazine. Are you the father-to-be?"

He didn't know it was *that* kind of interview. "That's me."

"Is it okay if I record you?"

"Yeah. Listen, are you sure you don't want to talk to the mother?"

"Oh no. Our magazine looks for fresh, new ways to explore the parent-baby dynamic. You're perfect."

"Okay. Hit me."

"So, what's it like to be expecting?"

That is fresh and new. Badge fell back onto the sofa, grabbed his drink. Cosmo and some girl talked just inside the room, their heads bent close. "Exciting, if kind of surreal. We live in this submarine of a tour bus, so even with the baby coming it's rock and roll around here most of the time."

"What's it like performing next to the woman who's going to have your baby?"

Betty's pregnancy had done nothing to dampen her performances. The drum riser had become her spot of choice during solos, a place she could fling herself down from. When she did it, Badge tried not to look. "It's about the same as before. You can't tell Betty to do anything for her own good."

"How far along is she?"

"Six weeks."

"That's early."

"The stick turned pink. That's all I know."

"Badge, tell me," Marcia said. "Are you two hoping for a boy or a girl?"

"We haven't talked much about it, but I'm leaning towards a girl. I have a boy already."

"You and—"

"From a previous marriage. This is Betty's— We'd settle for a healthy anything."

"Have you decided on names?"

"We really haven't. We promise to name it something."

"Great quote. And what does the little bundle of joy mean for the future of— What's the name of the band? No Fun Intended?"

"We don't see it as a choice between—"

"What I mean is, are you going to take some time off from performing?"

Just then, Betty walked into the room. She wore her grey sweatsuit, and her outfit from the show hung over her arm. She sat on the couch. Cosmo and the girl had migrated away. "I think the plan is to take some kind of break," Badge said.

Who is it? Betty mouthed.

Badge put his hand over the receiver. "*Modern Baby.* You wanna take it?"

Betty's eyes got big, and she shook her head violently *no.*

"So, when's the magical day?" Marcia said.

"Early March. We've got a few months of touring left, then we go back to L.A. and start making a home for our new family."

"Great. Well, I won't keep you any longer. Congrats to you and Betty. I wish you all the happiness in the world."

"Thanks," Badge said and hung up, dropping the phone on the couch.

"How'd you get stuck with that one?" Betty said. She spread her gig outfit on the couch, making sure the sweat dried with no wrinkles so she could wear it again tomorrow.

"Someone wasn't here." Badge's drink was tapped. He went to the booze table, poured another. "Where were you?"

"Fans," Betty said, not looking at him. She seemed to be taking on the attributes of motherhood, something in the slope of her neck as she tended to her dress, like her head spun in bliss thinking of her baby ... or someone else.

"Weird show, huh?" Badge said. He wanted Betty to bring up Vince. If it came from her, it meant so much more.

"I thought the set moved too slow."

"You didn't think the crowd was a little strange?"

Betty didn't move. From the back, she could have been praying, or waiting for the firing squad. "What do you mean?"

"I don't know." He took hit of his drink. *She knows and hopes I don't.* "Just something I picked up. Must've been me."

When Badge woke up in the hotel room the next morning, Betty wasn't there.

He grabbed his cigarettes and smoked while he waited. His life was becoming one long wait, for Betty, for the show, for the kid, for something to come along and take all this away from him. He was tired of it. He would ferret it out now.

He sat in the desk chair with the curtains open and watched blackbirds take off and land on a telephone wire. He brewed a pot of coffee. By the time Betty showed up, the ashtray held several butts.

Her eyes looked startled when she saw him sitting there, feet up on the air conditioner, the fog of smoke engulfing him. "Hey," she said.

"Where have you been?"

"Excuse me?" She had a false, cocked tone to her voice. It was the voice he knew she'd use to lie to him.

"I asked where you've been." He didn't turn from his spot in front of the window.

"The Internet cafe up the street. This place has no access."

"What's so important on the Internet for you to climb out of bed on a Sunday morning?"

"We're on the road. There's no such thing as Sunday morning."

"What were you doing?"

Betty set her computer bag down, sighed. It was a sound he remembered hearing from her in the studio, the track not coming together, her vocals bothering her. "I don't want to get into it. You got drunk last night."

"Get into what? You just went to the Internet cafe up the street."

"You're trying to make it sound like—"

"I saw him, Betty."

He thought he heard a gasp, a short, almost imperceptible escape of air. Maybe it was a random noise from the coffee maker, or maybe the ringing in his ears from last night's gig was playing tricks with him, but the sentiment of it—that the secret was out—cascaded through the room, through him and, he guessed, through her.

"What?" she said.

"I saw him from the stage." Badge flicked an ash into the ashtray. "He smiled at me."

"Okay," she said. "I met Goo at the Internet cafe."

"Right."

"I didn't say anything because I didn't want you to freak out."

"Why would I freak out?"

"I saw how you were in New York."

"How was I?"

"You acted like the jilted lover."

"He's your old boyfriend."

"That's right. My *old* boyfriend. And that's what I told him."

"Come on."

"It's true."

Badge sucked on his cigarette, blew out smoke. "You told him you're not interested in him."

"Of course I did."

"You told him to stay away."

"I told him I was with you."

Badge set his cigarette down. He felt vulnerable, like a depleted helium balloon, hovering just above the floor, easily kicked. He couldn't look at her for fear of giving in too early.

Betty slid her hands over his shoulders, bent over, her lips close, her breath the slightest warm breeze against his ear. "I told him I'm having your baby."

Badge grabbed his cigarette, took a long drag. He couldn't afford to be made a fool of. If she were lying, if she betrayed him with Vince, he'd never be able to live with having forgiven her. He mashed out his cigarette. "I don't want to see him again."

"Or what?"

He blew out smoke, felt the nicotine in him, the buoyancy it gave him. "If I do, we'll find out."

23

In Tallahassee, the crew unloaded at the Lilly Pad, a long, low, cinder-blocked club that must've been a strip joint at one time. Metal poles came up from half-circle stages at the edges of the room. Someone had painted the bar's logo, a giant alligator, over the faded outline of what must've been a curvaceous woman. This place had come together quickly. If the Lilly Pad was Tallahassee's idea of a good music venue, then it was seriously hurting as a rock and roll town.

Tad pushed Les's cabinet up the ramp that led to the stage, let out a puff. "Welcome to the jungle," he said.

Badge nodded from his bar stool. He was starting to feel the weight of life on the road. It had been sweltering all through the South. The stagnant air, the mundanity of the bus, the lack of anything to say kept him quiet most of the time. He found himself hanging out at the venues earlier than necessary, chasing down a drink before soundcheck, nursing it as the crew loaded in. Anything to get away for a while, a small chunk of time not dominated by Betty.

It had become impossible to break her away from the add sheets that revealed where "Calypso" was being played, the magazines that quoted her, the Internet chat rooms where people dished on her around the clock. It wasn't a problem during the shows. She still performed with the command of an astronaut, or the elegance of a matador, or the verve of a graffiti artist. She didn't so much play the music as release it, her voice destroying as it created, every scream like a wrecking ball that left perfect rainbows in its wake.

But away from the stage, lying in their hotel bed before she woke up, or staring at the horizon as the bus drove, Badge could see, if not lines of worry, where they would eventually settle on her face. She was taking it all too seriously, allowing to gnaw at her what she should've dismissed out of hand. Her pregnancy, the thing that should've been becoming more important to her, seemed yesterday's news, as relevant as a gig or meal or hotel stay from weeks ago. Holly, who'd never talked about kids until she was pregnant, had only gotten more interested as the days ticked by. With Betty, the subject didn't come up unless Badge brought it up.

"What do you think will be the last day of the tour?" he'd said. They were in their hotel room in Atlanta, and Betty was, as usual, staring at her computer, searching for opinions of herself.

"Huh?"

"We're booked through summer, last gig L.A. Do you think we'll make it that far?"

"Of course we will."

"That puts you at three months. How much longer after that?"

"The doctor said I have five months before I even have to start worrying about it."

"So we tour through October?"

"I don't know right now, okay? Jesus, you'd think you were the one having the baby."

Luckily, a happy occasion was right around the corner. Betty would turn twenty-two in a couple of weeks. No Fun Intended would be in Austin, and Glen had rented out the banquet hall at their hotel, arranged food and booze, made sure everyone would be there. Glen himself would fly in from L.A., as well as a bunch of folks from the record company. Shoulder La Back would play an acoustic set, learning numbers like "Happy Birthday" along with some of Betty's favorites. A party with friends, a show put on for her, plenty of chances to ham it up, it was exactly what she needed. Hopefully, once they headed back west, everyone would start acting like themselves again.

Tad positioned Les's amp stageleft, wiped his brow. "Badge, how long you been playing guitar?"

"Twenty-five years."

"So, if I start now, I could be as good by the time I'm fifty?"

Badge tried to muster a laugh but couldn't. He took a hit of his drink. "I imagine you'd be a prodigy."

"A guitar prodigy," Tad said. "That'd work."

"Of course, there's a quicker way."

"What's that?"

"Buy a bass."

That was when Badge saw movement out of the corner of his eye. Someone, a man, ambled up the main corridor, pushed his way through the double doors and out into the day. It looked like Vince. He couldn't be sure, but the texture of the buzz cut, the long gait, it had to be. Rage inflated inside Badge, and he bounded off his stool and out the door.

The sun had a starkness to it, and it brought with it the kind of punishing heat that had originally led to the invention of the siesta. Industrial plants surrounded Badge on both sides, but no vehicles came or went. Vince—it *was* Vince—rounded a corner, unaware he was being followed, and Badge took off after him. Badge rounded the corner and stopped when he saw Vince approach a waiting cab. Someone was standing next to the cab. Betty.

Badge doubled back, stood against a wall, peeked around.

The two were talking. Vince had his hands in his pockets, Betty looked at him, her arms crossed. It was impossible to tell what was going on. Then Betty gave him something, the pair hugged, and Betty jumped into the cab, which drove away.

Badge went back to the club, reclaimed his stool. Vince was back, Betty knew it. He threw down the rest of his drink, headed for the door.

When he got to their hotel room, Annelle, the band's Southeast radio promoter, sat at the table with Betty. Annelle's leather boots peeked out from beneath her jeans, and she held a stack of CDs against her chest. A freshly cracked tequila bottle sat on the table, its cork off, next to a shot glass.

"Hey," Annelle said.

"Vince," Badge said, glaring at Betty.

Betty looked out the window.

"That's my cue," Annelle said and stood up. She was one of the most seductive women Badge had ever seen, coils of short hair, long neck, hips that rocked like moored boats. Badge had always suspected Annelle had a crush on him, but it might've been Annelle's gift to make everyone feel that way. "I'd better get these CDs over to the station, but Badge, just so you know." She grabbed his arm, squeezed it. "Number three in all the fucking South."

"Awesome."

"I think we got a shot at *numero uno* next week." She smiled, a full-toothed grin. Not long ago, she was close to losing her job, unable to break three alternative bands in as many months, until No Fun Intended saved her ass. "Fraugarten's got to be on its last leg. They can't keep feeding that German shit to kids in Atlanta, can they?"

"Well, kids are the best because they do whatever you tell them."

Annelle laughed. "Well, guess what? Next week they're

gonna have the sudden urge to give it up for Betty." She kissed Badge's cheek and left.

"What about him?" Betty said, still looking out the window.

"What were you doing with him?"

"I wasn't doing anything with him."

"Why didn't you tell me he was here?"

"I just found out."

"You didn't know?"

"Not until he called."

"What did he want?"

"None of your business."

"You're cavorting with your old boyfriend, and it's not my business."

"I wasn't cavorting."

"What were you doing?"

She turned away. "He needed money."

"Christ. How much?"

"A few twenties."

"What for?"

"A Greyhound ticket back home."

Badge doubted it. At this point he had to. "What was he doing here in the first place?"

"I can't stop him from following us if he wants."

"Is that what he's doing?"

"Not anymore."

"And I'm supposed to believe that?"

Betty wouldn't look at him. "Believe whatever you want."

Badge went to the table, tried to look into her eyes but she wouldn't oblige. He grabbed the tequila, filled the shot glass.

"Annelle used that," she said.

"Whatever," he said and threw the shot down.

24

Annelle followed the band to Memphis, cruising by them on I-65 in her rented Lincoln Town Car, waving as she passed. After the Memphis gig, she offered to take anyone who wanted to go to the Palisades Hotel and Casino. "It's in Mississippi," she said. "Way out in the middle of nowhere. Everyone at the label swears by it."

"I'll go," Gaston said. With no travel until the next day, Gaston was ready to party.

"I'm in," Les said.

"No casinos for me," Flip said, looking despondent, a baseball fan turning down a trip to Wrigley Field.

"Good call," Betty said.

"What about you?" Badge said to Betty.

Betty crossed her arms. They were corralled in front of the Peacock Club where they'd just played to 500 loyals. It was the kind of gig they were seeing fewer and fewer of, intimate exchanges that created longtime fans. Despite the hour, Beale Street buzzed with people and traffic. Betty hadn't changed from her gig outfit—red leather mini, black top—and every once in a while someone whistled from a car. "I need a night off from you bozos."

"Anything wrong?" Badge said.

"A little sick. No big deal."

For all he knew, Vince was still around, waiting for Badge to let his guard down. "I'll hang back too."

"No," Betty said. "Please go."

"I don't mind."

Betty grabbed both of Badge's arms. "Get the fuck away from me for a while."

"Hormones," Les whispered as Betty walked away.

Later, when Badge climbed into Annelle's Town Car, Flip and Gaston were in the backseat.

"Don't tell Betty," Flip said.

"Everyone ready?" Annelle said. She had a half-filled glass between her legs, a drink stolen from the club.

"Where's Les?" Badge said.

"Bagged out," Annelle said. "Just the four of us."

"*Just the four of us*," Gaston sang, a nice, round baritone. Gaston was gussied up, new black polo shirt, crisp jeans, and his hair was greased back in what must've been a first encounter with styling gel.

Annelle eased into traffic. "Sounds like someone had some vocal training."

"I sing when I'm happy," Gaston said. "And at church."

"And when traffic clears," Flip said.

"Does that sign say 61?" Annelle said.

"Does that mean you can't see it?" Badge said.

Annelle laughed, beautiful rows of white teeth. Badge had seen her drinking just offstage during their set, dancing with Philly during "Calypso." Along Highway 61, redbrick buildings stood mostly abandoned. Streetlamps led into darkness.

"You ever been to this place?" Flip said.

"I never come to these parts," Annelle said. "If it weren't for you guys, I'd be sitting at my desk begging some programmer to play something."

"Memphis is a great town," Gaston said. "I used to hit it with Bill Bayou every few months in the seventies. You wouldn't believe the fun we had."

"Different now?" Annelle said.

"Better now," Gaston said. "Cleaner, neater, but— I don't know— Something's missing."

"We want it both ways, don't we," Annelle said. She was paying more attention to the conversation than the road, and the Town Car eased towards the shoulder. "I think I'm all street until I get around a Pottery Barn. Then I'm buying all this earth-tone shit."

"Paintings with apples," Flip said.

"You saw that one too?" Annelle said. "I so wanted that one."

The casino was upon them within an hour, a massive, luminescent building, curves of light drawing shapes in the night. It stood like a monument to a world brighter, prouder, more gaudy than the one they lived in. A parking lot extended out, a shuttle puttered to the casino. A group of cars bunched by the entrance, so close their owners could stumble to them with no problem.

"Wow."

"Whoa."

"I had no idea."

"Mississippi did it right," Annelle said. "Tennessee don't want gambling? Fine. We'll build a casino right on your border."

"Just like Vegas," Flip said. He was visibly struck, the scene offering its strange beauty to him at no charge ... for now.

"What do you want to play, boys?" Annelle said.

"Blackjack," Flip said.

"A friend of mine taught me craps years ago," Badge said. It was Reggie. One lazy summer afternoon the pair had gone to Vegas and spent a fruitless thirty-six hours at the tables.

"I'd love to play craps," Annelle said, "but I don't know a

thing about it." She glanced at Badge. "I don't suppose you'd want to teach me."

Inside, red velvet curtains hung at least a hundred feet from the ceiling. There was little action. A boomerang of blackjack tables extended one way, half of them covered. Rows of slots followed the curve of the wall. In the other direction, keno tables, roulette, some mandarin game. The craps area seemed to be where the action was. People crowded around tables, leaned in, cheered when something good happened.

"So," Annelle said. She wore a leather racing jacket that accented the slant of her waist. Her hips—nothing but her hips—eased closer to Badge. Flip and Gaston had already beaten a path to the nearest blackjack table. "You wanna take me to school?"

Badge had to laugh a little. The hotel's lobby was right through the door. "Come on."

"Come on, what?"

"You know I can't."

"But you want to."

"Good luck to the program director who doesn't want to play your record."

Annelle smiled, eased towards him. He could smell her, something close to cocoa butter but more expensive. He felt he could kiss her with nothing but a stretch of his lips. "It's only rock and roll," she said.

"I know, but Betty."

"You in love?"

"Maybe."

"If she cared that much, she'd've come, right?"

"I'm trying not to give her any reason to doubt me. This old boyfriend of hers is around."

"Vince."

"You know about him?"

"The crackhead."

"What?"

Annelle pursed her lips.

"What are you talking about?"

She looked away.

"Vince is a crackhead?"

"I didn't say that."

"Yes, you did."

"No, I didn't."

"Did Betty tell you that?"

The fire in Annelle's eyes died out, doused by the bucket of Badge's inattention. She backed away, slid a hand down his chest. "You want to obsess over that girl for the rest of your life, go ahead. But tonight it's either craps, or it's something else. Take your pick."

The four of them played blackjack at the same table. Their dealer—a Vietnamese guy with thick hair and no rapport—seemed to take pleasure in busting them. Gaston was up 200 early and lost it all back, each disappointing hit conjuring a "bah" from his lips. Annelle kept her chips in stacks in front of her, betting here and there, switching to a slot machine called "Crazzzy 8s," finishing one drink after another, waiting until the rest wanted to leave. Flip was down early and quickly, losing all his pocket cash within minutes, then finding an ATM and blowing that too. Badge barely paid attention to his cards, wondering how he'd play his hand with Betty later.

"He's trying to quit," Betty said.

Badge and Betty had just ordered breakfast at a diner called Phyllis' on Beale Street—formica countertops, cylindrical cream dispensers, padded booth seats. Betty, who'd woken up craving pancakes, ordered the Tall Stack. Badge ordered coffee. Nothing but coffee sounded good.

"They're all trying to quit," Badge said.

"What?"

"Your money is now in the hands of some drug dealer in Tallahassee."

"What kind of attitude is that?"

"It's reality. They've been trying to cure it for as long as it's been around, but it never works. An addict is an addict is an addict."

"You mean like you?"

Badge stared at her. A million arguments jostled in his head like dancers behind frosted glass. He leaned across the table. "I don't borrow money from people for booze. I don't lie, to you or to anyone else–"

"You can quit anytime, right?"

There was nothing he could say. If the girl wanted to try and save a drug addict, to feel the distinct way the heart breaks when the addict failed her, fine. Everyone had to do it once. Only fools did it again. "I won't be quitting tonight, that's for sure."

25

The next night, in New Orleans, after the band finished a raucous gig at Valentine's on Bourbon Street, Badge's adrenaline finally relaxed enough to turn his attention to Betty. When her cell phone rang, she went to answer it.

"You're kidding," Badge said. He was on his knees, on the bed, completely naked. His erection pointed up at two o'clock. Vince had already called once that day, needing someone to talk to during his "recovery."

"He's at a critical point," Betty said. In nothing but her tank top, she fumbled for the phone.

"*I'm* at a critical point."

"Goo?" she said, putting the phone to her ear.

Anger spun in Badge. It was feeling oddly similar to the one that had led to his erection, but somehow flip-flopping it, making the light dark, a photo negative of his soul. He grabbed the phone from her.

"Hey," she said.

Badge went into the bathroom, threw it into the toilet.

"What the fuck?" Betty said. Her eyes bounced from the toilet to him. "You asshole."

"That makes two of us."

"Who the fuck do you think you are?"

"The person you're supposed to care about."

"I sure as hell don't care about you right now."

Badge gathered his clothes.

"I'm all he has," Betty said.

Badge pulled on his pants. "That's sweet."

"I'd do the same for you if you'd let me."

Badge stomped into his boots, didn't bother to tie them. "Thanks anyway," he said and left.

The New Orleans night was hot and thick. Streetlamps dotted the road. Red and yellow neon signs illuminated storefronts. A heavy-dropped rain felt seconds away.

He turned up Chaise Street, meandered past businesses, each with steps leading upward. In New Orleans, the only way to go was up. Go down and the place would swallow you. A few strip clubs were open, backlit pictures of dancing girls in the windows. A boy tap-danced, extending his hand. This town could see right through you, smell your heart right out of you. Badge handed the kid some change before ducking through the door.

The inside glowed dark red. Almost no one was there. A stripper in nothing but a G-string danced on a stage for an audience of one. The customer was younger, skinny, buzz-headed. He sat very close to the stage, his legs spread, smiling up. The stripper, her hair beaded like Bo Derek's in *10*, smiled coyly, turned and let the kid have an eyeful. Soft club jazz played from somewhere. The kid probably thought he was going to get her number.

Badge sat at the bar, which was padded with red vinyl along its edge. The bartender—really old, with folds of skin dangling from his jaw—wore a white shirt, dirty at the collar, and a black vest. He nodded at Badge. "What can I get you?" His voice was thinner and higher pitched than Badge expected.

"Gin and tonic."

"Yessuh," the man said. With clinks and gurgles, he handled the bottles.

Badge lit a cigarette. "What do you do if someone gets out of hand?"

"Hm?"

"You know." Badge exhaled smoke. "What if that guy over there decides he wants to drag that woman out the door?"

The old man smiled. "This here's an easy place. Now, Bubba's up the street?" He dropped a lime into Badge's drink. "You play rough, you wind up at Bubba's."

"Is that right?"

"That's right." The old man slid the glass to Badge. "Being around as long as I have, you come to know a few things."

Badge took a drink. It was stiff compared to what he was used to, but that stiffness tasted good, like a bite from an exotic fruit, one that might be poisonous. "Tell me what you know."

The old man smiled. "I know you didn't come in here to talk to me."

Badge took a tug from his drink. He liked this old man. There was something redoubtable about him, a soothsayer, seeing your future, handing it back to you. "Okay. Why did I come here tonight?"

"Why does any man come here?"

"You answer questions with questions." Badge sucked down the rest of his drink, slid his glass across the bar. "Hit me."

"You don't want answers," the man said. He took the glass, dumped the ice. Badge took a drag from his cigarette. This was exactly who he wanted to talk to, this guy and no one else. The old man scooped ice, worked the bottles. "No one really wants the answers. The questions keep us going."

"So, what's the question?"

The old man tilted his head, poured. "How pleasant can life be for me in the next hour?"

"I'm gonna guess you have some idea how pleasant life can be for me in the next hour."

The old man set Badge's drink in front of him, leaned in. "Dominique," he whispered.

"Dominique."

"Bet your ass." The old man reached under the bar, slid a photo to Badge.

It was a Polaroid, swollen with age, showing a dark-haired girl in lace underwear. The flash made her face look blown-out, and her lips, puckered towards Badge, resembled nothing so much as a plum carefully sliced into, ready to eat.

"You're offering me this girl?"

"She's in back. I get her for you."

Badge looked at the picture again. "What's her story?"

"Same as everyone. Got in with the wrong crowd. From Carolina, I think."

"Carolina." Badge took a drink, looked at the picture. "Dominique from Carolina."

"You want her, I get her."

Badge set the picture down. "How much?"

The old man's brow wrinkled. "For you? Seventy-five."

"For an hour?"

"Maybe not quite that long. Maybe till you're satisfied."

Badge turned towards the room. The stripper had come off the stage and was chatting with the young man. She swayed to the music, ran her hand over his hair. Everyone's heart was on display in this town. Badge wanted to see Dominique's, to see if it beat like his. He spun back around. "I'll take her."

"Very good," the old man said. He tapped the bar twice, disappeared behind a curtain. "Dominique," he yelled.

Badge sucked his drink down to the ice, stared at the line of bottles behind the bar. Betty wouldn't care, and Badge might not care if she cared. He took one last tug and ducked into the bathroom.

When he came out, the old man was smiling. "She's ready. You got the money?"

Badge reached for his wallet, pulled out three twenties, searched out a ten and a five.

"And for the drinks," the old man said.

Badge rolled his eyes, took out another twenty, replaced the ten with it.

The old man lifted the barricade that offered access behind the bar. "You gonna have a good time."

The gin worked its magic as Badge walked down the hallway. Since he'd arrived in New Orleans earlier that day, he felt discombobulated. The city had a way of turning him around, like someone was repeatedly blindfolding him and dropping him at different locations. The wallpaper, flower designs, curled at the top. The place smelled of something slightly more pleasant than mildew and slightly less pleasant than cherry flavoring.

The hallway led to a dimly lit room, almost darker than if the lights had been out entirely. A bed, the sheets a mess, was the only furniture. A television, turned off, sat in the corner. On the bed sat a book, upside-down to mark its place. *I Never Promised You a Rose Garden*.

"Hello, hon," Badge heard from behind him.

Dominique stood in the frame of the bathroom door. She was shorter than Badge had expected, her face fuller. Her hair, grown since the picture, was styled in a new, chaotic way, a lion's mane. She seemed edgy, like something boiled just beneath her surface, something she'd never admit to him. She wore a robe, dark and silky. Badge couldn't tell its color in the dim light. "What did you have in mind?" she said.

The simplest route was the easiest to explain. "Guy out front seems to think you can make me feel better."

"We can do that," she said, the slightest hint of a Southern accent in her voice. She reached into the bathroom for her cigarette, took a drag. "Take your pants off."

"I was maybe thinking we could talk a little–"

Before he could finish, Dominique was upon him. She got onto her knees, started unbuckling his belt. "You go right ahead and talk, hon, as long as you don't mind if I–" She worked his pants down, got to work.

"So," Badge said. Dominique's spell enveloped him, sending waves through his thighs, little sparks as harmless as those from Fourth of July fireworks. "You like that book you're reading?"

"Mm-mm," Dominique said.

Badge felt softness in all the right places. He touched her hair but found it too sculpted. "There's this girl."

"Mm-mm," Dominique said.

Badge felt sweat build up on his head. "She's too young for me."

"Un-mm," Dominique said.

"But now my life's all tied up with hers, and I can't– I can't seem to– I can't come standing up."

Badge edged down onto the bed, and Dominique followed, continuing where she'd left off. "I can't see our lives together after this tour." He touched Dominique's head, ignoring the hairspray. He fell backward onto the bed.

"Mm," Dominique said.

"I don't know what I'd do if– I don't– Oooh–"

The release spread quickly from the center of his forehead to every extremity, like a water balloon breaking on a concrete floor. Dominique performed the finale in a way that was efficient to the task and that Badge could neither see nor imagine. He lay on his back, letting the world, all of its unanswered questions, creep back into him.

Betty was on the hotel rotary when Badge got back. She lay facedown, still in nothing but her top, her legs bent with her feet in the air. Badge grabbed his clothes bag.

"What are you doing?" Betty said.

"Getting my own room. Tell Philly to get me one from now on."

She looked at him, then said into the phone, "Goo, I gotta go."

"Don't bother," Badge said and slammed the door behind him.

26

The next morning, band and crew watched as Badge came out of his hotel room. They already seemed to know the events of the night before, like everyone on the bus was connected by nerve tissue and things registered with each of them at the same time. Then again, maybe people just talked too much. Badge walked past them, boarded the bus, headed to the back.

"So," Les said. He sat down next to him, slapped Badge's knee. "Betty finally wised up and got rid of you, eh?"

Badge said nothing.

"You know, if you want to share a hotel room for a while—"

"No, thanks."

"It's not a big deal. I get bored on my own anyway."

"It's cool. Don't worry about it."

"Well, if you change your—"

"I know it's weird for everyone. It's weird for me too, but it's just going to have to be weird for a while."

In Nashville, No Fun Intended were to play a relic of a ballroom called the Emporium, and a camera crew from MTV would be there to film the gig, the footage for a new show called *True to Life*. Glen had worked the phones for weeks to set it up, but Betty wanted nothing to do with it.

"MT fucking V?" Betty said. "Do they even play music anymore?"

"They play the hell out of our video," Les said.

They met the MTV crew at a Mexican restaurant just up Elliston. The director, Nolan, dark hair turning silver and his nose so sculpted it looked cartoonish, tried to impress Betty with his knowledge of L.A. punk. "The Go-Go's were the last thing we'd listen to back then. Belinda Carlisle? Please. It was all about X. It was all about the Germs."

"The Germs?" Betty said, incredulous. She stirred her virgin margarita. Badge liked that she'd ordered it, a reminder he was still part of her.

Nolan shook his head vigorously. "People think of them as this band of waste-oids, but they were fantastic when they first started." He took a hit from his cigarette, stared wistfully into his past. "I can't think of one band from the nineties that even came close to them. Maybe Screaming Trees."

"That good, eh?" Betty said, rolling her eyes.

"If I had a video camera back then, I'd be a rich man today."

Later, in the backstage room, Betty paced back and forth. "That phony wouldn't know 'true to life' if it came cascading out of his ass."

"It sounded like he knew a lot about the scene back then," Les said. Since New Orleans, Les had taken up the stance of devil's advocate. Badge, with no more leverage, kept his mouth shut.

"The Germs? Please."

"I always heard they were better than advertised," Les said.

Betty kept pacing, her arms locked behind her. She stopped, her eyes sparkling. "What was that store we passed on the way in?"

On Betty's direction, everyone piled into The Stitchin' Post. The walls were covered with pearl-buttoned shirts, denim pants, cowhide coats and any number of cowboy hats.

Mannequins were outfitted in the latest styles from Stetson and Wrangler. Novelty T-shirts–"Nothin' but Country," "It's a Country Thing, You Wouldn't Understand"–occupied nooks along the wall. A giant clock advertised Woonsocket's Chewing Tobacco, *The Snuff That's Ruff.*

Betty stopped them as they came in. "Pick out whatever you want. We're wearing it for the show."

Les looked around with something like horror in his eyes. "What if we don't want anything?"

"Have fun with it, for Christ's sake," Betty said. "Pretend we're making our debut at the Grand Ole Opry."

"And how are we gonna pay for this?" Philly said.

She flashed him a look that could've shriveled Saran Wrap. "With the band charge card. And don't go crying about it to Glen or I'll make your life really miserable out here."

Les found some red leather cowboy boots he seemed to genuinely like. "Reminds me of a pair I had when I was six." He also found a red and white western-style shirt and matching bandana.

Flip, going for more of a gay cowboy look, opted for a white western shirt, bright orange bandana, and white leather chaps. "Ride 'em, cowboy," he yelled, lisp and all.

Badge played along too, found a western shirt with a sequined outline of a Mack Truck on its back, and cowboy boots. It was good to see Betty like this, taking banality and turning it into something fun. It beat the hell out of the easy cynicism she threw around most of the time.

Betty grabbed four cheap straw cowboy hats, pushing one onto her head. "That'll do 'er," she said. "Cash us out, Philly. We'll see you over there."

When they got back to the Emporium, Betty searched out Tad and Cosmo.

"Set the stage up for semi-acoustic," she said.

"What?" Tad said.

"The semi-acoustic setup we use for radio, and put it all up front, right at the lip of the stage."

"We already soundchecked," Cosmo said. But one look from Betty sent him to his task.

Betty's outfit took the cake. She bought a red-and-white checkered shirt with red corduroy piping, a knee-length skirt with tassel-y fringe, and cowboy boots, stars and stripes on the toes. She managed to braid her dreadlocks into something resembling pigtails, and her cowboy hat was pushed deeply onto her head. It looked like she'd have trouble seeing.

They all took the stage, grouped together up front, looking like a post-apocalyptic version of the Carter family.

"Howdy, y'all," Betty said into the mic.

The crowd stood silent.

MTV cameras glided by, moving parts to a machine unaware of its own malfunction.

"'Calypso,'" one brave soul yelled.

"Why, shoot, partner," Betty said. "We'll play 'Calypsa' for ya real soon, but first, we'd like to do a little number called 'Yellertail.' Hit it, Buford."

Flip, in his white duds looking like a bleached member of the Village People, clicked out the intro of "Yellowtail," and the rest jumped in.

Badge expected the show to tank. He would've bet on it—the sound bad, the monitors screwed up, the band unprepared—but after a couple of passes through the intro of "Yellowtail" the four got their sea legs. The groove, scaled down to its minimum, felt great, as if the song was meant to be played that way. The rush of not quite knowing what they were doing was exactly what they needed. Hell, they could've been the Carter Family.

During "Forecast," a punker jumped onstage and danced hoedown style. During "Guess Me Not," the crowd held lighters aloft, swaying back and forth. During "Calypso," they sang every word, the loudest points, as always, coming at the word "Calypso." Twenty years from now, the song would remind everyone at the Emporium of this night during the summer of 2000.

The cameramen eased past the band, in front and behind, underneath and around, insects trying to get as close to the light as possible. The crowd cheered, which encouraged the band to play more, better, longer. When they ran out of songs, they resorted to "Heartbreaker," and the place went bonkers.

No one—not band, crew, MTV crew, or audience—knew whether they were at a hoedown, a rock show, or some kind of novelty gig. They simply loved it, loved being part of it. As the band set their instruments down, the crowd whooped like No Fun Intended had cured cancer or saved the rainforest or just kissed the bride. The four walked to the lip of the stage, wrapped their arms around each other, took a bow in unison. On their way off, Badge launched his cowboy hat into the audience, not caring where it landed.

27

In Cincinnati, Badge awoke to the sound of the phone ringing.

After the Nashville gig, the band had partied late into the night, and the fun continued during the drive north. They finally stopped at the Roadway Inn just across the Ohio River from Kentucky. Their Cincy gig would be at an amusement park called Coney Island, an all-day show featuring No Fun Intended, Shoulder La Back and a dozen local acts. They would go on last, the highlight of the show.

Badge was a hungover mess. He felt like he'd been peeled from plastic. Cars whipped by on the freeway just outside, whooshes so loud you would've thought they were spaceships. He picked up the phone. "Yeah?"

"Dad?" It was Malcolm.

"Bako," Badge said, sitting up. Malcolm had never called him on the road before. "Everything all right?"

"Just checking in."

Just checking in? He must've found the itinerary. "How's baseball going?"

"Fine. What're you doing?"

Badge looked at the nightstand, where his fifth of gin sat. He'd made a pact with himself that he wouldn't go through more than a pint a day. To save money, he'd quit buying pints in favor of fifths, and at some point decided that a pint equaled "about half" of a fifth. He liked this theory so much he avoided searching out its validity. "Getting ready for soundcheck."

"I saw your video."

"Yeah? What'd you think?"

"We liked it."

"We?"

"Me and Wylie."

"Who's Wylie?"

"He's in sixth. He has every AC/DC CD."

"You like AC/DC?"

"Hell yeah. The guitar player—not Angus—but the other guy? Do you know what his name is?"

"No," Badge lied.

"Malcolm."

Badge had always liked Malcolm more than Angus. Malcolm hangs back, plays the riffs, lets his brother have the spotlight. When Holly was pregnant, they'd pulled "Malcolm" out of the ether, but now he wondered if Malcolm Young might've had something to do with it. "I'm still calling you Bako."

"Can I get a drum set?"

He'd half dreaded this day, the day his kid would corner him with an interest in music and the last thing he'd want to do is say no. "I can't imagine your mom'd be crazy about it."

"She said okay."

"What?"

"She said to ask you, but if you're okay with it, she doesn't care."

So I get to be the bad guy. "What do you say we start with acoustic guitar?"

"Noo."

"It's cheaper, and your mom will like it better than you banging around on drums in the basement."

"She's okay with it."

"Well, I'm not."

"*Please?*"

"Worse things will happen to you than having to learn some guitar."

"*Nooo.*"

"You'll thank me someday."

"Wylie already has a guitar."

"Then you'll both have one. You can be Angus and Malcolm."

Someone knocked at the hotel room door, and Badge peeked through the curtains. Betty. "Listen, kid. It's great to hear your voice, but I gotta go."

"When are you coming home?"

"It won't be 'til the end of the summer, but know I can't wait to see you."

"Will you play here again?"

"Probably. It's killing me, but I gotta go. Be good for your mom, okay?"

Badge hung up, pulled on his pants, hid his fifth of gin, opened the door. "Come on in."

Betty wore a clingy sweatsuit that looked new. At last night's party, she'd started sing-alongs, but when everyone's attention switched to a game of Carolina, she got miffed and disappeared. Maybe she was lonely, looking for company.

"What do you know about Flip going to that casino in Memphis?" she said.

Badge ran his hand through his hair, which was more matted than he'd realized. "What am I supposed to know?"

"I heard he went to the casino with you and Annelle that night."

"Where'd you hear that?"

"Is it true?"

Badge remembered the kill-or-be-killed look in Flip's eyes, the fan of twenties he brought back from the ATM.

Betty stood there, arms crossed.

"Have a seat," Badge said.

"I'm going to lunch. Just tell me."

The part that gnawed Badge was that Betty had given Vince—the crackhead—money without batting an eye, and she'd turned Flip down just like that. "No," Badge said. "Flip didn't come with us."

"Really?" Betty said. "I just talked to Annelle and she said—"

"Annelle was loaded that night. She's probably screwing up names."

"So you're saying Flip wasn't there." She stared at him.

Badge felt his bottom lip curl ever so slightly into his upper one. If he were playing poker, his opponent would've called his bluff. "I don't know how much clearer I can be."

The suspicion in Betty's face dwindled. "Well, okay." And she turned to leave.

"By the way." Badge needed to keep her there, to keep the exchange going. It was the closest thing to a conversation they'd had in a week. "Since we're on the subject of money, I can't help but notice that, despite a string of sold-out shows, no one has mentioned giving the boys a raise."

"What?"

"I mean, what's it been, a month without an empty seat?"

Betty's face pursed, an exodus of any goodwill that might've been there. "You want a raise?"

"I don't want a raise. I said the boys might be feeling the pinch."

"The boys."

"Twenty sold-out shows in a row; they notice these things."

"And you're taking it upon yourself—"

"I just thought I'd say something."

Betty smiled, the endgame of acquiring new knowledge, of figuring him out. "You're right. The boys could use a raise. I'll tell Glen to get on it."

"I mean," Badge said. "We're not ungrateful. That extra crew you're bringing on board, everyone's happy about that." It had been announced after the Nashville gig, a new drum tech, someone to change heads, take the pressure off Tad and Cosmo during loadout.

"Crew member?" Betty said.

"Yeah. The one that's coming on in Chicago."

"Oh!" she said. Her eyes grew as big as bass guitar picks. She backed out of the room. "Yes! No problem. Listen, I gotta go."

Because of a contract signed months ago, No Fun Intended was scheduled to lead off for a local band called the Returnabees in Indianapolis. The Returnabees couldn't hope to fill even a tenth of the 1,400-capacity Acorn Club, but they insisted the bill stay as agreed upon. No Fun Intended sat around the bus, waiting for soundcheck. Flip worked on some rudiments, a practice pad between his knees.

"Did Glen say any more to you about the new guy?" Badge said.

"Chicago is all I know," Flip said.

"I hope he clicks with us."

"Someone else to change drum heads. That's all I care about."

When they arrived in Chicago, Badge learned just how much he wouldn't click with the new guy.

As the bus eased in front of their hotel, a Best Western in Wrigleyville, Vince waited for them at curbside. He stood as stationary as the lamppost and newspaper kiosk and the hotel itself. Chicago bustled around him, but his eyes were trained on the bus, his smile telling a story not of getting anywhere but of arriving, finally arriving.

When Betty saw Vince out the bus window, her face glowed. Badge remembered a time when she'd looked the same for him. They were in Oklahoma City, and Badge had returned from a search for dinner with a giant hot fudge sundae. He remembered feeling he'd nailed it better than she could've ever hoped for, that she'd love him forever.

Even before the bus came to a stop, Betty bounded out the door, and in an instant the two were wrapped in each other's arms, kissing on the mouth.

The rest of the band and crew watched. Nobody knew what to say. Badge looked for the nearest large, blunt object to use on Vince, or himself.

"Vince," Les said.

"Who's Vince?" Tad said, but nobody answered.

Part IV

Hurricane Badge

28

Badge stared out the bus window, watched in bafflement as Betty and Vince kissed openly in front of them. The air felt unnaturally heavy, like a stillness had settled upon Badge and was gently pressing him down with nothing but the force of its fingertips.

"I wouldn't blame you if you walked out of here right now," Les said.

"It's a job, right?" Badge said, and he grabbed his bag and stomped to the back of the bus, slamming the door.

He wanted to smash Vince's face in, to take his smile and not just turn it upside down but make it unrecognizable as a mouth. He looked around for something to throw and found nothing but Philly's clipboard, which hung from the wall. He grabbed it and launched it at the window. He punched the door, and the cheap wood gave easily, creating a hole. "Hey," someone yelled from the other side. Badge punched again, creating another hole, this one slightly larger than the first, its ugly sister. He cocked to punch again but the door flung open.

It was Gaston, who pressed Badge backward with his weight, tumbling them both onto the couch. Gaston pinned Badge, held his wrists with both of his hands, his giant belly like a medicine ball on Badge's gut. There was no hope of escape.

"Not on my bus," Gaston mumbled.

Badge searched for air.

"Wanna destroy shit?" Gaston's weight created a pain in Badge's back where it met the couch. "Be a real rock star and take it to the hotel."

The rest of the gang, Les, Tad, looked on. Badge wanted to ask them to get Gaston off him, but he had no air to speak with.

"Can you be calm?" Gaston said.

Badge nodded.

"Are you sure?"

He nodded.

Gaston eased off, spread his legs to accommodate the waist pivot necessary to get airborne, a Thanksgiving parade balloon inflating. "That door's coming out of your pay."

Badge didn't answer.

"And whatever work I have to put into it."

"Got it."

Gaston let out a breath, tugged down his shirt. "All right."

From the back window, Badge watched as everyone piled onto the curb. They and Vince eyed each other tentatively at first. Then hands were shaken. They talked a bit, about what Badge couldn't imagine. The civility of it was enough to infuriate him.

Betty smiled on from Vince's side, her eyes nothing but slits of happiness. Badge searched for some sign of guilt in her, of remorse, or at least of fear of his anger. But if she felt it she didn't let on. She held on to Vince's arm, an announcement they'd be sharing a life together for the time being, a hotel room, a bed.

Les, God love him, stomped right past them and into the hotel.

After the group dispersed, Betty and Vince lingered on the sidewalk. They were waiting for him, to plead their case, to tell him how it was. He'd sooner let Gaston back on top of him than give them the satisfaction. He waited in back until they took the hint and went inside.

In his hotel room, Badge drank straight from his bottle of gin, sucked it down in gulps, willed it down like a someone bench-pressing more than he'd ever lifted. He lay on his hotel bed, stared at the ceiling, a screen on which the projection of Betty and Vince kissing ran over and over. Somehow, he would make Vince suffer. If not today, soon. The kid was shit, and everyone—even Betty—would eventually smell it.

Badge startled awake. The light from outside had turned golden. He had no idea when soundcheck was, if he'd missed it. He threw on his clothes, ran out of the hotel. He made a wrong turn on Clark before stumbling upon the Coreus, their venue for the night. The club's marquee read NO FUN INTENDED in bold black letters.

Inside, everyone was soundchecking. Les and Betty fiddled with their instruments. Tad taped cords at Betty's feet. Flip popped his snare at regular intervals *pop … pop … pop*, waiting for Cosmo, behind the soundboard, to tell him to stop.

"You're late," Philly said.

Badge grabbed his guitar, strapped it on. He felt a weight on top of his head, like a bean bag threatening to slide off this way or that. If he managed to wake up in St. Louis with his job intact, it would be a miracle. He smacked out some chords, tried to blend in.

His eyes met Betty's briefly. Her hair was tied back in a beaded bun, and she wore zebra-striped tights he'd never seen before. A swallow traced its path down her throat. She seemed worried about something, an impending calamity: Hurricane Badge.

He didn't know where Vince was. Someone, maybe a few people, hovered behind the drum riser.

"Good," Cosmo said, his voice through the monitor, and Flip stopped hitting his snare. "Now let's hear the whole kit."

Flip broke into a complex samba rhythm that made focus impossible. Badge felt a tap on his back. Vince.

The overall effect of this guy standing next to him was like that of a mushroom, like Vince had popped up from some combination of the climate and moisture and the wooden planks of the stage. He was dressed in his usual getup of leather suit coat and black pants, but now he had a familiar red patch on his shoulder, "CREW." His smirking face was close enough to punch.

Badge edged away, looked down at his pedal board, not quite ignoring Vince but not acknowledging him either, how he might treat a reporter who'd somehow finagled his way into soundcheck.

"So," Vince said. He leaned into Badge's ear. "Funny how things change, eh?"

Badge struggled to hold his fists. He could make this guy into mushroom Stroganoff in one second.

"Well," Vince said. He again leaned into Badge. Amid all the noise of the drums, it must've looked to the others like the two were having a conversation, maybe making peace. "I just want you to know that, for Betty's sake, I'm willing to let bygones be bygones." Badge tuned his guitar, didn't look up. "We can start this whole thing over as though you and I never met."

Badge said nothing. Flip pounded away behind them. *Bam, koosh, bam-licka, koosh-koosh.* Badge's head filled with electricity, the drums, the rage, the intersection of drunkenness and hangover. He could feel Vince waiting for a response. If he hadn't known better, Badge would've thought Vince was playing at being his boss, an idea so far beyond the pale that Badge—if he was inclined to do anything—would've laughed in his face.

Badge wrapped an arm around Vince's neck. "Listen, fuckface," he said. His smile was the perfect camouflage. "I don't care what you say, or what you do, but in your short, happy life on the bus—before you fuck it up for yourself as you most surely will—if you cross me, or Betty, or anyone else on this stage or in this crew, I'll personally make sure nobody ever has to deal with you again." He squeezed Vince's head a little tighter. "Got that?"

Vince pulled away, his face wrinkled. "I'm sorry it has to be that way."

Badge, smiling, patted Vince once, twice, on the back. "I will fuck you up in front of your whole family."

"Okay," Cosmo said through the monitor. Flip stopped playing. "Badge, let's hear you."

After soundcheck, Les strolled over. "What do you say you and me have dinner?"

Les led Badge and Flip to a restaurant called Jacoby's, just up the street from the Coreus. The three found a table towards the back. Cleavaged waitresses in black outfits scurried around. Badge went to light a cigarette, but a waitress stopped him, pointed to the No Smoking sign.

"Sooo," Les said. "How's that for a fucking curveball?"

"What's the deal with this guy?" Flip said.

Badge rubbed his eyes, watched stars form, dissipate. "Ex-boyfriend," he said. He really wanted a cigarette.

"Didn't look 'ex' to me," Flip said.

"Shut up, Flip," Les said. "Badge, this is easily the most low-down thing I've ever—"

"Well, it's happening."

"And sidemen have no power out here, we know that."

"Flip," Badge said. "Betty knows you went to the casino that night in Memphis."

"What?" Flip said. "How?"

"Annelle told her."

"Did you say anything?"

"No, but if she asks, you weren't there."

"Okay," Flip said. "I wish I hadn't been there."

The waitress brought drinks. Badge hit his gin and tonic.

"What the hell did you say to him at soundcheck?" Les said.

"I told him this game isn't over yet."

"He's got no intention of being a drum tech, that's for sure," Flip said. "I tell him something and he barely listens."

"So, what's the kid doing?" Les said. "If he's Betty's boyfriend, fine, but—"

"He's a crackhead," Badge said.

"What?" Les said. He stared at Badge. "You know this?"

"He claims he's off it. Betty's giving him money."

"Jesus Christ," Les said. "He'll bleed her."

"Not if I can help it," Badge said.

"And what if he gets Betty into it?" Les said.

Badge sat up, felt the purifying energy of having someone agree with him. "What the fuck is Glen thinking having a crackhead on the bus? Does that sound like an element you want to bring into this thing?"

Les and Flip shook their heads.

"Glen should know about this," Badge said, "if he doesn't already."

"I'll tell him," Les said. "I've got no problem telling him."

"It'll sound better coming from you."

"Consider it done."

29

The next day, before soundcheck in St. Louis, as Tad re-soldered some of the connections of Badge's Stratocaster, someone looking very much like Betty came into the backstage room.

She wore the same clothes as Betty as the night before, walked with the same gait and carried the same bag and sported the same boots as Betty, but this person's hair was styled into sleek, pristine cornrows. The rows looked like thick bands of black licorice arching across her head, each one ending in a silver bead. "Some fuckhead got his hands on 'All, All the Time,'" she said.

Badge looked at her in amazement. This hairdo was shockingly bad. The silver beads were like tacky Christmas tree ornaments, and her pale scalp shone brightly between each row. It must've taken all day to style. It made him miss the girl he'd once known, who'd disappeared and been replaced by this tense girl with this tense hair. So much energy expended, so little reward.

Badge had managed to make it through Chicago without further incident, with the help of the backstage gin bottle. His drunkenness had formed a cocoon around him, encasing him in a bubble no one dared puncture. It was a nifty trick; stay drunk and people stayed away. He'd remember it.

Philly looked up from his computer. "What are you talking about?"

"It's all over the Internet." Betty flung open her laptop. "I found it online."

"Nice hair," Tad said, but Betty didn't acknowledge him.

"Like Napster?" Philly said.

"That's one of them," Betty said. "There are others."

"Is this what Lars Ulrich is always bitching about?" Tad said, but again no one responded.

"There was just that one cassette," Badge said. He'd all but forgotten about the song, which had made them all happy that night in Vegas. Now more than anything he wanted to hear it again. It felt like a lifetime ago, a better lifetime.

Betty tapped the keys of her computer. "Some guy nicknamed Cleetus McFleetus uploaded it, and it's been downloaded like a million times."

"I thought I heard someone yelling for it in Chicago," Badge said. He remembered the girls, the pair of them, teens or pre-teens, standing in the front row and screaming until their faces turned red. It had sounded like "all anodyne," and Badge didn't know what to think.

"It's all over the place," Betty said.

Badge thought of Cosmo, who'd recorded them that night in Vegas. "Maybe one of the hookers got it."

Betty's computer played music. The speaker was small, the tone making AM radio sound rich in comparison, but there it was, acoustic guitar, Betty's singing, Cosmo's shaker, "All, All the Time." It could've been a song buried deep on side two of a Jimmy Buffett album, a surprise masterpiece just when you thought all of the good ones were finished.

Betty took in the music with blinks of her eyes. She seemed worried that people might hear something she didn't get a chance to vet, that this tiny aspect of No Fun Intended might somehow blow her cover. Her voice sounded great, like someone down on her luck but still managing to see the good in life. Now she was the opposite, someone with all the luck in the world and no clue what to do with it.

"You guys did that in a hotel room?" Philly said.

"One take," Betty said.

"Glen's gotta hear this." Philly reached for his cell phone. "How many times did you say it's been downloaded?"

"I didn't get the number," Betty said. "It was way more than any of the others."

Philly disappeared out the door. "Glen, you're not gonna believe—"

"What are you gonna do?" Tad said.

"Find Cleetus McFleetus and crucify him," Betty said.

"Why do anything?" Badge said.

Betty looked surprised. It was the first time he'd spoken directly to her since Chicago. It was a nice opportunity to break the ice. If he were going to survive out here, he'd need to learn how to operate.

"What do you mean?" she said.

"It sounds great. Your fans want whatever they can get their hands on. At least it's something you can be proud of."

A smile crept across Betty's face. "That's exactly what Goo said."

Badge looked down. He couldn't stand that she—that anyone—could see the two of them as on the same side of anything. "What did Goo say?"

Betty strolled away, her hands locked behind her. "He just thinks this free-society stuff is the best thing ever."

"I didn't say that."

"Kinda sounded like you did."

"Who does the monitors?" Vince said to Philly at soundcheck. They stood next to the monitor board, its dozens of blue, red and yellow knobs belying its simple purpose. The venue, Shenandoah, was more rectangular than most of the places they played. The wings of the room extended way past the edge of the stage, where it must be hard to see. Badge set up a flanger he'd had in his gig bag for years. It might sound good at the end of "Calypso." It was time to try something new.

"The venue usually has someone for monitors," Philly said.

"And when they don't?" Vince said.

"Then Cosmo gets everyone set up before he does front-of-house."

"What if someone needs something during the show?"

"Then we deal with it."

Vince didn't speak, but his expression—wrinkled brow, doubting eyes—said it all.

"And Betty's guitar?" Vince said.

"Tad takes care of it," Philly said.

"Badge's?"

"Tad."

"Les's?"

"You got it."

Vince shook his head. "Ever think of hiring someone?"

"It's more complicated than that." Badge could tell Philly'd dealt with boyfriend-types before. "We could afford it. The question is, do we want to take on another personality?"

"Personality?" Vince said. "You don't like 'em, fire 'em."

"We wouldn't want to hire someone just to fire them."

Badge snorted out a laugh. Vince looked at him, eyes thinning.

"Besides," Philly said, "at the end of the day, keeping things small puts more money in Betty's pocket."

"And that manager's, I bet."

"You know it," Philly said. "Now, if you'll excuse me."

At the St. Louis show, Vince suffered a major gaff on his first night as drum tech. During "Breakfall," Flip's rack tom started to loosen, the drum edging down, and after some prodding from Philly, Vince rushed out to fix it. Having no idea what he was doing, he turned the nut the wrong way, sending the drum collapsing onto the snare. Flip shooed him away and, drumstick between his teeth, tightened the nut himself.

After the show, congregating on the bus as it headed to Kansas City, everyone gathered around Vince. "It's all changing," he said. His fuck-up from earlier in the night had been annoyingly forgotten. Badge sat with a copy of *Rolling Stone*, pretended not to pay attention. "Record stores are going under. Albums are getting cheaper to make. The Internet is the best thing to happen since who-knows-what."

"Except no one gets paid," Les said.

"You get a check every week for these gigs," Vince said.

"I've got this friend," Tad said, "who's got this great website with free songs, but no one ever downloads them."

"That's why Betty's situation is so perfect," Vince said. Badge could picture Vince and Betty talking about this while lying in bed, a raft bound for the New Music Age, imagining what they would make of it. It was better than what Badge could've been imagining about their nights together. "She gets a fan base on the record company's dime and sets herself up to run the whole thing. Two years from now, when everyone else is wondering what happened, Betty's gonna have an army of fans. 'All, All the Time' only makes it better."

"It wasn't me, by the way," Cosmo said. Betty had asked him about the stolen tape at soundcheck and Cosmo—eyes wide, mouth agape—was either completely innocent or the best liar Badge had ever seen. "That cassette's been missing for weeks."

"No one blames you," Betty said.

"I'm actually glad it turned up," Cosmo said. "I thought I lost it."

"Cosmo," Vince said. "You are the fucking man for getting out the recorder that night."

"We can all think free music is the coolest thing since the Beatles," Les said. He sucked tequila from the edge of his shot glass. He had a styrofoam cup of coffee on the table, bought as they left town. Coffee and tequila seemed to offer no contradiction to him. "But making records is the whole reason I do this. You're talking about it going from being an art to being a piece of marketing collateral, this chore we have to do to go on tour."

"The record's totally essential," Vince said. "Did you guys know you can make records in your house now?"

"You can *kind of* make records in your house," Les said.

"No," Vince said. "Bands are doing it all the time. You buy the right gear, convert a room into a studio, and make it right in your home. The thing pays for itself."

Les threw back his shot, let out a grunt. "Sounds like kids playing in the sandbox to me."

"Well get ready," Vince said, "because it's coming."

30

It was bound to happen at some point, but Badge didn't expect it so soon.

Coming onto the bus before the Kansas City gig, walking through the bunk area and opening the door to the back room, Badge saw on the couch, intertwined with each other in a way that reminded him of spiders or gymnasts or the yin and yang symbol, Betty and Vince in mid-embrace.

Vince's shirt was off and in a ball behind him. Betty's was well on its way, corralled around her neck. She still had her boots on, but her skirt was hiked up to allow access, which Vince was taking full advantage of, working his wrist like he might to crack a safe, testing the coils, listening for levers to fall. The smell as much as anything alerted Badge to what was going on. Both sets of eyes looked at him, miraculously without losing contact with each other's lips.

Badge shut the door, his brain zooming. He thought briefly of putting his fist back through the door, which Gaston had refashioned with planks of balsa wood, but he got his feet moving and got off the bus.

He marched up Pace Street. High-end apartment buildings towered to his left and right. Les had mentioned that everyone was going to an Irish pub up the street. Badge would go too. Anything to escape the images floating around in his head.

"Badge," he heard from behind. Betty. She ran to catch up.

"I'm sorry," she said.

"Fuck you."

"I didn't plan any of this."

"Who's idea was it to have him on the bus?"

Betty's mouth opened, but nothing came out. The silver beads in her hair sparkled in the sunlight. "I love him."

"Good Christ," Badge said and kept walking.

"I've loved him since I was fourteen."

"Great."

"You want me to lie?"

Badge stopped, ran his hands over his eyes. "I want you to want a life with me and our kid, but you want a life with him."

Betty sighed, wouldn't look at him. "Maybe this baby thing isn't such a good idea."

"What are you saying?" But he knew what she meant.

"If you and me aren't together–"

"Don't even think that."

"I planned on talking to you about it."

"I don't want to talk about it. There are plenty of things we can do that don't mean–"

"You're telling me you want this kid no matter what?" She looked at him, tears in her eyes. "You want this kid even if I'm with Goo?"

Badge didn't answer. He couldn't. There was none. "I gotta go."

The Irish pub was on the corner of a street lined with redbrick buildings, all uniform and classic-looking, completely within their element. The pub was livelier than the rest. People mingled on the patio.

His crew was easy to find, just past the hostess at a giant round table. Tad, Cosmo, Les, Flip, even Jonah, the bearded lead singer of Shoulder La Back. Every table in the place was filled. More people grouped around the bar.

"Badge," Les yelled.

They all made room. Everyone had a drink. Earlier that day, Badge had planned to scale back on the booze, but tonight was not the night. Cosmo had a large bowl of soup. "Clam chowder," he said.

"I need a drink," Badge said. Waitresses crisscrossed the room. "Which one's ours?"

"Cosmo," Tad said. "You could wait until we all had something."

Cosmo shoved a spoonful into his mouth. "Mmm."

Their waitress had walked up. "Could you take his soup from him?" Tad said. "He doesn't seem to know the rules."

The waitress, young, brunette, and not the least bit taken in, said, "Your food's coming." Then to Badge, "What can I get you?"

"Gin and tonic."

"You got it."

They all watched the waitress stroll away. "Steady as she goes," Les said.

"And she does go steady," Cosmo said.

"I don't know," Flip said. His fedora sat atop his head, the feather so ruffled it looked freshly plucked from a chicken. "This younger pussy. It doesn't work for me."

"What?" Jonah said. Only twenty-four, Jonah had the thickest beard Badge had ever seen, and his eyes sparkled like someone always ready to crack a joke.

"You're shitting me," Tad said.

"I'm serious," Flip said. "There's something, I don't know, sterile about it. They're pretty but not feminine."

"Fuck," Tad said. He leaned forward, thumped his head on the table. "Kill me if I ever get like that."

"Tell me this," Flip said. "What do you hold onto with these girls?"

"I know what *they* can hold onto," Cosmo said.

Betty's top off, Vince's hand moving.

Les motioned for another waitress, this one short, blond, wearing a black top that showed off her shoulders. "Can you get me a Maker's Mark? Anyone else ready?"

"Hit me," Tad said.

Everyone watched as the waitress ambled away, seeing what they would hang on to.

"I admit I like looking at it," Flip said.

"Ha," Tad said.

Les held his drink aloft. "Here's to looking at it."

The rest clinked glasses, and Badge looked for their waitress, waiting for his drink. He didn't have all night. *Maybe this baby thing isn't such a good idea.*

"Jonah," Tad said. "What was up with you and that chick in Memphis?" They'd all seen her—tall, wearing a black dress and a choker. Jonah and she had talked backstage, and everyone speculated after they left.

"Transvestite," Jonah said.

"What?" Tad said.

"Nooo," Cosmo said.

"I called that one," Les said.

"I kinda saw it too," Jonah said, "but I had to know for sure."

"How'd you find out?" Tad asked.

"How do you think?" Jonah said.

They all laughed.

You want this kid even if I'm with Goo?

Badge rose. "I gotta go."

"Why?" Les said.

"That chowder's making me sick. I'll see you at the gig."

Outside, the humidity kept everything low to the ground. The stretch of road next to him was busy, car noise drowning out everything else. Everyone was on the move, living life, except Badge.

Les caught up with him just before he turned the corner. "What's up?"

"Fuck it, Les."

"Fuck what?"

"Fuck Vince."

"I know it's tough on you."

"I just walked in on them fucking in the back of the bus."

Les registered this with a calmness that only slightly broke toward despair, something at the corners of his mouth. "I talked to Glen yesterday. He didn't know about Vince's drug problem. Now he does."

"What's he gonna do? The guy's already more a part of this thing than we are."

"Glen's gotten me out of some pretty hairy stuff in the past. We just need to hang tight."

"Fine, but I'm working on my own plan too."

"Your own plan?"

"Don't worry. It won't involve you. It won't even involve me."

Les shifted his weight, looked into the distance. "I gotta tell you, you're starting to sound more and more like a guy who's not heading for a happy place."

"Jesus."

"I'm talking about keeping yourself cage-free here."

"I hear you."

"Do you?"

"I do."

More cars passed, and then quiet descended. It felt like peace, when the bombs stop falling and you're reminded that life can be something other than complete chaos.

"See you at the gig," Badge said.

The cabbie pulled up to a boarded storefront at an abandoned shopping mall, what must have been a Von Maur back in the day, its gravel and cement facade promising all things eighties within. Badge had found the cab sitting in front of an apartment building, asked the driver to take him someplace where he "might score some rock." It felt strange saying "rock"–like he somehow didn't qualify to say it–but the guy didn't hesitate, got onto Rhonert Boulevard and headed to the part of town where chain stores sat back from the road.

The cabbie shifted to park, stopped the meter. "Eight-fifty."

Badge slid a twenty out of his wallet, held it up. "I don't suppose you'd want to wait."

The cabbie rubbed his hand over his neck, looked into the distance. There was no one and nothing around save an abandoned car–its windows tinted, its wheels gone–parked by the store's entrance. The cabbie looked at Badge in the rearview mirror. "Eight-fifty."

Badge searched in his wallet for a smaller bill. "You don't by chance know how this works."

"Get out and stand there. They won't leave you waiting long. When it's done, walk that way."

"You ever known anyone to have trouble?"

The cabbie blew a puff out his nose. "You sure you wanna be here?"

He handed him a ten. "Thanks for the ride."

Badge stood by himself in the abandoned lot, the sun disappearing quickly. The abandoned car's door opened and someone yelled, "What you want?"

Badge went to walk over.

"Hold up. What you want?"

"Rock."

Out popped a short, skinny boy, no more than sixteen. He walked like someone had just finished scolding him. "What kind?"

"The good kind."

The kid's lips curled into what might've been a smile. "You want speed?"

Badge had no idea what Vince liked. "Crack."

The kid signaled to the car. "Walk over there."

The passenger's side window rolled down. A tall, thin man sat in the seat, wearing sunglasses. "Fifty," he said.

Badge pulled out his wallet. "I need a pipe too."

"What I look like?"

"You know where I can get one?"

"Lotsa places. You'll want the one down by the college."

"Which college?"

"You want this shit or no?"

Badge handed him the money, and the man slipped him a small plastic bag. It held two "rocks," white like old snow, about the size of spit wads. He remembered the bags of marijuana he'd bought as a teenager, fat things, a lot more bang for the buck.

"Now get the fuck outta here," the man said.

31

On the bus ride from Kansas City to Wichita, Badge pretended to sleep in his bunk. He had the crack, and he'd chased down a pipe too. Now he had to keep his eyes peeled. Vince would stumble, and when he did Badge would make sure he went down and stayed down.

On short trips like this one, the bus rarely pulled over, so when Badge felt the gears shift he went up front. "What's up?" he said.

"Number one in the country," Betty yelled. She pumped her fist in the air.

"What?"

"Glen called," Philly said. "We have the number one song this week at Alternative."

"And number seven on the pop charts," Flip said. He did a little dance that was some combination of the cha-cha and air drums.

"We're celebrating," Betty said.

"How 'bout a truck stop?" Gaston said.

"Will they have Champagne?" Betty said.

"One way to find out," Gaston said.

A giant likeness of a Tyrannosaurus rex guarded the truck stop entrance. Inside, men shopped the aisles. There was no

Champagne, so Philly ran over to a liquor store across the street. Most of the gang bought lunch and sat together in the communal area. A few yards off, Badge searched a rack of sunglasses. He wanted to avoid conversation. Sunglasses would be essential from here on out.

"I love this business," Vince said. He chomped into his pizza like there was a prize for getting the most in his mouth at once.

"It's great when it works," Flip said.

"Not the way it is now," Vince said. He finished chewing. "The way it's *going to be*."

"What's gonna change?" Cosmo asked.

"Everything," Vince said.

Betty, a single taco as yet unwrapped in front of her, blew off her straw's paper cover, which landed in Vince's hair. "Ha!" she said.

Vince brushed it out, grabbed her taco.

"Give it back," she said.

"What're you gonna do?"

"Kick your ass."

"Good luck."

Betty swatted at Vince—rougher than Badge had expected—and grabbed his arm, digging her fingernails in.

"Fuck," Vince said, dropping the taco.

"That's right." Betty hopped up onto her chair, stood full up, extended her arms muscleman-style. "I rule with an iron fist." She twisted back and forth, her chair swiveling. "Number one in the motherfucking country, motherfuckers."

Everyone cackled. Two heavyset guys at the sub shop looked concerned. The people in the checkout line glanced and turned away.

"So what does being number one mean?" Tad said.

Betty flopped back into her seat. "Same shitty tacos, that's for sure."

"I love shitty tacos," Cosmo said and chomped into one.

"It means we can start doing things our way," Vince said, "start making this into what we want it to be."

"Does it include us?" Tad said.

Vince slapped Tad on the shoulder. "We wouldn't think of getting rid of any of you. I promise it's gonna get a lot better from here on out. More crew, more per diem. You'll see."

After soundcheck in Wichita, Badge tested his pedal board as Betty put the finishing touches on the set list. They occupied the giant stage of Wanderlust, a downtown hall with hardwood floors perfect for dancing. The rest of the band and crew had migrated away.

"Why am I starting to feel like I'm not part of this thing?" Badge said.

"Hm?" Betty looked at him. The cap of her pen was between her lips, making her look like one of those plaster clowns that inflate helium balloons.

"Vince's talking a lot about the way things are going to be. I just want to make sure I'm part of it."

Betty looked down at her list, kept writing. "Do you want to be?"

"Depends."

"On what?"

"On what the plan is."

Betty popped the cap onto her marker, stood up. Her eyelids sat low over her eyes. "I just landed the number one song in the country. Can we have some Champagne and talk about it later?"

"For example," Badge said. He didn't want to let her off the hook. It was hard to get her alone. "What's all this talk about the coming apocalypse?"

"What?"

"You know what I mean."

Betty put her hands on her head, walked in a circle. "Okay. Get it out. What do you want to know?"

"I want to know what the plan is."

Betty exhaled once, deeply. "The plan is we're leaving the record label."

"What? When?"

"As soon as this record's over."

"You're leaving the label that just took you to number one?"

"That's right."

"What about the second album, with tour support, you've already agreed to?"

"We'll get out of it."

"You'll get out of guaranteed money coming to you from a record company? Sounds like they're the ones getting out of it."

"You think they don't want my next record?"

"Take the money while it's there. It won't always be. Have you run this by Glen?"

Betty crossed her arms, stared straight at him. He could've been an old company hand, one foot in retirement, and Betty a feisty young CEO ready to clean house. "It's not Glen's decision."

"Yeah, too bad it's not."

"You old fucks." She launched her marker to the back of the stage. "You all act like you know everything, but you're not gonna know shit here in about three seconds. Everything's changing."

"So I keep hearing. You and Vince are like the first fucking family of everything changing."

"Rock and roll is going to be a boutique industry. Thousands of labels, millions of bands."

"God save us."

"What's wrong with that?"

"Ninety-nine percent of it is going to be shit."

"It's freedom, Badge. How can you be against freedom?"

"That freedom is going to put me and my friends out of work."

"Real musicians will always have a place at the table."

Badge laughed once. "Really? Who told you that?"

"Goo."

"Well, if the crack monkey says so, it must be true."

Her eyes thinned. "You bastard."

"*I'm* a bastard," Badge said, even though he knew he was.

"He's been clean for weeks. The band gives him something to focus on, something to look forward to."

Badge threw up his hands. "So turn the business over to him. Give the junkie the keys to your career."

"He's reformed," Betty yelled, and she threw the set list down, which floated leaf-like to the stage.

"As far as you know."

"Just because you can't go five minutes without a gin and tonic—"

"Whatever. He's your problem now."

"Fuck you."

32

After the show in Wichita, Badge sat by himself in the basement of Wanderlust, which served as a large, dark, almost chilly backstage room. He sat in an abandoned booth, away from the twenty or so people chatting each other up. The drugs were in his pocket, as well as the pipe. Betty had followed Vince into an adjoining room and closed the door. Badge's window might open at any moment, and he'd be ready.

A girl—young, blond—came down the stairs, wearing a blue flowered dress that looked secondhand. The girl spotted Les, who talked with Reed, Shoulder La Back's bass player, and eased her way over to them. Les offered her a drink—whatever was in his cup—and she took a long tug. The three talked, and the girl got closer to Les, touched him on his belly. Les leaned away, and when the girl pushed closer he begged off, escaping to the drink table. The girl scanned the room again. Her eyes lit up when she saw Badge.

"Shit," Badge muttered.

"Hey," she said, scurrying over. "You got any room for me in there?"

"Actually, I was just about to—"

She sat down next to him. "I loved your set."

"Thanks." Her breath smelled funny, something chemical

about it, like drain cleaner. Badge was cornered. He'd have to physically move her to get out of his seat.

"I love that guitar you play." She slid closer to him. "What kind is it?"

"Stratocaster."

She ran her tongue over her teeth. "And what's that long metal thing that sticks out from it?"

Badge had to laugh. If she were any more aggressive, he could file rape charges.

"What?" she said.

He rubbed his eyes. "What are you doing?"

"What do you think?" She slid her hand up his leg.

"Um, yeah," Badge said. Despite himself, he felt turned on, the dime store genie inside him needing little more than what she offered. "But why are you coming on so strong?"

"I was hired by Collin." Collin was the club owner, a redheaded guy who'd made a point of shaking everyone's hand at soundcheck. "He's real happy about the full house tonight and wanted to offer anyone in the band—"

"You?"

"Why not?"

Badge couldn't think of a reason.

"I'm Krista."

"Badge."

"So," she said. "Is your hotel nearby?"

Just then, Betty came out, slamming the door behind her, and Vince followed. "Hey," he yelled, but she didn't turn, bounded up the stairs two at a time. Vince seemed to want to follow but turned back into the room, slammed the door.

"What's wrong with her?" Krista said.

"I don't know. What's your name again?"

"Krista."

"Krista, do you like rock?"

She looked surprised. "You serious?"

"Yeah."

"Doesn't everyone?"

"Well, I got some."

"You got some?" She cozied up to him. "Then let's party."

"You wouldn't be smoking it with me."

"With who?"

"A guy who likes rock. I want you to smoke it with him."

Krista's face betrayed no shock. She was probably used to being asked to do weird things, for a price.

"I'd pay you," Badge said.

Krista slid a cigarette out of Badge's pack, lit it with bar matches. Her forwardness was gone, replaced by something cold, shrewd. "Is he here?"

"It's the guy who just came out that door."

"He didn't look ready to party to me."

"Well, he likes rock." Badge took out his wallet. "How can we make this happen?"

She sucked on her cigarette.

"Would a hundred do it?"

"All I gotta do is smoke it with him?"

"Yeah."

"Sounds too easy."

"It is easy, and you can keep whatever rock's left over."

Krista seemed to struggle to keep her cool. She exhaled smoke. "Two hundred."

Badge sighed. Betty could be back at any moment. He flipped through his wallet. "For two hundred you gotta get him high as a kite."

"He likes it, right?"

"He's been off it a while."

"How long?"

"Couple weeks." He folded the twenties together and, under the table, held them out to her.

She looked at the money, shrugged her shoulders, took it.

"Great," Badge said.

"I'm a working girl."

He reached into his pocket, pulled out the pipe, the plastic bag. "He's alone in that room right now. Just go in, take this with you, and do your thing."

She took the drugs, hiked up her dress, snapped the pipe into the strap of her underwear.

"No one can know I had anything to do with it," Badge said.

"Your money buys that."

Krista put out her cigarette, stood up, adjusted her dress without taking her eyes off the door. "If Collin asks, I sucked your dick," she said and was off.

As she disappeared into the side room, Badge felt something like a breeze drift through him. He was exposed. This girl could call him out, tell Vince who was behind the whole thing, and Badge would be forced to lie. He was in deep now with the vermin, where you'd as likely be consumed as trusted. He went over to the drink table, replenished his gin and tonic, feeling the looks of everyone around him. He took a tug from his drink, hoping it would refill him with a good dose of I-don't-give-a-shit, and went back to the booth.

Another minute and Krista came out. She seemed to want to leave, but Badge's stare caught her. She shuffled over. "Wouldn't do it," she said.

"Huh?"

"Got caught talking to the wrong people or something, and his girlfriend's pissed."

"You told him about the rock?"

"Yeah."

"And you got it out, showed it to him?"

"Yeah," she said. "I even took a hit. He wanted nothing to do with it. He was trying to get his cell phone to work the whole time. As soon as he saw the pipe he told me to leave."

"And you didn't try again?"

"He didn't want it."

"Like hell he didn't." Badge stood up, felt the full extent of his height. It bothered her, he could tell.

"Here," she said and dropped the twenties on the table.

"But you keep the drugs, right?"

"I don't want 'em."

"Then give 'em back."

"I can't give 'em back here," she said, glancing around.

"Bullshit."

People began to notice. Les and Reed watched. A couple Badge didn't know seemed nervous, too close to the drama.

Krista looked cornered. Then she hustled through the crowd and up the stairs.

Badge slid back into the booth, and everyone started chatting again. He knew they wanted him to leave, but he wouldn't. Fuck no, he wouldn't.

Les came over. "Everything okay?"

"That girl was trying to get me to smoke rock."

"I thought I smelled something like that."

"Whore," Badge said and felt his rage simmer, at Krista, at Les, at everyone in the room, and especially at himself.

33

Badge's hotel room in Oklahoma City, on the bottom floor of a horseshoe-shaped Holiday Inn, buzzed with traffic noise. The clover of on-ramps pulled cars off the interstate and ushered them towards the venue, Halberstam Pavilion and KRDO's Can't Beat the Heat radio show. A surprisingly gorgeous Saturday in August, all the kids were coming out. There would be bikinis, bermuda shorts, sunblock and just enough chaos to make everyone feel alive. Badge hadn't moved from his hotel bed for hours, his gin bottle half empty next to him. The phone rang, and without lifting his head he answered it.

"Dad?" Malcolm.

"Hey, Bako." Badge sat up. Where did this superhuman strength come from, this ability to pull himself out of any drunken stupor for his kid?

"I didn't mean to," Malcolm said, and Badge heard tears in his voice.

"What's happened?"

"I got in a fight."

"You got in a fight? Where did you get in a fight?"

"On the playground." The crying was replaced by a low whine.

"Was it Reese?" Reese was a skinny, cowlicked kid who lived

next to the playground. A year before he'd stolen someone's autographed Eric Karros Dodgers hat and only gave it back after dousing it with water.

"Yes," Malcolm said.

Good. "Were either of you hurt?"

"I broke–" Malcolm said.

"What did you break?"

"Garage window."

"What garage window?"

Badge heard shuffling through the phone.

"The *Parkers'* garage window," Holly said. She was livid. Badge realized he'd been called by his son as punishment. "His fist went straight through the window."

"I'll pay for it. Is Malcolm all right?"

"Two stitches in the web of his fingers."

"Good God." The kid had never been through something like this. "I'm coming."

"Don't," Holly said. "The doctor took care of it. He just can't play baseball for a while."

"That's gonna kill him."

"He's really not that disappointed. He's far more interested in drums these days."

"I told him to forget about the drums."

"I think drums are a good idea. Someplace to work out this aggression."

"I gotta say, Hol, that Reese is a little shit."

"We don't punch out windows in this house."

"Right. Let me talk to him."

"Don't worry about it. He's in his bedroom punishing himself."

Badge sighed. "So, how are things?"

"Fine. You?"

"Fine." Badge liked the sound of her voice, a pure vibration from better times. "Rock and roll. You know how it is."

"Do I ever." Annoyance creeped into her voice, one drip of black into a bucket of white. "So, when will Malcolm see you again?"

"I don't know. We're in Oklahoma tonight. I know that."

"Badge, you sound—"

"Drunk?"

Silence.

"Because if I sound drunk, it's because I am."

"Great," Holly said, a spoonful of black dumped into the white. "Your girlfriend must be proud."

Badge sat up. "I'm thinking about coming home for good. I want to come home and take care of Malcolm."

"Is that right."

"I'd take care of you too, if you'd let me."

A long pause, enough time for a truck's backup tone to start, stop.

"She dumped you, didn't she?" Holly said.

Badge flopped back onto the bed. "Yep."

"Too bad."

"Left me for a younger man."

"How awful."

"Different from you. You left me for an older man."

"I didn't leave you at all," Holly said, a ladle of black dumped in. "You left yourself."

"How is Mountain Man, anyway?"

"He's good, Badge. I gotta go."

"Gotta go, eh?"

"Dinnertime."

"I love dinnertime at your place."

"Not enough, apparently," and the line went dead.

That night in Oklahoma City, in the set change between bands, Vince had forgotten to secure Flip's kick drum, which meant the thing crept forward, which meant Flip had to reach farther and farther with his foot to hit the pedal. By the end of the first song he was leaning all the way back, almost parallel to the ground, trying to finish without missing a beat. Vince was nowhere to be found, so Tad had to run out and fix it.

The rest of their set, shortened to accommodate eight bands, seemed oddly safe, paint-by-numbers. They played in a clipped, indifferent way, and Betty offered no drama or between-song banter. The thousands of concertgoers, most of them far away, acted like it didn't matter who was onstage. For the first time in No Fun Intended, Badge had to try to get excited about playing. After "Calypso," some fans down front screamed for more, but Betty pretended not to hear them as she stomped off.

Afterwards, Badge sat on the couch in the backstage room, his sunglasses concealing his eyes. Les, Betty and Vince flicked beer bottle caps into a trash can, waiting for the crew to finish loading the bus. Badge had downed what was left of his gin and nursed a beer now. His drunkenness was loud in the room, he knew it, and people seemed to be ignoring him. He tried to pay attention to the other three but found it hard. He didn't know how long it'd been since he'd spoken.

"Who the fuck do they think I am?" Betty said. "Emmylou Harris?" During the set, a group of cowboy-hatted patrons had started line dancing, making her fume.

"Yeah, *she's* got no cred," Les said, rolling his eyes. He flicked a bottle cap, which hit the can and bounced away.

"They're just plebs," Vince said. After the set, Flip had gone looking for his drum tech, expecting a *mea culpa*. When Vince offered none, Flip grabbed the tequila bottle and disappeared.

"Well, that's the last one we do," Betty said. "I'm not out here to entertain every yokel with fifteen bucks." She downed some water and tossed the half-finished bottle across the room, where it swished in a garbage can. Tad, loading equipment outside, stopped short when he heard the thump.

Vince took a tug of his beer, a stabbing motion that bent his head back. "I'm thinking about an all-club tour. None of this mass market shit."

"Wait," Les said. "You think playing for less people is better than playing for more?"

"I think Betty should play for her fans," Vince said.

"Fans are from the sticks, fella," Les said. "And when it comes down to it, you and me and everyone else on this planet is from the sticks."

"It's not about where they're from," Betty said. "It's about them getting what I'm doing. What's the point of communicating when people only hear the wrong thing?"

"For seven years," Les said, "the only gig I could get in the world was with a cover band in San Bernardino. We played whatever people asked of us, metal, Motown, samba. Worked it out on the spot if we had to. People pay to hear your music, you respect it, because I'm here to tell you, it won't last forever."

"I can't get excited about people boot scooting to 'Calypso,'" Betty said.

"Well, you oughta be," Les said. He grabbed a beer and left.

"Jesus," Betty said after he was gone.

"It's okay," Vince said. "When we finish the tour, we'll be done with this senior circuit crap."

Betty couldn't help but motion with her eyes to Badge. He knew he looked catatonic, propped up on the couch, sunglasses on, his chin wanting to edge down.

"That lush is out cold," Vince said. He took a couple of ginger steps towards Badge, like he might to feed a squirrel. "Badgie. Badgie, you in there?"

Tad stuck his head in the room. "Bus leaves in ten minutes."

Vince rounded up the last two beers, and the pair headed for the bus. Betty stopped at the door. "You coming, Badge?" She almost yelled it.

"Huh?"

"Bus is leaving."

"I'm comin'."

"You sure?"

"I can make it to the bus."

With a grunt, he pushed himself off the couch, caught himself before he stumbled forward. *Talk about me like I'm not here.* He bent over to grab his beer and somehow wound up on his knees. He laughed at his drunkenness, his dumb luck. He was sure that being on his hands and knees was somehow Vince's fault. Badge grabbed his beer, pulled himself up. *I'll show you a lush.* He drank the beer in slow gulps, draining the bottle. Then, with the same underhand motion as Betty earlier, he tossed the empty towards the can, missing entirely, and the bottle shattered on the cement.

The crash startled him, and he staggered over to the can. Glass was everywhere, a Milky Way of stars on the floor. Next to him, a few items still needed to be loaded out. Betty's amp, Flip's cymbal case, a couple of gig bags. He couldn't leave the glass here. Someone would step on it and cut himself. The bus idled just outside. With a drunken exhale, Badge again got down on his knees.

He picked up the shards one at a time, using only the tips of his fingers. A few big pieces had gone all the way under Flip's cymbal case, and Badge got them, dropped them in the can. The top part of the bottle wound up in the corner, and Badge crawled all the way to it, threw it away. One sliver had bounded up into Betty's gig bag. Badge carefully picked it out and dropped it into the can. He did this until all the glass was cleared and by some a stroke of luck managed not to cut himself.

He got to his feet, looked down at Betty's gig bag, a black canvas thing forever unzipped at the top, all of her pedals and cords within. There was probably a few hundred bucks worth of stuff in there, enough to ruin a guitar player's day if it were lost or stolen. Enough for a drug addict to sell to a pawn shop.

Badge picked up the bag, looked at it, glanced both ways up the corridor. No one was around. In the distance a band blared away onstage, one he didn't recognize. They could've been the Beatles and he wouldn't have noticed. He dropped the bag in the trash can, gave it an extra push to make sure Tad didn't see it when he finished loading. *Talk your way out of this one, asshole.*

34

"Where's my cord bag?" Betty said.

They were at soundcheck at Terraces, a club that had once been Dallas's premiere live music venue. Badge had been to the club years ago to see Elvis Costello, making the trip across Texas for the chance. He remembered a line of people sitting on the wooden barrier along the balcony, their legs dangling over the edge. Tonight the place would be just as full, but no one would sit on the barrier. No one would think of it. That was how rock and roll had changed. A world full of the right people doing the right things at the right time. A kind of hell.

Terraces had slipped into disrepair over the years. The club's wooden floor was covered with a thick layer of black. A mural of a sun-drenched vista had been scratched to the point that it looked more like abstract art. The velvet curtains, tied at each side of the stage, were so ripped they'd become badges of honor.

"I got it ready last night," Tad said. He scoped the floor like he might to look for a small animal. "Vince, did you grab Betty's cord bag?"

Vince, half watching Flip change a drum head, looked annoyed. "It's around."

"I'll check the bus," Tad said.

Badge kept his head down, worked the tuning pegs of his Stratocaster.

Tad came back, a bewildered look on his face. "I can't find it."

"You *know* you packed it?" Betty said.

"I know I pulled it together." But Tad knew that wasn't what she wanted to hear.

"Christ," Betty said. "Philly!"

"You wanna borrow some of my stuff?" Badge said.

"No."

Philly emerged from the back.

"My gig bag's gone."

Philly looked at Tad. "You can't find it?"

"I checked everywhere."

"There's probably 500 bucks worth of stuff in there," Badge said.

"Someone must've seen me packing," Tad said.

"All right," Philly said. "I'll call the club. Betty, make a list of everything you need. Vince, you wanna run to Guitar World for us?"

Shane Alprin, the show's promoter, stood just offstage during soundcheck, smiling and nodding as the band played. He wore a toupee of dark hair parted severely to one side. No Fun Intended was his first sellout in months. "Let me feed you kids," he said after soundcheck. "What do you want? Steak? Ribs?"

"What's good?" Betty said.

Shane grinned, nodded. "Don't worry. I'll take care of it. Meet me upstairs in an hour."

Dinner came in four aluminum serving bins. Two held a medley of barbequed meats: chicken, ribs, pork. One had mashed potatoes, melted butter floating like sea foam on top. The last had half-cobs of corn, assembled crisscross style. Band

and crew created towering plates while Shane stood by, smiling around his unlit cigar.

"Stuff is hard to keep track of on the road," Badge said. In the onslaught of food, the lost bag had been annoyingly forgotten. He sat back from the table, pulled a foot onto his knee.

"It's really not," Tad said. "You just have to stay on top of it. I'm trying to remember if anyone was around."

"It's not your fault," Badge said. "If someone takes a shining to your stuff out here, needs it or wants it or whatever, they're gonna get it. I remember in the Famous Dead." He took a tug from his beer. A brief glance at Betty ensured she was listening. "We lost all kinds of stuff. Gig bags, cymbals, cash. Of course, we found out later who it was."

"Who?" Tad said.

"Raoul," Badge said. "Our bass player. Good guy, nothing wrong with him. He just had an unspoken goal to snort up Peru."

A few laughed. Betty's eyes got bigger. Vince's narrowed.

Badge pulled his cigarettes from his pocket, slid one out. "Eventually we caught him."

"How?" Tad said.

Badge lit his cigarette, dropped the match onto his plate. "One night Raoul was short coke money, so he stole our leadoff band's drum set."

"What?" Flip said.

"How'd he do that?" Tad said.

"He waited until after soundcheck, when everyone was gone." Badge smiled, shook his head. "He took it right off the stage."

"What'd you guys do?" Tad said.

"Their band's manager brought it to our attention. Raoul denied it. Convincing liar too. The manager dragged us all up the street to a pawnshop, where the drums sat in the window waiting to be sold." Badge took a hit of his cigarette. "I never thought Raoul would stoop so low, but that's what you have to understand about addicts."

"What's that?" Vince said. He looked at Badge like he'd eviscerate whatever he said next.

"The drugs come first. Always."

"Horseshit," Vince said.

"It's a sad fate."

"You're an expert, I suppose."

"You got something you want to tell us?"

"You want me to confess to stealing the cord bag? The fucking cord bag?"

"Not if you didn't."

"I'm not gonna dignify that."

"Badge, shut up," Betty said.

Badge took a drag of his cigarette, put it out on his plate. "Whatever you say, boss," he said and got up to leave.

Later that night, at a coffee shop next to the venue, Badge nursed a gin-infused Americano and watched people walk by.

To his surprise, Betty came in. She wore large sunglasses and a scarf around her head. She was getting good at disguising herself. Since Vince had come aboard, fans had become the enemy, high on her list of people she didn't want to deal with. Badge knew the list well. He was at the top of it.

Betty stopped when she saw him, then went to the counter, ordered, wouldn't look at him. When she got her coffee, she started back out the door but stopped at his table. "Sometimes I wish I were a sideman in this band."

"Really?"

She set down her coffee, sat across from him. "Just sit back and play."

"Doesn't sound like you."

"Probably not, but I think about it."

"It's hard being the boss."

"I didn't know I signed on to be the boss."

"Good thing you did," Badge said. "Anyone else would've screwed it up."

"I figured you'd say otherwise."

"People are lining up around the block to see us play. You did something right."

Betty smiled, went to sip her coffee but found it too hot. "Do you really think Goo stole that bag?"

Badge remembered when he was the one she confided in, realized how much he missed it. "What do you think?"

"He's been kind of a dick lately."

"How so?"

"In Wichita I caught him talking to two guys on the street. He swears he wasn't doing anything wrong, but how am I supposed to know?"

"Addicts say whatever they have to say."

"I don't want to have to worry about him every time he's out of sight." Betty slid her paper cup in little circles on the table. "I guess I'm starting to wonder—"

A group of girls—fans, no doubt—came into the coffee shop. Betty turned away, and the girls, oblivious, went to the counter. When they left, Betty let out a sigh, grabbed her coffee. "I gotta go."

"You don't have to."

"It's cool. I just needed someone to listen for a minute. See you there."

Before the gig, Philly popped into the backstage room. "Badge, you got a second?"

Philly led him to the outdoor balcony, where plastic tables and chairs were strewn about, a spot for employees to take smoke breaks. Below, a giant Dumpster was so full its lid wouldn't close.

"What are you trying to pull?" Philly said.

"Huh?"

"They found Betty's gig bag– You know where they found it."

"What are you talking about?"

"Come on. A barback saw you."

Badge couldn't speak. He looked over the horizon, the rows of buildings.

Philly took off his glasses, rubbed his fingers over his eyes. "Do you know how many guitar players would get on their knees and weep if they got this gig?"

Badge said nothing.

"And do you know what kind of trouble you'd be in if I told anyone what happened to that bag?"

Badge stared straight ahead. A bird flew by, going somewhere with purpose, direction.

Philly put his glasses back on. "I'm gonna tell Betty they found it backstage. That's all I'm gonna say, but if it happens again–and for Christ's sake it better not happen again–I'm gonna tell her something else."

The Terraces gig went so well Shane bought everyone Champagne, and they drank together in the backstage room. "You guys are the best thing that ever happened to me," Shane said, but Badge suspected the next band to save his ass would be the next best thing that ever happened to him.

Badge migrated to a little offshoot of a room, gin bottle in tow. He was tired of the nonstop banter. With Betty's gig bag found, she and Vince seemed on renewed terms, the two kissing long and heavy before she went onstage. Badge flopped onto the couch, shut his eyes, did his best not to listen to the noise from next door.

"Badge," someone said. A girl peeked around the corner. Her matted crop of black hair dangled with beads, exactly like Betty's old hairdo. She could've been the Ghost of Betty Past. "Remember me?"

"Sure," he lied.

"Tina Wang." She sauntered over to him. Badge had never seen a more accurate Betty likeness. Her dreads were all in place, and her clothes—white blouse, plaid skirt, combat boots—could've been designed with one eye on the photos from the band's album. "From Sacramento. You had me and my brother on the bus after the show. We played Carolina!"

"Oh yeah." Badge remembered the pair, college kids in sweatshirts and tennis shoes. "You look different."

Tina sat next to him, crossed her legs with a flip. "Yeah, well, that Betty. She did a number on me. Of course she's all cornrows now. I have to go home and get back to work."

"Keep it like it is."

"You're sweet."

Badge remembered some Web thing Betty had talked about, a site associated with Tina or her brother. "'Neil Young Must Die?'"

"Neil *Diamond*." She had a slight lilt to her voice, another new addition since the last time Badge had seen her. He wondered if she could adopt personas the way some people pick up accents. "Yep, that's me. I went right home after the show and started blogging about you guys. The site's gone viral. We had our two millionth hit last week."

"Wow."

"Which leads me to my purpose." She adjusted herself. "Things in the world of Internet rock are turbulent as ever. Rope Panda just launched a new site with instructional videos; Gravitate got Art Spiegelman to design their Web graphics; and Satellites from Yuma is out to trump them all with their Java-fueled MP3 player. If Betty wants to keep market share, she needs to up the ante."

"How can she do that?"

"Funny you should ask." She tapped Badge's knee. "I'm coming on tour with you to do some interviews. I want up close and personal, the day-to-day stuff, what goes on behind the scenes with No Fun Intended. Other sites are betting heavily on technical stuff—that's fine, let the geeks have their toys—but what they don't have is a bona fide star, someone who reaches through a monitor and grabs a viewer by the throat. What they don't have, in a word, is Betty."

Something thumped into the wall next door. Whatever it was splattered through the doorway. Betty yelled, "No fair, no fair."

"So, that's why I'm here," Tina said. "One week aboard the bus, see what there is to see, and report back. How's all this sitting with you?"

Badge took a slug from his bottle, looked at this young, pretty girl sitting next to him. She clearly hadn't been disappointed by life yet. Maybe Badge could be her first. "Tell you what." He slid closer, extended an arm behind. "You can interview me all you want if—"

"Great." Tina sprang up. "I'm glad you're on board. It makes it *sooo* much easier. We'll have great fun, you'll see."

35

In Austin, on Betty's twenty-second birthday, Badge offered to pick up Glen at the airport. It would get him out of any party prep duties, and it might offer a little break from the Betty and Vince show. Badge and Les had heard nothing from Glen, and they both wondered what was up. "If you don't see me after tomorrow," Les had said, wrapping his arm around Badge, "I'm probably at the bottom of Town Lake."

But Badge's suspicions melted away when he saw Glen emerge from the airport. He wore a watermelon Tommy Bahama shirt and what Badge wanted to call beach pants, white and billowy, tied at the waist. He carried a travel bag and sported leather sandals that looked like they'd been weaved by a master craftsman. This wasn't someone coming to Austin to fire anyone. It was an older guy getting out of the office for once.

"Badgerino," Glen said. The two hugged at the curb. Glen smelled of cologne, and Badge had to fight the urge to kiss him on the neck. "How you holding up?"

"Can't complain." Badge must've looked like a nightmare. He wore the same clothes as yesterday, and he couldn't remember his last shower. The three gin and tonics he'd already had that day were working their hazy magic on him.

"Sure you can, but you're not going to, are you. Let's get a cab."

Texas humidity weighed on everything, cars glided by. Glen looked rounder, less fit, but happy. The two, roughly the same age, had taken different paths in the music business. From Glen's haircut to the style of his clothes to the grin on his face, Badge knew which of them had made the right choices.

"Where to?" the cabbie said.

"Embassador," Badge said.

"Love Austin," Glen said as the cab pulled away. "I signed Full Bright out of here a decade ago. He was a mess of pain killers at the time, but once he hit the stage—" Glen made a whistling sound.

"How's Betty compare?"

Glen smiled. "Of course you want to know how he compares to Betty. Right now you want to know how everything compares to Betty."

The Austin skyline emerged in the distance, a bunch of tall buildings huddled together, protecting each other.

"So, how can I help you with your problem?" Glen said.

"My problem?"

"Your Betty problem."

Badge looked out the window. They passed rows of homes, small A-frames, one right after the other. He found it hard to believe people actually lived in them, had families in them, ate and slept and recreated in them. Life seemed irretrievably removed not only from himself but from everything else. "I don't think they have the cure for what I got."

"I hooked you two up in the first place because I thought you might be good together."

"Really."

"You keep her out of trouble, she keeps you out of trouble, and you both stay knee deep in the good stuff."

"The good stuff."

"I'm sorry it didn't work out. You have to know I'm sorry."

"Don't sweat it. I think our bigger problem is Vince."

"Yeah, Les mentioned the—" He took a hit from a pretend pipe.

"Betty thinks he's reformed."

"You think he's not?"

"That's my guess. Betty caught him hanging out with some street guys in Wichita. I don't know what you're thinking letting him on the bus."

"I don't get a choice anymore."

"Well, that's only going to get worse. The two of them are plotting to get rid of all of us. They want to go punk rock, do it all themselves."

"Punk rock." Glen shook his head. "Two words that mean you can do everything poorly and still call it art." He patted Badge's knee. "Don't worry about it. It's going to be all right."

They pulled up to the Embassador, a thirty-story building, high and thin. The lobby teemed with people. Glen motioned Badge towards the couch. "Wait for me a minute? I gotta check in."

Badge sat down, kicked his feet up on an ottoman. A group of four or five guys, what may have been another band, waited by the elevator. They took turns pushing the button, looking up.

"Fourth floor," Glen said. He was bagless now, and sweat came through his shirt, especially where the strap had hung. "The guy said the elevator just got stuck. We gotta take the stairs."

Their footsteps echoed on the metal stairs.

"We need to deal with this Vince thing before it gets out of hand," Badge said.

"We will." Glen was having trouble catching his breath. "Wait till we get to the room. I've had to pee since I got off the plane."

They found room 423. "I can't believe they don't have keycards in this place," Glen said. "What decade is it?"

Glen's room was almost exactly like Badge's—cherrywood armoire, matching headrest and coffee table—but Glen's had a Jacuzzi tub. "Planning a big night?" Badge said, motioning to it.

"It was the lowest room they had. I'm not hiking to the twentieth floor." He opened the mini-fridge, grabbed an Amstel Light. "There are two in here. You want one?"

"No."

Glen twisted off the cap, took a drink. Something changed in his face. "Why don't you sit down."

The silence was uncomfortable. It made Badge want to cough or sniffle. "I don't need to sit down."

"I think you should."

Badge didn't sit.

Glen shrugged, sat on the edge of the coffee table. It was as though, instead of attending a friend's birthday party, he was suddenly attending a funeral. He took another drink. "Betty wants you off the tour."

Badge stared at Glen, whose face was tough, a guy who'd done this before. What a fool he'd been to think Glen was happy to see him. "You mean I'm fired."

"You're fired."

"I'm fired," Badge said, and he smacked the Amstel Light out of Glen's hand, sending it to the floor. "I'm the best fucking thing that ever happened to that girl."

Glen watched the beer empty onto the carpet. "She doesn't think so."

"You gotta tell her."

"You try telling her anything lately?"

Badge stomped towards the bed, he didn't know why. There was nothing there for him. There was nothing anywhere for him. "She can't do this."

"She can fire me, she can fire you."

"Can't you say something?"

"I have," Glen said. "I fought like crazy for you, but it's over. She wants her life back."

"Her life with Vince? Glen, the guy is no good for her."

"I'll deal with him later."

"But you'll deal with me now."

Glen sighed. The funeral–quick as it was–had gone on too long. He was genuinely starting to feel remorse. He pushed himself up, meandered towards the window. "You've got a plane ticket waiting for you at the front desk, along with severance pay. You won't have trouble getting work with this record under your belt."

Glen took in the view, and Badge knew he wouldn't turn around. The coffin was buried. What else was there to see? "So that's why you made the trip."

"Part of the reason," Glen said. "It's also Betty's birthday."

36

Less than a minute after leaving Glen's room, Badge entered the hotel bar.

Windows made up all of one wall, causing the light from outside to blind him as he walked in. The place was empty, no candles lit, most of the chairs up. Badge sat on a barstool, waited for someone to help him. Noise came from the back, but no one seemed to know he was there. Maybe he wasn't.

A copy of a weekly newspaper, this one called *Bomb*, sat on the chair next to him. A few pages in and—of course—there was a half-page photo of Betty. Her hands were on her hips, her legs slightly apart, and she stared Superwoman-like into the distance. Before he could stop himself, Badge read the caption.

> Betty's songs have an exuberance that suggests hope, a tilt not backward toward death and drugs and nihilism but forward toward the future, what still might be. With Radiohead and other computer rockers the only meager threat on the landscape, Betty and No Fun Intended remind us that rock music, real rock music, is made by the people, for the people.

Badge dropped the paper to the floor.

A woman peeked around from the back. She looked to be in her mid-thirties and had brown hair like Debra Winger's in *An Officer and a Gentleman*. "Oh," she said. She had something in her mouth and finished chewing as she strolled up. When the chewing took longer than she expected, she rolled her eyes, motioned in an "I'm still chewing" way. "What can I get you?"

"Gin and tonic."

The woman nodded, reached for a glass. While mixing, she used her tongue to clean food out of her gums. Badge knew he should eat too, but instead he would drink. He would get spectacularly drunk. No one was left to give a shit, least of all him.

The bartender set a napkin down and his drink on top of it. "Four bucks."

Badge dug a twenty out of his wallet, set it on the bar. "I'm going to need another."

"That's what we're here for." She snatched up the bill and went to the register. The tag of her white blouse was flipped upwards. "In town for a gig?"

"Nope." He took a tug of his drink. She'd made it strong.

"Well, you might want to keep your eyes peeled. Famous people are about today."

"Yeah? Who?"

"Some singer. They're having a party for her in the theater room tonight."

"What's her name?"

"I can't remember. Betty maybe?"

"Heard her music?"

"There was some video on this morning while I was getting ready."

"What did you think?"

She set his change on the bar. "I didn't see the big deal."

He was starting to like this bartender. "I ask because I know her."

"You know her?"

"Sure. You wanna meet her?"

"What? No."

"Come on. How many chances do you get to meet a bona fide star?"

"You really know her? Does she always wear her hair like that?"

She was talking about Betty's hair in the video for "Calypso," her beaded dreadlocks pulled back into a semblance of a housewife's bun. It looked striking, and people showed up to the concerts expecting it, which of course meant Betty would never wear it that way again. "You really want to know something about Betty?" Badge said.

"Sure."

He leaned across the bar. "She's a redhead."

"*Nooo.*"

"It's true. Trust me, I know."

The bartender's eyes thinned and she turned her head, catching his drift. "You're trouble," she said, but Badge could tell this wasn't necessarily a bad thing.

Badge downed the rest of his drink. "Give me another."

They talked and Badge drank. Her name was Mindy, and she'd worked at the Embassador for eight months, the longest she'd ever worked anywhere. She preferred daytime shifts after getting robbed at gunpoint one night. She'd never married, didn't like boyfriends. Men made her feel "bought and paid for." She didn't mind kids, but wasn't necessarily pining for one either.

"What time do you get off?" Badge said. "You wanna help me find something?"

Town Lake was busy with joggers and bikers. A path meandered around trees. Mindy, still in her work clothes, saw it first.

"It" was a bronze statue of Stevie Ray Vaughan. Stevie wore a cowboy hat and a large poncho that came down in folds. He stared straight ahead, cowboy-like, and he balanced his Stratocaster against the ground. A thin bronze silhouette extended behind him along the pedestal, his "shadow." Badge had always wanted to see this tribute, not quite believing it existed.

"He looks sad," Mindy said. She hopped onto the pedestal, touched his eyes.

"The guy quit everything," Badge said. "Drinking, drugs. Then he died in a helicopter crash."

"You're a fan?"

"Not really, but I followed him, especially after he quit drinking."

Mindy reached for the low branch of a maple tree, plucked off a leaf. "I never cared for music."

"What?"

"People have been nuts for it all my life, but I never got into it."

"Where're you from?"

"Richmond."

"Texas?"

"Virginia."

"Remind me never to go there."

"It's a nice place." Mindy had the ability to miss or ignore any irony in what she heard, a quality Badge had known in a few people. He always thought them superior. "I bet I can count on one hand how many record stores we had."

Badge touched the fingers of Stevie's hand, which still held the heat from the day. "This is great."

"What?"

"Just that it's here. That this guitarist was so important to this place they erected a statue to him."

Mindy spun on the gravel as if on a dance floor, her arms spread.

"Wait," Badge said. "How does a girl who doesn't like music wind up in Austin?"

She stopped spinning, came over to him. "Music I can take or leave. It's musicians I can't live without."

Mindy loved to be chased.

Once their clothes were off, Badge's hotel room bathed in yellow light, Mindy scampered, all of the playful parts of her bouncing, to the other side of the room. Badge stalked her, edged her towards the corner, watched her eyes grow bigger with each step. She screamed as she tried to escape, taking a route over the bed, and he pounced on her, corralled her arms. The game thrilled them both. All night Mindy, like a wild horse, at once resisting him and begging to be broken, galloped away, and Badge was forced to recapture her.

Badge woke in the middle of the night having dreamt he'd missed a gig—a dream that had followed him throughout his life. The anxiety made him want to hurry out of bed. He supposedly had a flight back to Albuquerque that day, the ticket waiting for him at the front desk.

Mindy purred next to him, naked, her butt like bread dough sliced down the middle. A few hours ago, Badge had rolled off of her, foggy, heavy-limbed. They said nothing; nothing needed to be said. He'd gotten up to pee, then she did. They lay there, not speaking, listening to the occasional drunk stumble up the hallway until they fell asleep.

Carefully, Badge slid out of bed, found his bag. The night came unusually bright through the curtains, the lights of Austin radiating up to the window. In the bathroom, Badge put his head under the shower, put on some clothes. When he ducked into the hallway, the door squeaked loudly, but Mindy didn't stir. The girl who didn't like music. That was how he'd remember her.

The hotel lobby felt surreal, bright lights, nobody around. The front desk attendant—skinny, clean-cut—looked at him with guardedness.

"I'm 619," Badge said. "Do you have something for me?"

"You're Badge?"

"Yeah."

The attendant grabbed a manila envelope. "We were expecting you yesterday."

Muffled noise, live music, came from behind a set of double doors. Badge pointed. "Betty's party?"

"They started at eight. The catering staff left at one. A guy came out about a half hour ago. That's all I know."

Badge heard Shoulder La Back playing souped-up country. He knew he shouldn't care what was going on in there, but he wanted to know. "How can I get into that place without being seen?"

"Wouldn't have a clue," the attendant said and went back to work.

Badge reached for his wallet, pulled out a twenty, set it on the counter. "You sure?"

The attendant eyed the money, snatched it off the counter. "There's access from the second floor, but you didn't hear it from me."

Badge pushed through the doors and found himself on a U-shaped balcony. The wooden seats that made up the rows were bolted to cement. Below, on a stage lighted no differently than the rest of the room, Shoulder La Back played a Johnny Cash cover they seemed to barely know. Jonah hopped pogo-like as the rest of the band barreled through the changes. Fifty or so people cavorted around the room. A few looked like reporters. Three women whooped it up on the dance floor, one wearing a silver dress and high heels, the other two in bare feet. They were probably invited from the gig the night before. Despite the darkness of the balcony, Badge had to be careful no one saw him.

More people grouped around two tables in back, each covered with Champagne bottles and papier mâché centerpieces. Cosmo danced close with a girl. Tad, who wore one of the centerpieces on his head, sat with Tina Wang, her arms around his neck. Flip, with no shoes on, slid in socked feet on the wooden floor. The rest tossed back Champagne. Les and Glen were nowhere to be seen.

And, of course, there was Betty, Betty and Vince. You could tell they were the featured attraction, something in the way they stood off to the side and "received" people. Betty wore a zebra-striped top with a no-room-for-error miniskirt. Vince wore a new black sport coat, and he drank straight from a Champagne bottle. Birthday aside, this party seemed to be Vince's introduction to the world as Betty's new beau, the kind of introduction Badge had never thought to expect.

The band finished with a mess of noise. The guitarist went down on his knees. Jonah took a slug of Champagne, rested his arm on the mic stand. "Welcome to the top, Betty," he said into the mic. Tad stood on a table, his arms outstretched, like he was signaling to a passing plane.

Vince meandered to the stage, shouted. The girl in the silver dress glanced at him as she clapped. Vince said something to Jonah, and the two clinked bottles. Then he spun around, held his arms aloft, took it all in. Tad pointed at him. *You're the man.* It was Betty's birthday, Shoulder La Back was onstage, but somehow this was Vince's moment.

Then Vince saw Badge, who'd apparently moved too close to the balcony's edge. Vince's eyes locked on him, and he smirked, pumped his fists in the air. *I win. You lose.*

The silver-dressed girl leaned into Vince, and Vince grabbed her around the waist, bent her backwards for an impromptu dip. He guided her back up and held his hands aloft, a dance contestant after a flawless routine. The band continued making noise. Jonah bounced up and down, his arms swinging.

Betty, by herself in back, watched as the silver-dressed girl got close to Vince. Betty's face was still, someone reflecting on the path she'd taken, if she'd taken the right one. When Vince whispered in the girl's ear, Betty disappeared beneath the balcony.

Badge caught up with her at the other side of the hotel. Any fear she might have harbored of Badge showing up must have dissipated long ago, and now, face to face with him, her eyes widened. Nothing's really a problem unless it's staring you down late at night, after a few drinks.

"Hey," Badge said.

Betty rolled her eyes.

"Glad to see you too."

"What do you want?"

"To say goodbye?"

"Goodbye," she said but didn't leave.

"Off to Lubbock?"

"Yep."

"You won't need a guitar player once you get there?"

"Glen's taking care of it."

"Yeah, Glen does take care of it, doesn't he."

She stood on the first step of the stairs, looking down at him, her miniskirt hugging her legs. In her zebra stripes, she could've been the queen of some jungled territory, an island off the coast of Africa, rich in gold. Badge wanted to throw himself at her feet, profess his loyalty, but he couldn't. She'd be gone before the first words came out of his mouth. "But can this new guy give you what I can give you?"

"He's just finishing the tour. We'll get a replacement later."

"You don't have to do that."

"Yes, I do."

"I know things have been rocky lately."

"They've been more than rocky, Badge. They've been crater-like."

"And you know when it started."

"I know when it started, and I know where it ends. Go home. It's over." And she turned to go upstairs.

"You're having my baby," Badge said.

Betty looked at him with just a hint of pity in her eyes, the way she might look at a peasant. "That's a technicality."

"What do you mean?"

"A baby is the woman's first." She put her hand on her stomach.

As a visual it was hard to refute, but Badge said, "That's not the whole story."

Betty rolled her eyes, started up the stairs.

"I wouldn't count on me going away."

"Then you'll give me no choice."

"What choice?" he said, but realized what she meant.

It was then Badge heard "Hey" from behind him.

Vince hustled through the lobby, Tad behind. Vince's eyes narrowed, and his face shriveled like he'd eaten something sour. "Look who showed up." He was drunk. "Tired of hanging out in the bleachers?"

Badge had a fistful of Vince's coat before he knew what he was doing, and he slammed him into the wall once, twice. The move felt perfect, all anger, vendetta. Vince coughed, but a split second later he smacked at Badge, the fight in him ignited. His boots kicked at Badge's shins, his knees at his groin. Badge wrapped his hand around Vince's throat, squeezed hard, pushed him against the wall. He could break this kid, strangle him or snap him in two. He'd like it. Vince stared back, eyes hate-filled.

Badge pummeled Vince's face. Voices called from behind,

Betty screamed, but Badge could barely hear it. Vince's arms and legs flailed as Badge punched, to no avail. Someone grabbed Badge from behind, pulled him backward.

When Badge broke loose, the world froze. Vince lay motionless, blood all over his face. Betty looked shocked. Tad stared at Badge, breathing heavily. The hotel attendant, who must've come over during the skirmish said, "The cops are on their way."

Feeling the game changed, and drastically against him, Badge hustled out the revolving doors and into the night.

Part V

Thank You, Good Night

37

Outside, there was no sun. The storefronts across the street were dark, barred. A dozen streetlamps emphasized how far Badge had to go to get out of sight.

He ran left. A transient lay curled in the entryway of a church, a lone car puttered by. Badge remembered Vince's face, the swelling around his eyes, his nose like a runt potato. He ran towards the lake, the neon signs nothing but blurs.

He rested around a corner. A neighborhood store, closed for business, was dark save a lighted placard advertising cigarettes. Badge ducked into the store's entryway, took out the manila envelope. Inside was a plane ticket to Albuquerque scheduled to leave that morning, along with a check for five thousand dollars, "Thanks, Betty" written in the memo section.

He folded the check, slid it into his pocket. He dropped the rest into a garbage can. He couldn't take the flight. For all he knew, cops would be waiting for him.

A city bus clanked around the corner. Badge eyed it as it went by, took off after it. "Hey," he yelled. The driver, a skinny man with dreadlocks, pointed to the corner.

Fluorescent lights shined in the bus's interior. Badge dropped a few coins in before noticing blood on his knuckles. He switched to his other hand.

The driver glanced up. "That's plenty."

"Huh?"

"It's only a dollar."

Badge put the rest of his change in his pocket. "How far do you go?"

"Everyone gets off at Howard."

He took a seat in back, kept his head cocked towards the window. The bus turned on Guadalupe, going what Badge took for north. As the buildings changed to the gentrified type, he allowed his tension to ease. He was free—for the moment.

At a cross street, an older drunk man wearing a cowboy hat got on. He looked briefly at Badge and sat behind the driver, nodded off, coughed. His coughs grew in frequency, every second or so, *cough ... cough ... cough.*

"Hey, old man," the driver said. "You gonna die on me?"

The old man didn't acknowledge the driver but quit coughing.

The next morning, after sleeping in a patch of trees behind a grocery store, Badge bought a car, a powder blue '64 Plymouth Valiant, the kind a restorer might be interested in if its body weren't so shot, flakes of rust breaking off of its fender like dirt clods. The vinyl passenger's seat was torn up the middle, and the inside smelled of antifreeze, but he didn't have time to be picky. "Drives like a dream," the salesman said, a guy named Weed. "Don't let the engine noise fool you. That's just how they sounded back then."

"I got cash," Badge said. The check had just been cashed up the street. "How soon can we get the paperwork done?"

Weed ran his hand over his mustache. "For cash, I don't see why there has to be paperwork."

As he drove through Austin in his new car and felt the distance of the day from the night before, Badge couldn't make himself leave. He wondered how hurt Vince was. Who was to say he hadn't slept it off, taken a shower and climbed back on his horse? Badge's right hand, his weapon of choice the night before, hurt, and he steered entirely with his left.

The front entrance of the Embassador was busy with people. The sun prompted sunglasses all around. Badge's bag was probably still on the balcony. There was no way he could risk getting it.

He circled the hotel once, twice. The band's bus sat out front, no sign of anyone. He parked where he could see, waited.

Around noon, Les came out, followed by a quick succession of band and crew, each stuffing his bag underneath and climbing aboard. Tad emerged with Tina Wang, carrying both of their bags. Gaston started the bus, a loud chugging.

Betty came out wearing a baseball cap and soul-concealing sunglasses. She carried both her own and Vince's bag, used her momentum to toss one underneath, then followed up with a less ladylike move to stow the other before stomping back to the hotel.

She came back out with Vince. Vince wore the same clothes as the night before, but over his face, right over the top of his nose, like a starfish clinging to a rock, was a giant white X. They'd been to the hospital. Badge had broken Vince's nose.

"See what you get, fucker," Badge said.

Vince walked slowly, holding Betty's arm. He could've been an old man being helped along by a dutiful, if annoyed, nurse. It took a while, but the pair managed to get aboard. Gaston slammed the door, and the bus eased away from the curb.

Badge watched as the bus got smaller and smaller, and felt an emptiness grow inside of him. He turned the ignition. Before leaving town, he stopped at a liquor store, where he bought a case of gin and put it in the trunk of his car.

In Lubbock, he parked behind No Fun Intended's venue for the night, the Lubbock Gas Light, a square, grey thousand-

seater with a gravel parking lot and no windows. Badge parked
in the back, a stand of trees behind him. No one from the bus
would think to give the Valiant a second look. The sun shined
over the plains. He sucked on a freshly christened bottle of gin,
drifted off.

He startled awake when a taxi pulled into the parking lot.
A tall, shaggy-headed man got out of it, guitar case in tow. The
rent-a-guitarist. Leftover metal guy, you could tell. Tank top,
tan arms, snakeskin boots. Betty would flip when she saw him.
Badge could've been ready to play himself if his hand didn't
hurt so badly. The gin helped.

A while later, Les came out of the bus.

"Les," Badge yelled.

Les started towards him but doubled back. He reemerged
with Badge's guitar case, scurried over. Badge opened the door
to his back seat. "You better get outta here," Les said, sliding
the case in.

"Hello to you too."

"I'm serious. They were talking to the cops yesterday."

"Fuck it, Les."

"You're gonna think fuck it when they catch up to you. I
could get arrested just for knowing your whereabouts, which
I don't."

Badge eased back into his seat. He could tell by Les's
expression that he didn't look good. He lit a cigarette. "How's
Vince?"

"Bemoaning his fate."

Badge puffed out a laugh.

"Broken nose, fat lip, some cut behind his ear that needed
stitches. Once that nose heals it'll be crooked."

"Poor kid."

"You fucked him up pretty good. I'm not sure I'd be so
casual."

"How's Betty?"

"She thinks everything's gonna be better from here on out."

"Wait 'til she gets a load of my replacement."

Les shook his head. "Got lost on the way to the White Lion concert, is my guess."

"If I didn't know better, I'd say Glen is exacting revenge."

"For what?"

"For firing him."

"They fired him?"

"I told him Vince and Betty were out to replace all of us."

"The tour's only got a week or two left," Les said. "I wouldn't be surprised if we all got–Holy shit."

Les had just noticed Badge's hand, which lay like a dead fish on his lap.

"It's fine," Badge said.

"Fine, my ass. You need to see someone."

"Dr. Tanqueray," Badge said, holding up the bottle.

Les glanced at the bus, where nothing stirred. "Give me your keys. We'll get you to a doctor. You're too drunk to drive anyway."

They found a clinic downtown next to an enormous dome. They had to wait an hour, Badge's hand wrapped in an ice pack, nothing to do but crave a drink. Sick people disappeared behind swinging doors. No one ever came back.

When Badge's number got called, Les shook his good hand. "I gotta go to soundcheck, but do me a favor. Get your lame ass home to your kid."

"I will," Badge said. "Have you heard anything about the baby?"

"Like what?"

"I don't know. Betty's been talking about ... Have you heard anything?"

"Nothing. Actually, I can't believe how little it comes up." He patted Badge on the shoulder. "Get fixed up and go home.

There's nothing out here for you anymore. There might be nothing out here for any of us anymore."

A dark-haired nurse led him to an X-ray room. She put his hand on a metal plate and disappeared. After a *beep* she led him to another room, where she left him. Badge's hand throbbed. He hadn't had a drink in over an hour. The room was too bright.

The doctor came in, pudgy, with round glasses. He looked from the X-rays to Badge and back. "Your wrist is fractured."

"*Fuck*."

"You'll need a cast."

"I can't do a cast right now."

"Skip the cast and you'll be in a lot more pain for a lot longer, not to mention risk permanent damage."

The cast took forever. The nurse made a big deal about washing him. "A lot can grow in six weeks."

"Six weeks?" Badge pulled his arm away.

The nurse eased his arm back down, wrapped his forearm in cotton and added wet strips of fiberglass. The cast heated as it dried, and it was all Badge could do not to rip the thing off before it hardened. "What color of gauze do you want?" the nurse said, and he glared at her.

On the way out, the receptionist offered to go over his bill. Badge waved her off, handed her a credit card.

"You can fill your prescription up the street," she said.

"Here." He dropped the slip on the counter. "You take it."

38

It was dusk when he got back to the Lubbock Gas Light. People drove into the lot, their cars like filaments drawn to the magnet of the show. They parked in a semblance of where they thought the painted lines ought to be. Badge watched from his driver's seat. *Park wherever you want. There are no rules. Never have been.*

He kept having to find new positions for his cast, switching it from his lap, to his side, to a jimmy-rigged armrest. It was starting to make his head swim. The thing stretched from around his thumb to just under his elbow, and he had to fight the urge to stick his fingers in and pry it off. His cigarette smoldered in the ashtray. The only way to take a drag was to set his bottle down.

Badge popped open the car door, climbed out. There was a rock show here tonight, right? He'd buy a ticket if he had to, maybe work his way up to the front, demand to play. That could be his new role in No Fun Intended: band vampire. No matter how many nails you pound in his coffin, he keeps coming back. He took a last tug from his bottle, dropped it to the ground. He started towards the venue when he heard his name from behind.

It was a young woman, eggplant-shaped, in bermuda shorts and high-top tennis shoes. She wore glasses, and something about her mouth suggested it never quite shut. "You're Badge, right?"

"Who wants to know?"

"Melinda. I've seen every No Fun Intended show from here to Tampa. What happened to your hand?"

John Lennon once said, if a fan chases you down, never stop and never speed up. Just keep walking in the same direction at the same pace. Badge started for the venue. "Got it caught in a door."

"Wow." Melinda kept up with him, pulled along by the same force that drew everyone towards the venue. "You can't play like that, can you?"

"They got someone else."

"He can't be as good as you. You're one of my favorite guitarists ever. I put you right up there with Richard Lloyd."

Badge stopped, looked at her. Her glasses reflected the streetlamps. "You like Television?"

After some commotion at the gate—the doorman didn't want to let Badge in, and it took Melinda to convince him ("*Yes*, he *is* the guitar player. Look at the poster!")—they found themselves in a packed lobby. A line snaked back from the beer garden, intermingling with the restroom line. People grouped in front of the main doors, creating a bottleneck.

"How are you able to fly to all these shows?" Badge said.

"Not fly," Melinda said. "I rented a car."

"What do you do for a living?"

"Braid horse manes," she said, as naturally as if she'd said "waitress" or "work at a bank."

Teenagers teemed by the merchandise table. The image on the T-shirt featured Betty in her best Pat Benatar pose, Badge and the others fanned out behind her, a gang ready to attack. "You're lucky to have such a cool boss," Badge said.

"He's okay. I'm the best, so he pretty much has to do what I say."

They meandered to the main doors, waited to enter. Standing still was Badge's most difficult task. The sea of heads ebbed and flowed. He needed someplace to spread out, where his drunkenness wouldn't be so loud.

"Do you want to sit with me?" Melinda said. "I usually go all the way back."

They climbed the stairs to the balcony. People sat on wooden benches. Melinda found an empty row and shuffled over. Guys at opposite ends shined spotlights down on the curtain that cloaked the stage.

"I met Betty in Huntsville," Melinda said. "She was real nice. Signed my ticket stub. Which reminds me." She took out her ticket. "Would you?"

"I don't have a pen."

"I got one." She handed it to him.

Badge went to sign the stub.

"On the front. That way when I get it framed I won't have to choose which side."

He signed the ticket sloppily, his cast making it all but impossible.

The lights went down, and the crowd whooped. Everyone stood up, and so did Badge, his cast trying to tip him over. He hadn't been this drunk at a show in years. He remembered seeing Aldo Nova in Albuquerque when he was in high school. He and his two friends, Nick and Manuel, drank a fifth of whiskey in the parking lot. Manuel spent the concert vomiting in a trash can. Nick passed out well before Aldo hit the stage. It was Badge's duty to make sure they both got home that night. Whose duty was it to make sure he got home?

Despite the surge of energy, Melinda offered no sign of enthusiasm. She stood motionless, her high-tops slightly apart, her hands tucked in her pockets.

"*All right*," came the growl over the P.A. "*Are you ready to rumble?*"

The crowd whooped, and hands shot up. The spotlights did figure eights on the curtain. Melinda hopped onto the bench so she could see better.

"*Ladies and gentlemen ... NO ... FUN ... INTENDED!*"

The curtains slid open, and there stood the band. Betty was up front with her Gretsch, looking more frail than he'd ever seen her, slightly bent under the weight of her guitar. The new guitarist stood stageright—like he belonged there as much as anyone—his purple Jackson too high on his torso, his bushy hair ridiculous. Les manned the other side, a bearded, stageleft bookend. Flip adjusted his snare. Badge couldn't believe how pro they looked; the glistening chrome of Flip's hardware, the gravity of Les's persona, the big Gretsch hanging from Betty. Jealousy curled inside him like smoke.

The band broke into "Calypso," and the crowd seemed to stretch into the air, like they'd all suddenly grown a foot taller. It was too rumbly where Badge stood—the bass got trapped in the rafters and lingered too long—but he could feel the power of the music, the jolt it was for everyone in the place.

Betty's cornrows drooped over her cheeks. They seemed to be prodding her, a red cape to a bull, but she wasn't taking the bait. Her eyes—Badge could tell even from this distance—levitated between wakefulness and sleep, here and not here. It was a look he associated with bluesmen, waiting for the music to, God willing, take them away. Betty sang.

> It was Friday, it was my day
> My sit around get high day
> My don't ask why day
>
> And where'd you go to steal that careless smile?
> I haven't seen one like it
> In quite a while

Badge felt the texture of her voice, the weight of the words.

And if I never seem to go with the flow
It's all I know
Calypso

And if you're pulling everything from the past
You're always last to know
Calypso

Badge tilted his head back, felt the bass reverberating in his ears.

The guitarist played a solo, a jerky, erratic thing that included an Yngwie-like ascension, a series of whammy-inflected bends, and a Satriani dive-bomb. It was a complete bastardization of what Badge had played on the record, and Betty glared at the guitarist like a tiger ready to devour. It should've been Badge up there. That solo was his, the music too.

When the solo ended, Melinda tapped Badge's shoulder. "You're way better than that guy."

The band picked up intensity as it came to the bridge.

And if I see this whole thing through
And I do what I gotta do
Will I see you?

And if I wind up on TV
And if I give to charity
Will you see me?

Betty repeated the chorus, and the band built to a controlled chaos. Flip rumbled the floor tom, Les pounded his strings, the guitarist played something gauche and ridiculous, but Badge didn't hear any of it. He was already in the parking lot, searching for his keys.

39

Badge followed the bus for days.

In Denver, the band played the arena where the Nuggets usually played, and Badge listened from outside, not wanting to get caught by security with an open container. He sat on the ground, his back against the giant dome, his cast in his lap. He felt the thump of the band through the wall, pretended to finger the chords. The clouds above threatened rain without ever quite following through.

In Salt Lake City, Badge paid to get into the show and sat by himself on the second floor balcony. The crowd couldn't have numbered more than 400, and Badge had to be careful not to be spotted from the stage. He hid his flask in his pants, took furtive swigs. After he got drunk, he set the flask on the table, daring someone to do something about it.

In Idaho Falls, Badge didn't have to leave his car to take in the show; the local alternative station played it live on the air. He fell asleep in the front seat, vaguely remembering "Calypso" as he drifted off. The next morning, his battery dead, he had to chase down a landscaper to give him a jump.

In Spokane, Badge ate fried chicken and threw it up in an alley behind a grocery store.

In Tacoma, the band played an outdoor pavilion where the audience could watch from the shore of Puget Sound. Badge stood amid the crowd, smashed on gin, his boots caked with mud, his cast like a traction weight on his arm. When he couldn't stand to look at them anymore, he bent his head back and looked at the stars.

In San Francisco, he called Reina.

"To what do I owe the pleasure?" Reina said. Her voice cut right through him, a blade sharp as a laser.

"I'm in town." He spoke from a pay phone in North Beach. Some kind of block party was going on behind him, a swing band, at least ten musicians. "Are you around this weekend?"

"I could be. What's in it for me?"

"What do you want?"

"Who'd have thought I'd be hearing that from you?"

"Things have changed."

"How's it going with Betty?"

He didn't want to get into it over the phone. She might sense his desperation and shake him loose. Then he'd lose out on what *he* wanted, a sympathetic ear, a shower, maybe a place to stay. "Can we meet someplace?"

"That bad, huh? Where're you at?"

"Columbus Street."

He felt her pause, perhaps considering her options. "I can meet you at Vesuvio in an hour."

"Where's that?"

"Ask anyone. They'll point you."

Reina showed up in a sweater that came off her shoulder, tight jeans and heels. She looked more harried than Badge had ever seen her, something anxious in her eyes. They were on the second floor of Vesuvio, looking down on the alley where the Beat writers used to carouse. Reina sat down. "You look like a nightmare."

Badge had done his best to pull himself together. Not good enough, apparently. "It's been a rough couple of weeks."

"Is that when she threw you over?"

"I'm choosing to look at it like I quit."

"Daddy quitting Mommy-to-be's band."

"That's about it."

"It'll make good copy."

"I knew you'd help me see the upside."

"So," she said, "are you going to tell me what happened to your arm, or are you going to leave me to guess?"

Badge had tried to keep the cast under the table. He wished there was a way to skip that part of the story. He held the cast up, looked at it, the rattiness of the gauze, the chewed-away look of the thumb area. "A little incidental contact."

"With who?"

"Betty's boyfriend."

Reina's lips got thin, trying unsuccessfully to corral a smile.

"I'm glad this amuses you."

"Forgive me. It's just a far cry from the way you were in D.C."

"Things were different then."

"They sure were. You treated me like I was some kind of plague."

"Was I that rough?"

For a split second, Reina looked right at him, a slight unevenness in her eyes. Yes, he'd hurt her, hiding her from the gang in D.C., not giving her a taste of the game she used to master. Badge didn't know hurting Reina was possible. "If you knew how rough I've been treated lately, you wouldn't sweat it," she said.

Their waiter, a guy in a black vest who seemed determined to ignore them, dashed by, and Badge waved him down. "I'll take a gin and tonic."

"Vodka martini," Reina said. "Two olives."

"Got it," the waiter said.

Reina sighed, probably wondering what she'd gotten herself into. "So what now?"

"What I need more than anything is a shower and maybe someone's couch to crash on."

She looked out the window to the alley where Kerouac had probably thrown up. "They have showers in hotel rooms. And beds."

Badge said nothing. He didn't want a hotel room, the loneliest places on earth when you have nowhere to go.

Reina slid onto her elbow. "You buy this round, I'll buy next."

An hour later, they drove to Reina's in her Lexus. Three gin and tonics mingled in Badge's head, giving him a break from his thoughts. The stereo played some band he felt he was supposed to know but didn't. The music had all of the trapping of rock music—singer out front, distorted guitar, cymbal crashes that made you blink—but with a precision Badge didn't like. It could've been the soundtrack for a video game, one set in outer space.

"I hope I'm not ruining your night," Badge said.

"You're actually getting me out of something." Reina drove with a quickness Badge would've found impossible in such a busy city. In North Beach, the block party raging, he'd parked his Valiant just to get out of traffic.

"What?"

"Charlie wanted to talk MP3 coding at his place."

"Who's Charlie?"

She didn't look at him as she whizzed through an intersection. "Charlie's something I wanted to get out of."

Reina's apartment was surprisingly small. One main room, one bedroom, one closet-like bathroom, one skinny kitchen.

An abstract painting took up most of one wall. A leather couch left barely enough space to walk by. The windows looked south at Twin Peaks, radio towers like space stations. Everything in San Francisco was giant and abstract. Badge could've been on some other planet, where practicality was a just an excuse to show a little style. "Nice place," he said.

"I like it." Reina dropped her purse on the couch, took off one heel, then the other. "I've never been one for collecting stuff. That was Monty's thing." She angled into the kitchen, flipped open a cupboard. "Is wine okay?"

Badge nodded. "Don't do much entertaining?"

"Not here." She pulled down two glasses.

"Well, thanks for having me."

Reina poured the wine. "You're not just anyone."

"Really?"

She strolled over to him, shorter now, somehow more manageable without her heels. She handed him a glass. "You know about life on the other side."

"The other side?"

"Come on. Back when it was all good."

Badge took a drink. A police siren came from down below, someone in trouble, not them. "The music."

"And other things." She drank, edged closer to him. "I guess I'm a little jealous of you."

"Why?"

"Being so close to the fire after all these years."

"Not so close anymore."

Reina smiled. The police lights from outside reflected off her eyes. They were barely two people, so close in age, proximity, experience, shared desire. She flipped away, headed towards the bedroom. "I'm going to change. You can help yourself to the shower."

Badge pillaged the bathroom cabinet for something to cover his cast, found a plastic grocery bag, tied it in a knot at his elbow. After his shower, he helped himself to a hair brush, a razor, a toothbrush still in its package. Clean, finally. He was beginning to wonder if he'd ever be clean again.

Reina sat on the leather sofa, swiveled the liquid in her wineglass. She didn't turn when Badge came out. "What a world," she said.

Badge worked his boots onto his feet, which he needed to cover up his dirty socks. "That it is."

"Tell me," she said. Her head pivoted back on her neck, like it had just doubled in weight. "When exactly did rock music become the land of computer geeks?"

"I don't know." He sat on the sofa. Reina still wore her red sweater, but in place of her jeans she had on white cotton shorts, a string knotted at the top. "But if that's true, that's pretty much the end of it."

"End of it? I got news for you, fella. We've been at the end of it for a while now."

"I'm not so sure."

"Well, you're the only one."

Badge reached for his pack of cigarettes.

"Please," Reina said, holding up her hand.

"Oh." He set the pack down. "No problem."

"The smell stays in the curtains forever."

He couldn't help but smile. "So rock and roll isn't the only thing cleaning up its act."

Reina smiled too. "You got me."

Badge touched her shoulder, felt her accept—or at least not reject—this gesture. He ran his hand around the back of her neck, and Reina eased back into his grip.

Badge lay like a slain warrior on her bed, his shirt off, his casted arm above and out of the way. He was drunk, light-headed, one orgasm to the wind. They'd worked quickly on the couch, so quickly Badge hadn't gotten his pants—or boots—off.

The sheets of her bed felt soft on his back. They were the best thing he'd felt in weeks. Well, second best.

Reina, in her red sweater and nothing else, pulled one of Badge's booted feet up. She planted it on her belly, went to work on the laces. He didn't remember this kind of attention from her back in the day. Maybe it was a new way to charm, something that helped her in her business life.

"So what's the deal with Charlie?" Badge said.

She seemed to hesitate, then continued unlacing his boot. "Charlie's fine for what he is."

"What is he?" But what he really wanted to know was *What are you?*

"Politician, congressman, someone we need on our side." She popped a boot off, dropped it to the floor.

"A congressman."

Reina pulled his other foot up, started untying.

"So, your company sends you in to—"

Reina stopped unlacing, stared at him with just a hint of heat. He imagined her having to give the same stare to the musicians she'd represented back in the day, bands who wanted to take time off the road, lead singers who wanted to direct their own videos. "Let's not spoil this with a lot of talk."

Afterward, they went up to the roof, a fenced-in square just above Reina's apartment. The air smelled like ocean: salt, decay. Lone Mountain was a silhouette against the night sky. Neighborhoods, houses upon houses, made the city seem impossibly crowded. It was cold, windy. Badge needed more clothes.

"So what's next for you?" Reina said. She'd slipped into a long, hooded coat with little on underneath. She must've been cold too.

"Gotta catch up with Betty."

Reina walked to the edge of the fence. In her coat she

looked like a poor, huddled mass. "I don't think that's your best move."

Badge found his cigarettes, flicked one out, lit it. His options were so limited he didn't know he had a best move. "I have to know about my kid."

Reina crossed her arms. "Your kid."

"That's right."

"This is about your kid."

"That's part of it."

"What's the other part?"

Badge pulled his cigarette from his mouth. A few possibilities jostled in his head—Betty, the band, pride—none dominated. "Isn't the kid enough?"

"Could be. But you already have a kid in Albuquerque, and after getting kicked out of your band, instead of going home to your kid, you've spent two weeks on the road following Betty with a case of gin in your truck."

Badge felt betrayed. She'd been as culpable as he was, if not in these exact sins, similar ones. "I'm not allowed to be concerned about—"

"Of course you are, if it's the truth."

"It's the truth."

"Come on."

"Okay, Reina. You're the one with all the answers. Why am I out here?"

Even in her long coat, she cut the figure of a formidable debater. Badge could see her in some meeting, eviscerating someone's point, forcing everyone to see things her way. "You're out here because in some way or other it buys you another night before you have to admit you have a problem."

Badge felt the truth of her words, but he puffed out a laugh.

"What's funny?"

"You're getting all worked up."

"I'm telling you this because I think you need to hear it."

"I quit cold turkey eight years ago."

"And you started back up."

"You think I can't quit again?"

Reina stared at him, her arms crossed.

"Where is this all coming from? We just screwed ten minutes ago."

"We did, and now I wish we hadn't. It's the last thing you needed."

"Fine, I'll leave." And he started towards the stairwell.

"Don't," she said.

Badge stopped, thankful he didn't have to follow through. He stood there, took a drag of his cigarette. His exhale was sucked away by the wind. "You sure know how to make a fella feel welcome."

Reina looked off into the distance, at the city beneath them. They were at the top of it. Only one way to go. "Finish that thing. It's freezing out here."

40

The next morning, Badge lay on the couch, watching out the window as the sun arced across the sky. Reina was gone for the day, some business or other. "I'll be back tonight," she'd said. "There are directions to your car on the table. If you don't move it, it'll get towed."

He thought about what Reina had said the night before. The physical effects of quitting would be the hardest. He hadn't had a drink in over twelve hours, and he could feel his cells starting to murmur. Fear of what came next threatened to keep him awake, but the sun eventually found him on the couch and he drifted off.

He woke in a panic, his fingers wedged between the cast and his arm. The thing made him feel confined. He felt like he might need to be rid of it, like it might weigh him down in some unforeseen emergency. He sat on the couch, digging his fingers under the cast. He needed to know he could get out of it if he had to.

Following Reina's directions, Badge hopped on the number one bus and went downtown. He knew he looked crazy, sitting by himself, rocking back and forth. He couldn't quit trying to bend it back, to scratch underneath it, to get it off him. A beautiful San Francisco day, clouds floating by, and all he could think about was this thing on his arm.

In North Beach, he found his car, a parking ticket under its wiper. He drove around until he found a drugstore.

Inside, fluorescent lights glowed white. Badge found the medicine aisle, lots of pills, each box promising relief. The next aisle had shaving accessories. Badge grabbed a pack of razor blades, the old-fashioned kind. The lady behind the counter wouldn't look at him when she took his money. Not her business.

Sitting in his car in the drugstore lot, Badge worked a blade, softly at first, then more forcefully, lengthwise down the cast. If he could just put a crack in it, it would ease his mind enough. But once he broke through up by the elbow, he snapped the cast all the way down.

His arm felt like hard rubber, a new toy that needed breaking in. He still couldn't bend his wrist, but the relief of getting it out of the cast proved worth it. Freedom. How could he ever live without it?

Reina came home just as Badge was ready to leave. To keep away from the wine in Reina's cupboard, Badge had stayed out all afternoon, bought some clothes, a striped shirt that reminded him of the seventies, pre-washed jeans.

"You look great," Reina said.

"Overdue."

"What happened to your cast?"

Badge held up his lame hand, which had the scrunched appearance of a moth yet to emerge from its cocoon. "Wasn't helping much."

"I hope you're well enough to go out."

"Actually, I was about to leave."

"Without saying goodbye?"

"I can't imagine you want me hanging around much longer."

"Don't be silly. I got us reservations at Kokkori."

"That's not necessary."

"I want to do it."

"Reina, I don't need your pity."

She looked askance at him. "Have you ever known me to do anything out of pity?"

They sat in the middle of a dimly lit dining room. All of the two dozen or so tables were full. People scurried about in the kitchen behind glass windows. A plate of olives, many different kinds, sat between them. Every customer in the place drank. Badge kept his hands under the table, his good one gripping the table leg.

"You all right?" Reina said.

"Sure," he lied.

A silver-haired waiter came up. "Can I get either of you something to drink?"

Badge squeezed the table leg.

Reina, seeming to pick up on the reason for his angst, said, "We'll stick with water."

The waiter nodded, disappeared.

"Thanks," Badge said.

"You're sobering up."

Badge nodded.

She grabbed her water glass, extended it. "To sobriety."

After dinner, Reina ushered him to the hotel up the street. The Courtyard ran at least forty stories. Its elevators, two of them with neon blue tracer lights, could be seen gliding up and down from outside.

"Where are you taking me?" Badge said.

She tugged on his good hand. "You'll see."

The lobby boasted a red and gold rug, a marble front desk, a huge chandelier. "Looks expensive," Badge said.

"You better believe it."

"Are you sure it's necessary?"

"Hm?"

"We could just go back to your place."

"Oh," Reina said. "We're not– Just wait."

They climbed into one of the elevators. People milled about outside in the dusk. A few cars glided by. When the door closed, Reina turned towards him, grinned like a cat. "We're here."

"Huh?"

"This is where I'm taking you."

"You're taking me to an elevator?"

She eased closer to him, a gumdrop falling into his mouth. She slid her hands around his waist. "I want you to fuck me in the elevator."

"What?"

"You heard me." She kissed him, seductively, which lit a candle in him.

"You're kidding." He felt her hand slide down, a dolphin playing in warm water. She wasn't. "You want me to fuck you in the elevator?"

"Yeah." Her lip parted, her eyes half-closed.

"I'll fuck you in the elevator."

They went straight up into the San Francisco night, enjoying the current passing between them, removing all that was unnecessary. This was what he would miss most when he went home to Albuquerque, which he'd do first thing in the morning. Not sex, or Reina, or risk, but the vitality of them all rolled into one. There was no denying something was happening in that little room, and anyone who came upon them might've been offended or aroused or mortified, but regardless of how they claimed to feel, it would be the highlight of their night, whether they knew it or not, the thing that most likely would resurface ten or twenty or thirty years from now as a memory, a dream, or a powerful notion, making their breath quicken, their hearts swirl.

41

When Badge woke the next morning, Reina was already gone. There was no official goodbye, but she'd known. They'd both known. It was time for Badge to get on with his life.

He left San Francisco with the sun shining, traffic on the Bay Bridge a notch above stop-and-go. It was only his second day of sobriety, but his quivers had already diminished, and his wrist didn't feel half bad. A new, different life lay just over the horizon, one time zone away. He imagined lazy mornings with his kid, afternoon baseball games. He found a radio station playing jazz combo music, which lasted until Pleasanton, when it morphed into Jesus talk. He turned it off.

Malcolm would be on his agenda, but with fifth grade just underway, not until the weekend. Badge would need money and quickly. He could try to get in a cover band. His right hand wasn't ready yet, but it wouldn't be long. Maybe a couple of weeks.

When Badge came to the exit for Bakersfield, where he was supposed to turn east to go to Albuquerque, he headed south instead, towards L.A. and the last show of No Fun Intended's tour.

He drove his Valiant up to the Avalon Ballroom, a 2,000-seater in the heart of West Hollywood. Posters out front revealed Crosby, Stills and Nash would play there, as well as the Goo Goo Dolls. The big time. It was hard to believe they'd made it this far, a shame he'd had to let it go. He barely had a hand left to grab on with.

He drove around to the lot, parked in a spot not far from the bus, which sat along a fence. Being there at the end might be just the tonic that he—that everyone—needed. No one stirred by the bus or anywhere else; it was early. Badge eased back in his seat, waited.

But as time passed and the reality of what he was doing took hold, Badge felt stupid. He put his keys in the ignition, sat there, waiting for the final inspiration to give them a turn and drive away. Not only had the pain in his wrist come back, it brought with it a sharp, tingling sensation, almost like his arm had fallen asleep. He rubbed his eyes, waited for the feeling to go away. His mind rushed to the contents of his car's trunk, the last two bottles of gin untouched from the case.

He climbed out of the car, looked back at the trunk. There was no way he could have this moment with Betty if he were drunk. One taste and it was over. But the cloying reach of those bottles drew Badge to the back of the car.

He stared down at the trunk. The blue paint had faded to light blue over the years. An indented circle around the key's slot, protected from the sun, still had the original blue color. Badge stood there, almost like he was visiting a gravesite, feeling the weight of what he was about to do.

He slid the key into the slot, and the trunk's lock disengaged. The lid opened, letting out a breath of spare tire smell. Badge could feel the monster gearing up inside him. With a quick push of his hand, he could've kept it in, but that would've taken something he didn't have now.

Badge helped the trunk lid up and, just as he remembered, there were the gin bottles, two of them, in random slots of the twelve-pack box. He wrapped his hand around the top of one.

It reminded him of the handle of a cigarette machine, like the one he'd helped Holly with that night at the Pixie so many years ago. Back when he'd still had something to lose.

He slid the bottle out, held it up in the light. It looked foreboding, like it held nitroglycerine. What part of his life hadn't been poisoned by this stuff? What tiny bit of his misery couldn't be traced back to the contents of one of these beautifully crafted bottles? For reasons he'd never understand, this liquid wanted to kill him, and for the first time in his life he realized he had to kill it first.

With a roadhouse swing, Badge shattered the bottle, causing a spray of liquid on the cement that looked like a meteor. He grabbed the other bottle and did the same, this meteor longer and straighter, extending well into the lot. Glass littered the two splotches, a milky way of jewels reflecting the sunlight.

Badge took off towards the street, with its storefronts, restaurants, people and plenty of walkable blocks to occupy his time before the show.

He didn't come back until sunset, the Hollywood Hills coated with gold light. The Avalon's lot overflowed, and people meandered to the front entrance. Badge could hear Shoulder La Back playing inside, more a rumble than anything, what sounded too loud even in the parking lot. Badge wouldn't go to the show. He'd seen enough of No Fun Intended. He just wanted it over.

The bus's inside lights were on, the shades drawn. Badge hooked the thumb of his bad hand into his jeans, hoping no one would notice, and knocked on the door.

Flip answered wearing a furry brown hat with bear's ears sticking out of its top. His eyes widened when he saw Badge. "Duuude."

"What's up, Flip?"

"Welcome home, buddy. Climb on up. Have a drink."

The bus swirled with people, energy. There were at least a dozen crammed into the small front compartment, talking loudly, tossing back drinks. Most of them struck Badge as record company people. Three or four Champagne bottles were about. A lava lamp—a new edition since he'd been aboard—did its groovy thing on the top shelf.

Philly's face drooped when he saw Badge, and he squeezed past everyone to get to him. "What brings you here?"

"I just wanted to say goodbye to Betty."

"Great. It's just that the show's about to start. Why don't you stop by afterward?"

"I won't be here. I'm leaving for home."

Philly came closer. "Betty's warming up in back, but she'll be done in a few minutes. Would you mind waiting outside?"

"I'm not here to cause trouble."

"I know, but I need you to do me this favor." Philly angled his frame again, an effort to force Badge down the stairs. "I need you to wait for her outside."

"Hey" came a voice from down the hall.

It was Betty, emerged from the back. She wore a miniskirt, combat boots, and a tight red Shoulder La Back T-shirt. Her cornrows were gone, replaced by a stringy black mess, like the Scarecrow from *The Wizard of Oz*. She looked at Badge with a surprising amount of calm, how the family matron might look at a long-lost uncle who'd shown up on Christmas Day. Everyone in the room froze, seeming to know, or at least sense, the drama. The stereo played reggae music, soft, bouncing.

"You got a second?" Badge said.

Betty looked at him. If she felt venom, he couldn't see it. "Philly, how long till we go on?"

"A few minutes."

"Outside," she said.

In the parking lot, the air felt temperate, tolerable, the kind of night when, with a little luck, things could go right. Badge didn't want to screw this up. He tucked in his shirt, held his lame hand behind him.

Betty came out of the bus with a reluctant plunge, how she might step into a high school class she didn't want to attend. "So," she said.

"Thanks for seeing me. Philly was ready to throw me out."

"Philly gets his orders from Glen. I get mine from me."

"How's Vince?"

She looked down, ran a boot over the pavement. Still no venom. "Vince went home."

"Really?"

"He went through the roof every time the bus hit a bump."

"I'm sorry."

"I took him to the hospital that night. Six weeks he's gonna have this thing on his face."

"I'm sorry. I know that's not much, but it's all I have right now."

Betty shifted her weight, her arms still crossed. "Is that it?"

"There's the matter of our kid."

She sighed, strongly. Badge almost felt the breeze.

"I just want you to know," he said, "that no matter what you decide I'm–"

"It's over," Betty said.

"Huh?"

Her eyes closed, reopened. "There is no baby."

"Oh." Badge couldn't help but take a step forward, in anticipation of catching something, but there was nothing to catch. "How–"

"Not my choice. It happened after the Salt Lake show. I went to the emergency room."

"I didn't know."

Tears welled in Betty's eyes, and she wiped them quickly, expertly.

"You didn't even stop the tour," Badge said. "You went right on–"

"There was nothing to do but hang out at the hospital and feel sorry for myself. I just needed to–"

"Betty," and Badge came to her, wrapped his arms around her. He felt this small, frail girl cry on his shoulder. His own tears came, and he let them fall into her hair. *There's no baby, no Badge and Betty. This is the last of it.* He squeezed her harder, knowing what awaited him after he let go.

The bus door opened and out came the rent-a-guitarist. He seemed especially tall to Badge, his shoulders like cliffs under his tank top, his cowboy boots giving him an extra inch he didn't need. Something in his approach made Badge let go of Betty. He backed away, wiping the tears from his eyes. The guy came right up behind Betty and, without taking his eyes off Badge, slid his hands over her shoulders. "Everything all right, babe?"

"Yeah." Betty wiped her eyes. "No big deal."

Babe?

"Gunter," she said, "this is Badge, our former guitar player."

Gunter?

"The infamous Badge," Gunter said, extending a hand.

"Wait," Badge said. It was all doing somersaults in his head. The math didn't add up, then suddenly it did. He looked at Betty, pointed at Gunter. "You're fucking this guy?"

"Badge, don't–"

"Wait," Badge said. "You're fucking this guy right after– While Vince is–"

"Listen, pal," Gunter said, his voice deep, prepared to stomp on whatever Badge said next. "What Betty does is none of your–"

Badge moved towards Betty, an effort to freeze this intruder out, but Gunter got in front of her, pushed him. "You don't wanna do that," he said. He raised his hands to eye level, crouched down. "I know Tai Kwan Do."

"Betty," Badge said, his disappointment in her complete. "You fuck this asshole?"

And that was the last Badge knew of the night. He felt the kick land squarely on his face, felt his head bounce on the ground, the rough feeling of the pavement. Then all went black, a restful sleep, one that promised dreams too deep to remember upon waking.

Epilogue

2001

Badge sat on a stool in what Reggie called "the warehouse" but what was really a converted meeting room. Packing supplies took up most of the space. Bubble wrap, a peanut machine. Boxes of computer chips were stacked along one wall. Fluorescent lights glowed, as well as Badge's computer, shining blue in his face. He'd managed to get the last of the orders ready in time for the overnight guy. The guy had scooped up the stack with his cart and disappeared out the door. Badge had yet to learn his name. It was too hectic most of the time to bother.

Reggie popped in. He was a slimmer Reggie than he'd been most of his life. His newly featured cheekbones made his face look longer and, frankly, older. Marjorie, Reggie's health-conscious new wife, was responsible for this sea change. At their wedding reception, Marjorie forced everyone to eat a no sugar, no trans fat, gluten-free meal. They didn't even have a cake. Badge and Malcolm had to stop at Whataburger on the way home.

Still, a great couple, Marjorie as quick-witted as Reggie reserved. Whenever Marjorie saw Badge, she invited him to dinner, even though he rarely took her up on it. By the size of the inner tube growing around his waist, he'd've been wise to accept once in a while.

"The big night," Reggie said.

"The concert," Badge said.

Reggie scanned the room. "Well, everything's done for today. Why don't you get out of here?"

"I'm just the chauffeur." Even though Badge had sworn off rock concerts, the announcement of Jeff Beck coming to the Revolution made him ignore his stance. His clothes for work that day—black T-shirt, black jeans, black boots—were strategically chosen to blend in at the show. "Something I'm doing for the kid."

"Whatever," Reggie said. "See you Monday."

Badge climbed into his pickup, flicked on the ignition. A beautiful Albuquerque night, cool, what might have been the beginnings of fall. He loved this time of year, the days getting shorter, the heat of summer losing a battle of attrition. He could almost imagine himself still in high school, driving along I-25, the Albuquerque skyline out his window, a concert in his plans for the night. He would let himself enjoy it, his first ever with his son.

The job with Reggie had worked out surprisingly well. When Badge came back to Albuquerque, broke, beaten, Reggie had taken pity on him. He offered to bring Badge into the business on the condition that he try Alcoholics Anonymous. This made Badge wince, but in retrospect it had been the right choice: two years without a drop, his cravings diminished, his chance at a decent second half of his life increasing with every sober moment.

And even though Reggie had given Badge the job as fulfillment manager on blind faith, Badge had proven his worth. The company had doubled in size since he'd started, and Reggie never had to so much as pick up a tape gun.

Badge would never forget, over a year ago now, calling Malcolm from a truck stop on his way home. His nose was so swollen he had to breathe through his mouth. "Betty isn't my girlfriend anymore," he'd said.

"I told the kids at school I knew her," Malcolm said.

"Well, you still know her. I'm just not in her band anymore."

"Who's band are you in now?"

"No one's. Your dad's in no one's band, but your dad really needs to see his son tomorrow. So that's going to have to be enough."

Holly had been a little easier on him. Badge sat on her couch, his face swollen, and told her of Vince, of getting thrown out of the band, of the miscarriage. He couldn't look at her as he spoke. She'd been through this type of drama with him before. It had led to their divorce.

"You're quite a marvel," she said.

"If that's what you want to call it."

"The other option is asshole."

"Hopeless is what I've been calling it."

"Naw." Holly stood up, grabbed his shoulders, looked at him with something close to love in her eyes. "You're not hopeless. I won't let you be hopeless. You're my son's daddy."

Badge took the I-40 exit. He had to get all the way out to Malcolm and Holly's and then back downtown before the leadoff band started. It was amazing how he'd all but excised rock and roll from his life, his guitars and amps locked away in the basement of his apartment complex, no contact with the people from his music days. He'd begun to wonder if it had all really happened to him when, a few months after coming home, Les called.

"I'll be in town tomorrow," he said. "You wanna meet up?"

"Sure," Badge said, "but not for a drink."

"Cool," Les said.

The pair met at a downtown restaurant called Chao, which was next to Rosa's, a little adobe venue where Les would play that night.

"Glen found me the gig," Les said. His appearance hadn't changed—flannel shirt, gaunt cheeks, beard down to his crotch. "Lesbo singer. Sultry, more cocktail-y, but boy, sexy. You can't not look at her when she sings."

"She on a label?"

Les shook his head. "Rich parents. They're trying to buy their way onto the charts."

"Can they do that?"

"That's all that's left. If you want to survive, you have to find someone with a little talent and a lot of money who wants to be the next Madonna."

"And Glen's part of this?"

"I suspect he's just playing out the string, waiting for the last of it to dry up. He'll wind up on some beach somewhere." Les took a drink of tea, herbal like Badge's, no kick at all. "Did you know Flip got back with the Gentlemen's Septet?"

"Wow."

"They asked him back on."

"Is he gambling?"

"Under control, as far as I can tell."

"Good," Badge said.

"And Tad and Cosmo are still out there. I saw Tad on the road with Moleskin last month. He and Tina are expecting."

"Good Christ. Another Tad."

"That's what I said."

A pause spread out between them. Badge could've filled it easily with "So what do you know about Betty?" But he wouldn't let himself.

Les seemed to sense the window too. He took another hit of tea, looked into the distance. "Albuquerque's nice. I can see why someone would want to live here."

Badge walked into Malcolm and Holly's house to the smell of chili cooking. Holly was nowhere to be seen, so Badge ducked into the kitchen, found the pot. Its lid was off, and small dots of brown were scattered about the stovetop. He tasted it with a wooden spoon. Meat, beans, chili powder, perfect. He rarely ate anything but takeout, the Chinese restaurant across the street from his apartment staying in business on his nightly visit.

Chinese food, autumn nights, his son every other weekend, he'd learned to love it. People died wishing for less.

Sounds of an acoustic guitar came from Malcolm's bedroom. It wasn't much of an effort, just the scratchings of someone trying to make sense of the instrument. Badge had bought Malcolm the guitar for Christmas but had never known him to actually play it. Malcolm's favorite music deviated from his dad's. Creed, Korn, Limp Bizkit. They were fine, but Badge couldn't stand the lyrics, stretches for something profound, high school kids trying to impress their English teacher. When Badge heard Jeff Beck was coming to town, he bought two tickets. If the kid was into music, he wouldn't slide into adolescence without getting a dose of what a real player sounds like.

"You ready for the concert?" Badge called down the hallway.

Crunching sounds, probably the kid stomping on junk on his floor. Malcolm was at the age when it was almost impossible to get him to do anything, especially for his own good. "Mom wants to talk to you," he said.

Just then, Holly popped in through the sliding glass door. She wore garden gloves and had little dirt rings on her knees. "Hey," she said, pulling off the gloves. A strand of hair escaped from the tie in back. She was aging well, and Badge wondered if she'd somehow done it on purpose, getting back at him by showing him what he'd given up. "Marlene from work's kid wants to go to the concert. He's about Malcolm's age. I told her I'd ask you."

"Sure."

"Good. I'll call her and tell her you're on your way."

"You're sure you don't want to go?"

Holly picked up the phone, dialed. "I never did get that guy," meaning Jeff Beck. "I pretended to like him because you did."

He wanted to approach her from behind, slide his hands over her shoulders, kiss her neck, but he knew better. "The ultimate sacrifice," Badge said.

"Marlene?" Holly said. "Badge and Malcolm would love to

have Travis along ... So he'll be ready in a half hour? Great." She hung up.

"So instead of you we get Travis."

"Malcolm wouldn't want Mom along anyway. I'm surprised you're allowed to go."

"I bought the tickets ... Malcolm?"

"*Yes*," Malcolm grumbled.

Badge pointed up the hallway. "Is this what you're getting from him most of the time?"

"If I got this most of the time, I'd call it an improvement."

"At what point do we get concerned?"

She shrugged, which nicely highlighted her neck, the pit at the base of her throat. That may have been Badge's favorite part of her, he was late to realize. "Let's just keep being good examples and see how it goes."

"You are a good example," Badge said, but caught himself. "I mean, if it doesn't go without saying."

Holly smiled, walked back to the sliding glass door. "And Badge. Make sure Malcolm is nice to Travis."

"Mom invited *Travis?*" Malcolm said. He was getting taller, his head almost reaching the passenger's seat headrest. Something in his face seemed stretched out, more serious, but the severity was undercut by the swoop of hair across his forehead, shellacked there with hairspray. Malcolm pulled a foot up onto his knee as Badge started the car. A new pair of Vans, blue with a white stripe, had suddenly become necessary for the concert. That must've been what the big search was about.

"What's wrong with Travis?" Badge said, but Malcolm was too appalled to answer.

When they got to Marlene's house, Badge realized what was wrong with Travis.

The kid came bounding out of the house as Badge pulled up, a towheaded blond, a little heavy, his lips forming a permanent smile. Badge realized Travis committed that unpardonable sin in the age of cool: he looked a little too excited about everything.

"Thanks, Malcolm's dad," Travis said as he climbed into the backseat. He carried a stack of magazines.

"You're welcome, but what are those for?"

"Each one of these has an article on Jeff Beck. I'm going to get them signed and sell them on eBay."

"Well," Badge said. He pulled into the street. In this part of town, rush hour intensified as it got later. "I ought to tell you, Travis, I can't promise we'll hang around long enough to get autographs."

Travis's eyes—Badge could see them in the rearview—slanted toward despair.

"But that's okay. It doesn't mean we can't have a good time. In fact, it's funner to go to a concert without having to worry about that stuff."

Travis looked out the window, crossed his arms. The reflections from passing cars whipped across his forehead. "Can I go home?"

The support band had finished by the time Badge had gotten Travis home and they got back to the Revolution. Badge and Malcolm made a beeline to the balcony stairs. One stairway followed another.

"Nice tickets," Malcolm said.

Their seats were smack in the middle of a row, halfway up the balcony. The stage looked as far away as the end zone to a kick returner. People sat too close to both the left and right of them. "Let's go up higher so we're not pinched in," Badge said.

There was nobody in the last few rows save one couple, doing their best to keep to themselves. For some reason, Malcolm chose a seat missing an armrest.

"So what's the deal with this guy?" Malcolm said.

"Jeff Beck? He was in the Yardbirds. He influenced more guitarists than you can count."

"He influence Angus Young?" To Malcolm, all roads led back to AC/DC.

"No, but just about everyone else."

"Then how come he's not more famous?"

"He's pretty famous, but maybe not obsessed with being on the covers of magazines and stuff."

"Just like you, right?"

Badge would someday learn to love this adolescent version of his son, smart mouth and all. He grabbed Malcolm around the neck, the only kind of affection his son allowed him anymore. "I think I just prefer being with my kid."

With no announcement, the band mosied onto the stage, and the crowd whooped. The musicians appeared dressed for an aerobics workout. Tight clothes, tennis shoes. Then Beck strolled out, his vintage Stratocaster strapped over him. He looked like a rocker. Skin-tight black T-shirt, high-laced boots. Everyone settled into their instruments, and after a rousing British "Hello" from Beck, the band started in on the first number "Earthquake."

Badge had heard the song a few times, the first track off the new album, which he'd bought in hopes of familiarizing himself with the material, but he'd had a hard time engaging with it. Something too modern about it. Still, Badge was surprised by how present the band was. The drummer, playing a complicated kit reminiscent of Neil Peart's, expertly guided the beat. Jeff's guitar was mixed up higher than the rest, giving the songs a brittle dimension. Still, the music was dulled by something, a sense Badge could see behind the curtain, through the seams. It was a curiosity. Pleasant, not vital.

Not so for Malcolm. The kid leaned forward, his shins against the seat in front of him, doing everything he could to take it all in. Badge remembered, in junior high, doing the same at a Peter Frampton show.

The band finished "Earthquake," and Malcolm hooted and hollered. "What album's that on?" he said.

"The new one."

"Do you have it?"

"I do."

"Awesome."

The band started the next song, one Badge didn't recognize. He didn't have the patience for any more new Jeff Beck songs. He'd catch the classics at the end of the show. "I'm gonna get something to drink. You want anything?"

"A beer?"

"Like hell."

"Soda?"

Badge went down the stairs. Despite the thump of the band just beyond the wall, people still hung out in the lobby. Badge went to the concession stand, bought Malcolm a soda, himself a water. He was heading back up when he saw the sign: *No food or drink in theater*. He pocketed the water, stood at the base of the stairs, drank Malcolm's soda. A large-screen TV played a simulcast of the show. The bass player looked older but not entirely out of place onstage with a rock band. His black hair was buzzed almost to the point of being shaved, and his sunglasses reflected the stage lights. Beck worked gracefully at centerstage, moved with smooth motions, stomping to the beat of the song, sliding up his Stratocaster to draw out high notes. He still played like he cared. Badge couldn't play at all anymore. His wrist, which had never quite healed, wouldn't let him.

A group of girls, none older than fifteen, huddled behind Badge. One, tall, in rainbow stockings, smoked a cigarette. "I can't believe it," she said.

"She left him?"

"Dumped him."

"No way."

"That's what it said on her website. Something about irreconcilable differences. There's this open letter where she goes on about getting it back to the way it was."

"Wow. I thought they'd be together forever."

"Nothing's forever in punk rock," the tall girl said, a pup imitating the world-weary groan of an old dog. "I just hope she kicks ass again. Her first record changed my life."

"Mine too."

"You're not old enough to have your life changed."

When Badge made it back to the balcony, the band had just finished "The Pump."

"Where's my drink?" Malcolm said.

"No drinks in the balcony."

"What?"

"I brought you a water. Keep it low so the bouncers don't see it." Badge couldn't believe he was smuggling water into a rock show. Times had changed.

The band kicked into the next song, "You Know What I Mean."

"Yes," Malcolm said. He pumped his fist. "I know this one."

Badge liked it too. He remembered playing it on his parent's stereo console, his headphones on, staring down as the record spun, lost to everything else. "This was one of your grandpa's favorites," he said, but Malcolm didn't hear him.

The band played on, and Badge drifted away. For some reason he remembered going to see Albert Collins when he was fourteen, the only kid in a room full of adults. He stood up front, his arms on the stage, watching the guitarist as the rest of the crowd danced. That was the day he learned what he wanted to do with his life. Nothing could be better than playing guitar onstage, towering over others, people's faces shining up at you. If only it were that simple.

And the band broke into "Dirty Mind," and Badge remembered, years ago, dancing with Holly on their wedding day. Holly wore white taffeta and, embarrassed by all the attention, pulled him closer. He felt her through every cell of his body, falling in love anew with every second that ticked by.

And the band played "Psycho Sam," and Badge remembered Betty writing a song in the practice room, squatting on a stool, hunched over a notepad. That was when Badge knew there was something inside her that ruled her, in the face of which Badge was irrelevant. It also made him long for her, like he might for an expensive toy in a store window, one his parents couldn't afford.

And the band played "Cause We've Ended as Lovers," and Badge remembered hearing the track one night at his dad's apartment. They'd just finished eating, and both of them lay on the couch, listening to the music, watching the sun set.

And the band broke into "Behind the Veil," and Malcolm cheered like he'd never heard anything so cool. What did the future hold for his kid? Would he really take up guitar, or was it just a phase, something to be forgotten as soon as the first girl winked at him? Badge almost hoped it was a phase.

Almost.

And the band kept playing, songs Badge didn't remember or had never heard before. But they were all in there, somewhere deep inside of him, and deep inside his mom, and his dad, and Malcolm, and Holly, and Betty and Reina and even Vince, melodies that would break your heart.

The prequel of *Badge, Ghost Notes*, as well as the single for *Badge*, "Calypso," are available at www.artedwards.com.

Badge Version 1.0 February 2014

I would like to thank Raquel Edwards, Deb and Andre Shapiro, Bret and Chris Glass Hartley, Karen Karbo, Valerie Williamson, Dan Berne, Christine Fletcher, Laura Wood, Charlotte Dixon, Kevin Burke, Connie McDowell, Debbie Guyol, Maura Conlon, Rebecca Kelley, Dana Cuellar, Mark Russell and Michael Zeiss for their insight during the writing of *Badge*. You helped make these pages sing.

And finally, I would like to thank those who contributed to *Badge*'s Kickstarter campaign: Sharon Schultz, Bob Dato, Rob McNelly, Dan Berne, Jay and Cindy McDougall, Brian J. Henderson, Jim R., Tom Socha, Brent Scarano, Kristi Houlberg, Kelly Eastman, Leisa Maranell, Polly Thune, Joel Benge, Ben Jenkins, Sunny Welker, John Principale, Robert Rich, Karen Karbo, Sandy Berrens, Deb Kutrieb, Matt Hancher, Stephan Cox, James Hass, Clay Cassells, Brian Horen, Duke Haney, Jeff "Smoke" Adams, Rebecca Kelley, Colleen Strohm, Gary Brent Bennett, Colby King, Heather Arndt Anderson, John Veltkamp, Marcia Kuma, Sharon Marie, Barbara Higdon, Uli Kirchler, Joy Cone, Mark Russell, Oregon Writers Colony, Dan Bauer, Mark and Judy, C. M. Fletcher, Peter Lubin, Cheryl Strayed and Brian Lindstrom, Sue Potter, Michael Zeiss, Karla Lodge, Loren Deck, Megan DiLullo, Nico Holthaus, Kathleen Achor, Sarah Gilbert, Kyle Nickerson, Laurel Hermanson, Craig Simmons, Dana Cutler, Zonal Rick, Steven Birnbaum, Esther Smail, Scott Brower, Gene Burnett, Charlotte Dixon, Zoe Zolbrod, Jason Roberts, Kim Schimmel, Tom Bache, Matt Stetler, Torey Olsen, Lisa Randall, Becky Palapala, Christi Suzanne, Jesse Eastman, Frank Lamanna, Brian and Louise Valentine, Robert Joseph, David Lindenbaum, Gloria Harrison, G. Xavier Robillard, Kathryn Harter, Kyle Krenz and Larry Altman. You helped make these pages exist.

CPSIA information can be obtained at www.ICGtesting.com
Printed in the USA
BVOW02s0802111213

338502BV00010B/1/P

9 780979 906688